SOFIE

Stephen D Butler

Butler's Homestead Publishing

STEPHEN BUTLER

--- For my dearest friends taken too early ---
--- Nombat, Prince, Beefnburger and Sparky ---

-1-

Feet striking hard concrete she ran, beating a staggered staccato rhythm. Sofie was free. Small, blood splattered footprints littering her path, she was spurred on by primal fear and jubilant exultation. She ran as fast and as far as she could, the skin on her feet worn bare by impacts and abrasion. Unicorn tee shirt, stained with abuse and torn by rough hands. Never again would she face his sick desire. Never again would she suffer his chastising whip.

Rowlands Castle is a picturesque English village as nice as any other. On the southern coast it sits, outside the South Downs National Park, north east of Portsmouth harbour. Its only unique feature is a long village green bordered by roads and by rail. In all other aspects its builders followed the same design as countless other country towns. It's only lacking the ubiquitous river to be found in most villages.

It's the sort of village where shoplifting is a high crime and graffiti is limited to a few lewd teenage etchings on bus stops. The average age of residents nearing the high side of seventy years. However, in this sleepy open air retirement home a traumatised innocent leaves her macabre trail of reddened prints.

Just one hour ago Sofie had been three and half miles further north in the even sleepier hamlet of Compton. An Edwardian farmhouse snugly nestled by woodland and by downs was her home. It lay at the end of a wooded track well away from the tarmac roads of civilisation. In this idyllic setting she had spent many happy summers exploring forests and investigating fields.

Sofie remembers spending many sun dappled days amongst the foliage, searching for badgers and trying to convince a local squirrel of her friendly intent. She had thoroughly explored the undergrowth and fashioned many a secret den beneath the strong boughs of a proud English oak.

She gathered piles of rocks and sticks for a purpose long forgotten, played in rivers by industriously building dams and chasing crayfish. The adventures she imagined day after day were enhanced by the worlds she visited at night through the pages of her books. The stories of Wilbur the pig, Black Beauty, Aslan, Bigwig and Hazel all woven into her reality with ease.

Running in terror through darkened and deserted village streets those memories seemed so distant, as if they had been experienced by some other little girl. Some other girl who had played, laughed and even enjoyed her life.

Sofie had attended a small village school. Built in 1906 from red bricks it still had the original white sash windows and a slightly leaky slate roof. The buildings architecture providing an atmosphere of severity and discipline to the educational proceedings. All the classrooms had seen many cohorts of well behaved students come and go year after year.

Every teacher past and present seeming to extract authority from the aether. Parents and teachers alike had strongly resisted any attempt to modernise the building. This meant that the school had escaped the councils unceasing obsession with cheap plastic renovations.

On Friday the seventeenth of July Sofie attended her last day of middle school. You may remember from your own education the last day of middle school is a curious affair indeed. A day of sadness and also great expectation. With classmates and friends heading to different high schools It's a time to remake yourself and a time to cast off the childish past.

On this day there is one question of upmost importance. 'where are you going next year?' The answer to this single question opens doors to new friendships as it closes on old ones. If a classmate is going to the same school as you they can be considered for continued friendship, otherwise they are likely to be forgotten and discarded.

Sofie herself sadly learned that her best friend would be attending a private academy to the north, while Sofie would be attending the local comprehensive next year. Separated by only thirty miles their continued friendship was as good as over. It wouldn't have been dealt a more significant blow if either child had relocated to Australia.

Ask Sofie now though and she cannot remember a single friend's name. Memories, grey and indistinct they have blurred together and been mixed up by more recent events.

As the last bell rings and the school day ends, children spill out of every possible door onto the sun baked playground. Anyone seeing this exodus would be reminded of a bee hive disturbed by an intruder.

Her educational program complete, for now, she could begin to live in a world much bigger than the one offered by daily lessons and repetitive routine. Promises are being made as these students say their farewells, most of which are a lot more final than intended. Summer meetings and secret adventures planned, Sofie says her last goodbye as she climbs into the back of a large black 4x4.

This car was provided by the nice people at her fathers work and was to return Sofie home one last time. It is at this moment where her memories become clear, as if now etched into steel. The smell of the leather, clearly recalled. The drivers smart dress and peaked hat remembered. Every fine detail from the mileage to the water spots on her window, Sofie took in everything. She was pleased, her legs now long enough to allow proper knee articulation around the seats edge.

Pressed firmly into the jet black seating as they accelerated away, Sofie enjoyed the sensation. She ran her hands along the fine white stitching, the needlework seeming impossibly neat. Familiar sights of her journey home observed as if through new eyes or for the first time. Something had changed, she felt more alive, more grown up.

Trees and hedgerows bordered the country lanes, looking as if they were flying past at great speed. This always excited Sofie but soon enough even this distraction lost its appeal and she brought her attention to the long road in front of her.

Roadkill is a common enough sight in the countryside, but when Sofie saw the vibrantly beautiful wings of a male pheasant, twisted beyond natural configuration limits, she felt a profound sadness.

"Hey kiddo what's wrong?" said the driver.

Sofie grasped for an explanation and in a much smaller voice than she expected said nothing more than "The pheasant".

With a repressed laugh the friendly but professional looking driver replied

"Aww well don't feel too bad little Missy, surely you have seen dead birds before?"

Of course she had, but why did it affect her so much this time? Perhaps with a new chapter in her life beginning and the endless opportunity in front of her Sofie had obtained a new understanding of how it must feel to face an untimely end. Perhaps it was just the distinctly gruesome cause of death that had befallen this unlucky pheasant.

Trying to comfort Sofie the driver had pointed out that pheasants are bred in their hundreds for sport.

"Only a matter of time until one toff or another gets busy with the twelve gauge Little Miss. Then bang, two barrels of good news and it's nighty, night anyway, see?"

Sofie decided, although well meaning, this man who had driven her these past years knew little of dealing with children.

The 4x4 tore down small country roads, disturbing fallen leaves and detritus with its turbulent wake. Sofie began to feel a novel sense of anticipation as they drew ever closer to her family home.

When Sofie was three her mother had died. Her father, Tom, would be there to welcome Sofie home today. Tom had done an excellent job of looking after her and providing for them both. He was a computer engineer or something like that. Sofie was not exactly sure. He had always been kind and Sofie loved him with all her heart.

On top of being instrumental in her creation he had helped her grow and learn, he had spent many hours making her into the sweet and kind girl she was today. All of her best memories had involved him and his unwavering devotion to her.

The 4x4 took a sharp left onto the dirt track that lead to her house. The unexpected sideways force making Sofie smile and refocusing her attention on the present. After bouncing through puddles and skidding slightly on the gravel driveway the car finally came to a complete stop outside her home.

Sofie jumped out and slammed the mud stained door behind her. Waving goodbye to the driver Sofie thought he seemed sad to be dropping her off. She felt a warm sense of sympathy for the driver, assuming he would miss their daily trips together. 'After all' she thought 'I am an extraordinary little girl. I'm sure I would miss my own company if I could somehow be away from myself' With that paradox in her mind she skipped across the driveway to her familiar front door.

Sofie was so full of excitement and anticipation. It was wonderful, beginning a six week holiday but here again she was distracted by the feeling of newness. It had been with her all the way home despite pheasants and high speed turns.

This was the same heavy green door she had approached many times. She knew every detail of the weathered and worn cast iron stags head knocker. Still she looked upon it all today with new eyes. She observed the smallest details with fascination. The paint beginning to crack, faded and peeling where it caught more sun. The annoyingly unsymmetrical stained glass porthole. She was still too small to see through the tiny lead inlay window but knew exactly what she would see if only growth would oblige in her desire for additional height.

The hinges offset to give the illusion of symmetry. Sofie had discovered that hinges are set this way so that observed from an adults height they appear to be evenly spaced top and bottom. She had remarked to her father that from a child's perspective it looks most peculiar.

'Why am I obsessing over this door?' she mentally chastised herself. The thought of seeing her father staying her hand just one moment longer, she began to knock.

She could hear her father's purposeful stride and solid footsteps approaching the door. Sofie's excitement grew. After much clicking, clunking and de-latching the door opened. Raising her arms and screaming 'Daddy' Sofie anticipated a doorstep bear hug.

It is undisputed fact that a father's hug is the best in the world for a little girl. Her feet left the floor as Sofie's heart soared. The unpleasantness with the pheasant totally but temporarily forgotten.

-2-

Police Community Support Officer (PCSO) Caroline May, shoulder number one zero seven seven was engaged in the commission of her duties, foot patrolling Rowlands Castle, Hampshire, England. Looking at her phone Caroline thought to herself 'At just after zero three hundred hours on the eighteenth of July jack shit happened.' She continued walking the streets and she crossed paths with a small black cat.

Sitting atop his garden wall, the keen eyed black cat observed the lady's meandering progress past parked cars. His garden as well manicured as any other on this street. He was thankful that the humans spent so much time tending the lawns and planting their little flowers for him too poop behind. His gaze followed the frustrated looking woman. Her pantomime actions and strange way of speaking aloud to no one, intrigued him.

Caroline instantly warmed to the cat, stopped her walking and asked, without any need for response

"Why kitty, why did they stick me in this dead end town on

this dead end shift?"

The cat shifted slightly at being addressed directly.

"Its because of these" she said cupping her breasts "they can't have a beautiful and intelligent lady around, it threatens their boy's club" then she added sourly "Bastards"

Caroline was not greatly beautiful or even overly intelligent. Average in many respects she had shoulder length brown hair tucked neatly into a ponytail. Slightly underweight but not skinny, in socks she stands at five foot and a quarter inches. She did have a large bosom, especially for a girl of her petite size. This fact alone had given her an overinflated opinion of her looks.

She received a lot of male attention. Wanted or otherwise, every double take, glancing eye and outright comment about her boobs had given Caroline the impression that she was a rare beauty indeed. Desired by all men and she suspected most women to.

Caroline could have been a wonderful person, she has a caring and empathetic nature. She loves animals, the taste of some and the company of others. She is artistic and has little time for spirituality.

Only one thing has stopped her from achieving anything in her life. Caroline has been constantly told that she is a victim. If anything goes wrong in her life one friend or another would, without the slightest knowledge or context, reassure her that it 'wasn't your fault,' or 'you were discriminated against.' Over and over again this message had been drilled into her.

During Caroline's teenage years her father had died while serving his country. Two tours of Iraq had gone well but he never returned from Afghanistan, leaving thirteen year old

Caroline an orphan. She had been taken in by her opinionated aunt and began to learn all about the patriarchy with their 'systematic oppression of women'.

Caroline had done poorly in her exams just over two years later. She couldn't see the point of continuing with education and decided to follow her father's example. She would pursue a career in the army, not just the regular army, Caroline was heading for the special forces.

She had been denied entry into the infantry and rejected by the police. She was even declined for a personal security licence. Learning that the Police's community support team was looking for a 'diverse and inclusive workforce' she had applied and bent the truth a little on her application form. Caroline had decided on some affirmative action of her own. One little lie about where her relatives came from, great grandma had swapped Kent for Kenya.

When the community support officers had accepted her application she had screamed so loudly her neighbour had come down to check she was ok. The police's human resource team had overlooked the fact her grades were more suited to a career that involved little or no responsibility.

During the ten week training course her instructors had quickly realised Caroline was abrasive, lacked any social skills, had grandiose delusions and believed that her lack of success was entirely the fault of anyone but herself. One of the police trainers had jokingly commented that he had never met a woman more perfectly suited for a role as a PCSO.

After graduating Caroline was assigned to Barry Tutton a PCSO mentor from Red Hill in Hampshire. Along with fellow newbie Robert Winslow, Caroline would spend the next three months gaining practical experience from Barry and the rest of the local team.

Barry had been a senior PCSO for three years ever since he had retired from the police proper. Caroline had made such an impression on Barry during her first week that she had been 'promoted' to night shift. A position that came with 'a lot of responsibility' and was 'an opportunity to advance' it even came with a new torch.

Barry had bought the D-cell Maglite himself from a local camping store on the high street and submitted the required paperwork to request that a night time PCSO patrol was set up. He had stated that the increased level of knife crime could be tackled by having an officer on the streets at night.

His request had been granted, despite the complete lack of any knife crime locally. There hadn't been a recorded incident involving a bladed weapon in any of the surrounding villages for at least ten years.

Well, apart from the time when one Miss J. Writhlington had reported a youth for carrying a knife. The youth, as it transpired was a forty five year old mother of three. She had just bought the offending article to replace a recently broken cheese knife. She had been spotted waiting for a bus and reading the description printed on to the sealed plastic pack that this deadly weapon came in.

Needless to say the PCSOs had sprung into action upon receiving this report and after a minor confrontation had confirmed that no one was in danger. They could not however, say the same for the lady's Brie collection.

The silky jet black cat was still sitting patiently.

"I mean" whispered Caroline "what would Rob and Bazza do if I kept showing them up by catching all the bad guys" She continued to her new found confidant "These men are all the same. Scared of what a real woman can do"

It was at this point that the cat was distracted by a most interesting leaf and his attention began to drift.

"What I wouldn't give for some action," she said "I don't mean that in a harsh way, like, you know. I just want something to happen."

The cat began to stretch and rose to its feet having had quite enough of this shrill and self obsessed human. He began to walk away towards that leaf 'no strokey strokes?' he wondered.

That was how Caroline would spend most of her summer nights, patrolling beautiful but empty streets and talking to locally sourced, unresponsive, free range wildlife. She only ever saw Barry and Robert at the daily meetings where she was always tired and more unpleasant than usual.

The meeting scheduled everyday for eight o'clock, the end of her shift and the beginning of theirs. Each morning she would conduct a handover and relay any pertinent information about the previous nights walking before heading home. Caroline would also see them at the start of her shift for a much briefer encounter.

With the money she had inherited from her father Caroline had bought a small flat just outside Waterlooville, a little town near Rowlands Castle. This meant she had no rent to pay and was in a much better financial situation than most people her age. The council tax and various bills had been a problem from time to time but she got by.

Her flat was in a converted three story townhouse and she often fantasised about buying the other two flats, kicking the neighbours out, knocking through a few walls and returning it to a single stately dwelling.

Once home, she would draw thick, heavy curtains and eat

various varieties of pot noodle alone on her inflatable couch, surrounded by the refuse of a life that had floundered. Her small apartment was a study in missed opportunity and failed expectations. The many projects started and never finished were stuffed into closets. Equipment for the hobbies she enthusiastically began and inevitably bored of stacked in spare rooms with forgotten fitness machines.

She had an extensive DVD collection, being too stubborn to understand the utility of streaming services. They ranged through many subjects but centred mostly around special forces documentaries. Today, she selected one of her favourites, a program about SAS selection. As she drifted into unconsciousness and slid slowly from her PVC throne the dulcet tones of an angry sergeant lulled her to sleep.

A long and lonely six weeks had passed, it was the evening of Tuesday September the first. Caroline awoke with a fresh outlook and a new attitude. It hadn't been an overnight epiphany at all, she had spent every long night shift that summer patrolling the empty streets with only a cat and her thoughts for company.

The hours spent on self reflection had been uncomfortable for her, but in her mind she had accepted the truth behind her 'promotion'. Spending those six weeks in solitary contemplation she had more than enough time to reassess the events that had lead her to where she was now.

She showered, dressed and brewed an extra large thermos of black coffee. Admiring her newly tidied flat she resolved to talk to Barry, apologise for her behaviour and ask politely if she could come back onto day shift. Before leaving for work she looked at the picture of her father which she kept on a dresser. She picked up his green beret carefully clutching it to her chest.

"Don't worry dad," she said to the picture "I will make you proud, I promise"

Once again patrolling but in a great mood tonight she saw her black furred friend. Caroline had christened him with the name Pickles. Over the weeks their relationship had grown. Pickles had no interest in Caroline's early offerings of dry noodles, no matter how much she insisted they were chicken. He had quickly adjusted his attitude when she started to produce fish scented meat treats. He reasoned that the moist morsels were well worth enduring the unrelenting tirade of weird noises this woman made at him.

"Pickles my friend," Caroline said "I think I might be seeing a little less of you."

Although Pickles could not fathom her meaning he did sense a more agreeable demeanour and began to purr as she produced another of the wonderful treats.

Caroline's talk with Barry had gone much better than she had expected. He had been feeling guilty about binning her and Rob was starting to get on his nerves. Barry had agreed that for two nights each week Rob would be covering nights and she would work the day shift.

Barry had actually tried to scrap the night shift altogether but the police liaison officer felt it was serving a good purpose. In the six weeks it had been active there had not been a single report of knife crime. With this response Barry found himself unwilling to explain the truth behind his original request and as such they were stuck with his pointless night shift. He broke the news to Rob over a pint in the pub one night.

Pickles had taken to following Caroline as far as the viaduct, a good two hundred cat lengths from his domain on Woodbury Lane but the risks were well worth it as he usually received a couple more chunks of heaven when they parted ways at the bridge.

Tonight however a thick metallic smelling fluid caught his attention and he began to lick the red substance eagerly from the pavement.

"Come on pickles," Caroline cooed "want another kitty tweet?"

Pickles didn't respond he was obsessed with the delicious red nectar that speckled the concrete.

Caroline had only ever known the cat to have an interest in the treats and strokes. Crouching to examine, what had caught the cats most singular attentions she saw a child's footprint partially outlined. 'Was that paint? Red Paint?' Caroline reasoned that the cat probably had more sense than to lick at paint.

"Oh my god." she exclaimed.

The realisation hit her. It was blood. There was an injured child and guessing the child's direction, she broke into a run. Feeling as if she had matched wits with Sherlock Homes Caroline sprinted towards the Green. Nearing the post office on Redhill Road she dropped her prized Maglite. Stopping to pick it up and catch her breath she saw the foot prints take a right onto the Green. Filling her lungs with air she could see a particularly well defined footprint.

The toes were pointing towards her. Mentally smacking herself she let out an audible groan and turned back towards the viaduct. Jogging at a more sustainable pace back towards Pickles who still contently licked at the red patches.

Following the prints, some blurred some perfect but most just a splotch or two, under the viaduct and onto Finchdean Road. The trail swung left into a car park that went behind a large white pub. At the back of the poorly lit, open air parking spaces was a green recycling point. The partially smothered sobs of a child were coming from behind the clothing donation bin.

Caroline got closer and rounding the corner was assaulted by a smell, the girl stank of excrement. She was wearing a torn and stained Unicorn tee shirt. Sofie lay in a ball naked from the waist down. Exhausted, terrified and ready to die she was crying so deeply that Caroline's approach went unnoticed.

The Child seemed to explode as Caroline touched her shoulder. Sofie kicked out into the darkness towards Caroline's hand. Sofie tried to get to her feet and flee, she was panicking. Sure she had been caught, her legs were too exhausted to stand.

Sofie tried desperately to crawl to safety. Two of her fingernails ripped from their beds as she clawed frantically trying to grip broken concrete. She grabbed at weeds and bushes kicking up dust and debris in her attempted escape.

A brilliant light came on and Sofie could hear the voice of a woman. It sounded kind and soothing to her. In her manic state and with an adrenaline befuddled brain Sofie thought maybe the spirit of her dead mother had come to save her. Turning slowly towards the blinding light she could see an angel.

Caroline stopped pointing the bright torch directly into the child's eyes, realising she was blinding the girl.

Sofie could now see a bit more as her eyes adjusted she began to make out what she thought to be a police uniform. All of a sudden Caroline was being enveloped by the girl's small ragged arms, while their owner sobbed uncontrollably.

Something had happened. This was big this was important. Caroline knew she had to call this in, she needed a medical team and back up. Well trained, she took out her mobile and dialled three nines.

-3-

Thomas Anderson put down his little girl at the door to their country home ever so carefully. Gently placing her small feet upon the unyielding flagstone floor as if he worried about breaking her.

"How are you Sofie?" asked Tom, while he began to inspect the girl's every aspect "Did you have a good day?"

Sofie wriggled as her hair fell all over her face and got in her mouth, struggling to be free from his parental diligence.

"Yes Daddy, Why must you insist on looking me over?" with a shy smile she continued "every day it is like you have never seen me before or imagine I have met with some tragedy at school."

Tom began turning Sofie by her shoulders to the left and right. Still engaged in his appraisal.

"Sofie you are just so perfect," said Tom "I can't believe how fantastically you have turned out." with a wide grin "I want to remember this and every moment forever my perfect little girl."

Sofie unceremoniously deposited her heavy school bag, laden with dense technical manuals, upon the reception hall floor. Kicking off her pink plastic sandals she skipped towards their kitchen, intent on raiding the well stocked double breasted fridge. The kitchen in this country home was unusually large and exquisitely laid out.

Tom had built the cabinets and surfaces himself, not from some chipboard kit but rather, by hand with locally grown oak. The floor was made of solid stones and supported a large dark green Aga. Brass fittings and copper utensils occupied every nook and most of the crannies.

A truly monumental white stone sink sat beneath a window with such a grand view as to make any man jealous. In the middle of this culinary palace was a marble topped island. With two stools, a small vegetable sink, under counter storage and hanging rack above adorned with Analon cookware.

This is where Tom found Sofie already engaged in devouring the sliced ham he had bought that morning at the local cafe come shop.

"Hey slow down Sofie," chastised Tom "I bought that for both of us."

Sofie had never tasted ham so perfect and through pork laden teeth exclaimed.

"This is the best ham ever Dad."

The Shop in Compton stocks all manner of locally produced goods. Being primarily a cafe two thirds of its floor space is dedicated to the steady stream of hikers and cyclists that frequent it during the summer months. However, during the cold winter and wet autumn the cafe had taken to selling a few odds and ends to its local customers. This business decision had seen the cafe flourish, providing needed income during the much slower off season.

They had expanded their range and local artisans had petitioned the owners to sell their crafted goods. No finer selection of sausage rolls, pies or indeed cakes can be found anywhere south of Yorkshire itself.

The cafe overlooks a village square, of sorts, it has a little old well at its centre. The well provides a perfect spot to enjoy any selection of baked goods from the shop.

Any visitor to this slice of English history will be heartily disappointed by the pub. Not because it is a bad pub, in fact it's a charming and friendly establishment as welcoming as any in England. The problem being that it seems to align its opening hours with a long forgotten lunar calendar only known to the elderly male clients it services.

If you are lucky enough to visit while the pub is open you will find a particular breed of man in that bar. The type whose life is etched deeply upon his soil worn hands.

Tom retrieved a loaf of sourdough bread, also purchased in the Compton store, and set about making sandwiches. After a long day at school a well constructed sandwich will nullify the hunger of even the most active ten year old.

Sofie could smell the faintest trace of cordite in the air.

"Have you been hunting Daddy?" she asked.

Tom stopped his busy sandwich preparation and looked up to meet Sofie's brown eyes.

"How on earth did you guess that Sofie?" said Tom.

"I can smell your shotgun,"

It hung above the kitchen door well out of Sofie's reach. Tom was meant to keep it in a gun safe but he didn't see the point.

"That gun was fired almost two hours ago." he said.

He thought to himself how amazing her sense of smell was to detect traces of cordite so long ago expelled.

Sofie was quite pleased with her dad's reaction. She felt clever.

"So, did you get anything?" she asked "Are we having it for

dinner?"

Tom smiled and explained he had come across a brace of pheasants on the edge of a small wood near Finchdean. The birds would require hanging for a week or so to let the flavours develop properly.

"we will eat them once they are ready." he assured Sofie.

Looking up he noticed Sofie had stopped eating, her fist still full of ham she was looking rather meek. Sofie was remembering the gruesome roadside fatality.

"I'm not sure I will want to eat pheasant any more Father."

The business with the birds, quickly forgotten as sandwiches were washed down with lashings of lemonade. Once finished Sofie retreated to her room where she would read her treasured books and await the call for dinner.

Pink, so much pink, curtains, bedding, furniture, toys and even the carpet sang out in a myriad of tones derived from that most feminine of shades. Sofie was infatuated by the garish and jarring contrast her room gave to the rest of the house. She felt quite assuredly that her room was in fact the only one that showed the slightest hints of belonging in this century. The rest of her home resembling a scene from the pages of a James Herriot novel.

Sofie loved to read and grabbed a well thumbed copy of Prince Caspian by C.S. Lewis. She sank into the bright, fluffy bed and began to reread the tales of Narnia. A story she knew well but with each and every reading the story seemed new and fresh to her. As if she remembered the story but was reading the words for the first time.

"Sofie." called Tom up the stairs.

She marked her place and began her descent, pulled forward by smells that could have enticed even Aslan himself to their dinning table. On the dark wooden table sat a thing of such beauty and boundless delight that Sofie felt she may burst from excitement. Staring open mouthed at the home made dish it took her father's voice to break the spell cast upon her.

"It's only pizza Sofie." he said.

Sofie felt that was a completely ridiculous statement.

"Only pizza" she said in dismay "Dad, one does not simply confront a girl with pizza and expect no excitement"

Having quoted her favourite, if somewhat ancient, meme and enthralled by the melted cheese masterpiece Sofie felt this was the best moment of her life so far. With six weeks of holiday ahead and nothing even slightly dire to concern her little world, Sofie would later wish that her predictions of a enjoyable and exciting summer ahead had been even slightly correct.

The two sat at the table eating happily, Tom content to finally have his little girl all to himself and Sofie almost exploding with joy as she gobbled down bread, sauce, pepperoni and cheese.

"So, Sofie what do you want to do tomorrow?" Tom asked.

Sofie looked up, unable to reply, mouth hard at work.

"It's the first day of summer," said Tom "we should do something together?"

Through breadcrumbs and with sauce stained lips Sofie said one word "Zoo" then continued her efforts in the swallowing department. Sofie knew she was misbehaving, eating in such an egregiously unladylike fashion, she was however surprised that her dad didn't seem to mind. In fact he seemed amused at his little girl contentedly mimicking the eating habits of a Gannet chick. Trying to swallow slices intact and making a mess the likes of which an artisticly inclined pig would be proud. She didn't care. Sofie was sure this was the best pizza she had ever eaten as surely as if it had been her first.

The next day Tom and Sofie would pay a visit to Marwell Zoo. With all the wonderful animals it has to see and experience. Sofie's fondness for Aslan would find her singularly intent on her effort to see the lions.

It would be one of the last happy days she experienced this summer and Sofie wished she could revisit that day spent wandering the animal enclosures.

-4-

At three fifteen a.m. the flashing blue lights of a police car swung into the car park behind The Rowlands Castle public house. Ambulance and Dog unit just moments behind them. Doors slamming, the police officers rushed to Caroline's seated figure. Survival blankets in hand they tried to wrap Sofie's body in the silvery sheets.

When Sofie saw that the attending officers were male she became, if possible, more agitated and afraid withdrawing from them to bury herself in Caroline's ample bust. Sofie's wailing cry tore at the night's still air once more.

PCSO Caroline May said "back up guys she's terrified."

The two male officers retreated and Sofie's wails began to ease and Caroline tried to sooth the petrified bundle in her arms. As if any more proof was needed this girl embodied everything wrong with the male species. It was a man who had done this, a man who had destroyed the purity of this little girl's world.

Whispering such nicety's as "it's okay, It's going to be ok. I'll look after you" It was in this moment that Caroline knew she would do everything in her power to make sure that whoever had hurt this girl would be brought to justice. Nothing would stop her and nothing would save the, as then unknown, male from her wrath.

The paramedics arrived in a shower of flashing lights and with Caroline's help a pretty young female medic called Sam coaxed Sofie into the back of an ambulance.

The Police were talking to the publican who's initially hostile attitude, at being woken by them so early in the morning, had softened considerably once he understood what was happening. He had neither seen nor heard anything. The first thing he had known of the incident was the loud banging on his flat's door by the two uniformed officers.

The publican's portly wife Marge was frantically making cups of tea, for what else should one do in an emergency. As she scrambled for cups and tea bags her mind was busy constructing a story that would consume village gossip for the next few days. In this narrative her husband and she had been instrumental in this unknown child's rescue. Sheltering the poor girl until the police arrived.

No one knew what dark forces had pursued this girl but Marge could readily guess at what happened. The rumours about sex offenders being rehoused nearby had been circulating for years. Confirmed in part by tabloid fear mongering and the ever advancing march of the rumour mill.

Sofie sat in the ambulance with her knees pulled tight to her chin surrounded by blankets and medical equipment. Sam started running preliminary checks.

Caroline asked Sofie "hey sweetie, can you tell me your

name" No reply, "where did you come from" again no reply, not even any indication the girl had heard. Caroline inquired where she lived and countless other unanswered questions. Sofie was effectively mute.

Sam looked over to Caroline her face devoid of colour. Sam had seen this before, the tell tale bruising and damage to Sofie's genitals told a shocking but obvious story. She told Caroline "We have to call in the specialist officers."

Caroline acknowledged and not knowing how else to proceed began to stand in an attempt to exit the ambulance. This caused a violent reaction from Sofie, it shocked Sam to see the formerly silent girl squealing like a wounded animal. Sofie lunged for Caroline's arm grabbing at the retreating PCSO. Sofie forcefully shook her head and Caroline gave up on leaving.

Sam had satisfied herself that Sofie was in no immediate medical danger from any of her wounds so she went to tell the police officers to radio for the sex abuse team. When Sam returned to the ambulance she had been furnished with two cups of tea and a plate full of biscuits.

Marge's worst fears had been confirmed by what she had overheard. Sam's request was no more shocking than the paleness of her face. Confronted with the awful reality of this situation Marge had given up on the rescue story. Marge now hoped instead that tonight's activity would go unnoticed by the ancient and judgemental neighbours.

Another twenty minutes passed before Judith Chaplin added her police vehicle to the ever growing number behind the pub. Judith had trained as a sexual violence officer just three years ago. She had spent seventeen long years in uniform patrolling the streets and had been passed over for promotion many times. Judith felt the sexual violence team would be a good way to move up the ranks a little.

In the last three years though she had dealt with some disgusting and depraved jobs, it made her hate the work more than any small gripes about promotion had. After a couple of really violent incidents close together Judith had brushed with full blown depression.

The mental health support for officers in this line of work being passable at best. After tonight little would shock Judith again apart from the hourly rates that the private therapists would be charging her.

Judith assessed the situation and planed her next step. With Sam's preliminary medical suspicion of rape on a minor the next step was to get the girl to the crisis centre and in front of a doctor. No amount of training or psychology could separate this child from her saviour though, Caroline would just have to come along for the ride.

The sexual abuse crisis centres are staffed around the clock by highly trained specialist doctors. The centres should also have a number of social workers on call at all times. Well, they used to but the city council has driven its childcare team so hard and so far, for so long that social workers are only expected to last six to nine months in the job. Underpaid and overworked has never been so aptly applied.

With case loads for individual staff well exceeding government recommendations and at dangerous levels for many years now. It is only a matter of time till children begin to suffer. The fact that they hadn't already is a testament to the amazing front line staff who go above and beyond their duty. Regularly skipping holidays and working unpaid overtime has become the rule, no longer an exception. Day in day out these people trade their physical and mental health for a cause they firmly believe in without reward or recognition.

Judith's car sped away towards Cosham, its damaged and

broken cargo on board, just as the canine unit finally arrived. Driving one of Hampshire constabulary's newest vehicles, sergeant Garry Atkins arrived with his canine partner secured in a specially designed dog cage.

Piggsy knew she had work to do. Piggsy was excited and Piggsy was ready. The shaggy German Sheppard leapt from the back of Garry's car ready to protect or hunt she loved her work. Her friend and master was securely holding an extra long black webbing lead that fastened to her collar.

Having been briefed and after refusing the proffered cup of tea Gary showed Piggsy to the green recycling point. She sniffed around and could smell fear pheromones thick in the air mixed with some kind of weird blood and other bodily fluids. Piggsy knew her job, she had been well trained and she would follow the blood like smell.

Trivial at first, Piggsy could even see the trail of marks and drops through the village. Leading along Redhill Road, across to The Green and towards The Fairway, a road that doubled back to parallel The Green.

Garry and Piggsy followed the trail past glass fronted high street shops and into red bricked, slate roofed suburbia. From the Fairway they went left and headed North along The Peak. It was only a hundred meters along this road that the blood like trail had finished, or started depending on your point of view.

Piggsy was a clever girl and she had realised the blood scent was also mixed with the smell of urine and human scat. She could follow this trail just as easily and continued north galloping paw by paw.

At Greatfield Way it was a right turn then a left onto Bowes Hill. The headlong chase continued. On the corner of Wellsworth Lane and Bowes Hill Piggsy became lost, the scent trails overlapping and criss crossing. The Strange animal that had left these markings had run back and fourth as if they had no objective in mind.

Investigating a little further along Wellsworth Lane, Piggsy found that the smells continued this way to the East. The hunt was on again. At the end of Wellsworth Lane a large private residence with thatched roof and swimming pool loomed but was quickly behind them as the duo headed into open countryside. The intrepid sleuth and her master headed over field and fence north towards Finchdean they ran.

A torrent ensued as the sky opened, depositing water that had until this afternoon enjoyed its floaty existence in the English channel. Ripped from the waves by the Sun's energy only to be condensed again by it absence. The droplets rejoining their fellows to fall once more upon the earth. Slamming into the ground and pounding the soil till sodden and seeping. The drops begin a slow but inevitable journey back to the sea once more. Through muddy fields and fast flowing rivers the water was fated to retread a journey old and familiar.

The rain itself posed no problem for Piggsy but it stirred up a cacophony of smells, obscuring any one particular scent. She whined and looked about inquisitively for her prey. It was no use she had lost the trail.

Garry, realising they had failed, put in a radio call to the two lads at the pub. Ten minutes later he could see his shiny new car being driven along Dean Lane towards him. The pair were picked up now, soaked to the skin and just two hundred metres south of Finchdean. A tiny village that holds many of its own secrets.

-5-

It was finally here, today was the day that excitement filled the air, this morning they were going to go see the lions. Sofie had, in her eagerness, rushed her dad out of the door at eight o'clock promptly. She had dragged, pushed and pulled at his clothes until he had occupied the driving position. Sofie jumped in the passenger seat making circular movements with her hand.

"Lets go come on move em out" said Sofie

Forty minutes long the journey had been insufferable. Sofie was agitated by her need to be first through the Zoo's gate. Their car rounded the corner into a deserted car park and Sofie's heart fell. Her mind grasping for explanations, surely the car park would have been busy if not full? There were only twenty minutes till the gates should open.

Sofie settled on the most pessimistic scenario, a catastrophe must have befallen the zoo forcing its closure. Tom parked the car within feet of the shuttered ticket booths.

Sofie was confounded and her tiny shoulders slumped in a general malaise. She was sure that nothing had ever disappointed her as much as this dismal day.

"Sofie what time is Marwell Zoo meant to open?" Asked Tom.

To her mind this was a spiteful question to ask. As if the loss of her days fun was not blow enough to her mood, now she must contend with her dads pointless questions.

"Nine a.m." She spat "every thing opens at nine, everyone knows that."

The darkness of Sofie's mood kept her arms crossed and head down, she took a while to notice that Tom was trying to draw her attention to his phone.

He childishly wagged and waved the backlight screen in her face. 'Ten A.M' the website proclaimed. 'No, it can't be' she thought. 'Everything opens at nine', but there it was in black and white. 'Ten till four every day'.

"Well that's just silly" said Sofie bitterly. She was relieved beyond measure but that brought with it a feeling of guilt. "I'm so sorry Daddy" she said in hopes of forgiveness.

Deciding that honesty was the best approach "I know you told me to check but I got distracted by all the stuff on the website and forgot, I assumed they would be open at nine though."

Over the next hour and twenty minutes Sofie regaled her father with endless facts and a great amount of trivia that she had learned on the Zoo's excellent website. Knowledge poured forth from the recesses of her memory on every animal and exhibit.

The car park slowly began to fill as ten o'clock approached, the queues began to slowly grow. Sofie and Tom were first in line to buy their tickets. Sofie was literally shaking with anticipation and excitement.

Once through the gates it was all Tom could do to keep up with his energetic little Sofie. She wasn't intentionally misbehaving by running off but she had become so overwhelmed by the impending fun that Sofie quite forgot her manners. She ran straight for the lion's enclosure, stopping only to check signposts and ignoring all the other animals they passed. Sofie only gave a passing glance to the penguins, her favourite birds, resolving to return later to ogle their funny little ways.

Tom had learned, from Sofie's trivia lesson, that the lions were a recent addition to the Zoo's collection and there was some doubt about how long they would be at the Zoo. Tom's naturally cynical mind wondered if that was indeed true or just a fear of missing out tactic that the Zoo's marketing department had devised in an attempt to maximise the profit from this year's school holiday.

Tom finally caught up to Sofie.

"you mustn't run off like that Sofie" he said coughing and now leaning on his knees for support he realised that his life as a computer engineer had not kept him in any sort of athletic condition. Tom wasn't overweight like so many in his profession but he also wasn't getting his daily dose of cardio either

"Please stay with me ok Sofie? It could be dangerous if we get separated"

This request barely registered with Sofie's conscious processes, her full attention transfixed on the golden brown creature standing proudly before her. Sofie was sure the lion was a friendly one just like Aslan but no amount of pleading had convinced Tom to allow Sofie to take part in the 'meet and greet' VIP experience package.

Tom seemed to see one of the brightly coloured adverts for this overpriced gimmick every couple of metres around the Zoo. The privileged child could get a bit closer to the animals or have a more involved encounter, if you paid an exorbitant fee.

With some of the non venomous snakes a brave child could hold them for photos that came at an extra cost. The Penguin Adventure involved feeding them sardines from a bucket while inside their enclosure. There were lots of furry rodents available for petting and pictures. Exotic parrots could be placed on shoulders and coaxed into speaking.

Sadly, in a forgotten corner of the Zoo's picnic area stood one lonely goat, often overlooked in these surroundings. Petting him was free of charge yet seldom enjoyed by either child or goat. It had been many months since his photo had been taken except by accident.

The lion's enclosure had a small cage in the middle that was accessed by a brick lined tunnel. A keeper would take the VIP through the tunnel and throw meat scraps out to attract the beasts.

Being honest with herself Sofie thought it was not that much better in the small cage with the keeper than out here, observing the majestic cats from the path. Both the general public and the VIPs were separated from the lions by steel bars anyway. She couldn't help but feel a little shard of envy when one of the biggest males took a fierce swipe at the VIP cage. The terrified children of rich parents were in no real danger.

One little boy did learn why the Zoo's staff had taken to keeping a supply of fresh towels and cheap undergarments just out of sight in the tunnels entrance.

"Next up Penguins" Sofie shouted in a maniacal fashion. Imitating a stereotypical penguin waddle with both arms pressed firmly to her sides and heels together she left the lions behind and tottered off towards her flightless feathered friends and their glass sided swimming pool.

Tom was much happier with this method of travel. He was easily able to keep up and his heart rate was not skyrocketing above the one eighty mark. He felt bad about refusing Sofie's pleadings at the lions cage. She wasn't to know he could easily afford the overpriced attraction.

It was his fear that had made him refuse her request not fiscal responsibility. He was being irrational but didn't like the idea of Sofie in that tiny cage. He also didn't trust her to obey the warnings about keeping fingers inside the protective bars. Sofie was just so naïve, he knew she would want to pet the great cats and would probably end up losing an arm. On the other hand what harm could a penguin do?

He would send her in to their chilly domain with as many sardines as she could carry. 'Hang the cost' he thought even if kilo for kilo these sardines were going to cost more than the finest Russian Caviar.

As it turned out, penguins could do an awful lot of damage. The staff dragged Sofie from the pool she had fallen into. Tom belatedly realising that sending an excited thirty kilo ten year old laden with five kilos of assorted fish into a pen containing over thirty hungry penguins, had in retrospect been a kind but bad decision.

The viciously cute birds registered the new addition to their environment, as one they descended upon an unbalanced and ill prepared Sofie. Taken all at once the birds combined weight was ninety seven kilos.

Tom and the Penguin Keeper had realised their mistake simultaneously. This was an adventure that should have been undertaken after the penguins had enjoyed their breakfast.

Still wet but wrapped in a warm Zoo towel Sofie was returned to Tom's safe keeping. "Sorry Sofie" he began in an ashamed voice.

She looked up at his downturned eyes

"Sorry?" She said "Why are you sorry that was amazing."

Sofie's jubilant tone immediately lifting Tom's spirits

"They were all over me Dad, didn't you see dad? One even hit me in the face with his flipper"

She recounted the experience excitedly in explicit detail.

In Tom's mind he had pictured Sofie methodically feeding the occasional bird one at a time. Crouching down and being excited as the gentle creatures took a fish every now and again. With her extra large stock the experience would have lasted Sofie many minutes.

In Sofie's opinion there was no greater fun to be had anywhere. Being dog piled by thirty mackerel crazed penguins would be the highlight of her day. It was a brief but also memorable occurrence.

The rest of the day had flown by for the pair in a whirlwind of fur, feathers and scales. Sofie had visited the lions no less than three separate times and even shared her sandwiches with a moody but appreciative goat. Just after closing Sofie had reluctantly left all the zebras, giraffes, meerkats, monkeys and more behind.

She trudged to their car laden with gift shop treasures and a free souvenir towel. On the way home Sofie had set about asking her dad if he liked or disliked each and every animal. Tom's favourite had been the snow leopard. Sofie agreed the white spotted cat was definitely a top tier feature but she had preferred the penguins overall.

Exhausted Tom was not sure which of them would sleep better tonight.

-6-

The next morning Tom set about filling his expensive coffee machine. With the practised ease of a true caffeine addict he brought it to life. After much hissing and spluttering the machine's work complete, he sipped at a strong and bitter mug of the finest coffee ever to grace the intestines of a rainforest tree cat.

They are called Civets and the coffee beans that they eat are gathered after being digested and deposited on the rainforest floor. Undamaged by the internal workings of these mammals the beans are dried, roasted and then sold to the best cafes

Tom was making the first sleepy steps towards breakfast when his tablet began to ring.

"Hello Tom" A posh and business like voice said. "I am just checking in old chap. How is everything going your end?"

Tom would be working from home over the next six weeks, his career in programming allowed him a lot of flexibility.

"Hi Pat. It's great, amazing in fact". Tom began recounting every detail of his time with Sofie since leaving the office on Friday. Patrick listened politely to Tom's rambling description of lions and penguins.

The pair had worked together for over twenty years now and were as well versed in each others' social lives, or lack of, as they were in the minutia of complex algorithms. Patrick had known Sofie all her life and he cared about her a lot. If either of the men had been religious then Patrick would have been named Sofie's god father.

Patrick was technically Tom's 'boss' but the working relationship was closer to a partnership. Both men had played equal parts in the success of their company. The work they had done together, secured various military and government contracts.

"Listen Tom" said Patrick shifting his tone "I know it is Sunday but could you be an egg and get me a report by email? Just a brief update on our little projects progress? I have a few of her majesty's finest dogging me for more information"

Tom had no objections, Patrick had given him a direction and a purpose, even a new chance at life.

"Yep no worries I will send it over after breakfast though. Ok Pat?" Tom could hear his friend saying

"good man, good man"

Tom hit the red icon and ended the call. Tom's work came with some serious risks. Not sure how law enforcement or the greater world would react to their current project, the thought of government backing gave Tom a little relief from the worry.

Over those last twenty years their company's security clearance had moved swiftly from secret to top secret and beyond. In a market saturated with tech startups and silicon millionaires Tom and Patrick had set themselves apart by not asking or answering any unofficial questions.

Realising he was just staring past the white tiled wall Tom grabbed his favourite Analon skillet and set about breakfast anew.

Bacon is a most curious passion. Even the limpest of offerings found in plain plastic packets on discount supermarket shelves can, once cooked, produce an aroma which will wake the deepest of sleepers. It is an unfortunate man though who knows only the smell and not the truest taste that should accompany it.

Hear someone proclaiming that they 'like the smell of bacon but it doesn't ever taste as good' you can be assured that this person has never had the good sense to buy locally produced, traditionally raised and cured rashers.

It is a similar story with the simple egg. The shop bought variety resembling the home grown ones in shell shape alone. For this reason, Tom had constructed a small chicken coop at the end of his garden. He heads there now to search inside the straw filled milk crate nesting boxes that hopefully contain a vital part of his and Sofie's breakfast.

The kitchen door that leads to the small patio and much larger garden was already open. A mild fog surrounding his thoughts he tried to remember. He had definitely closed it, he was sure of that. He was also sure he had locked the door. He glanced at the decorative wall hanger where last night he had placed the tiny brass key.

The brightly painted wooden cockerel had two hooks instead of feet and they were empty, the key was gone. Instantly a cold sweat erupted from him. If someone wanted to know anything about his work there was no better way to get that information than by taking Sofie. This nightmare scenario had plagued Tom's more paranoid thoughts almost daily.

"Sofie." called Tom. No reply. "Sofie" he calls again, this time as a yell with fear seeping into his voice. He was half way up the stairs but could already see her pink palace devoid of princess. Jumping the last few steps and barging into the room calling again and again. He checked bathroom and closet. No sign of his darling Sofie. In a blind sprint and only wrapped in dressing gown he descended the stairs two at a time then ran outside bellowing for Sofie. Only crows in the distance returned his screeching tone.

Wrinkled by fear his panic stricken face scans the world.

"Where is she" he says through gritted teeth, anger beginning to build inside himself.

The worst sort of rage anyone can feel is the one directed internally. Blaming himself for careless actions and knowing it was his own fault that this tragedy had beset him. The lack of an external target making the anger build to a crescendo inside him. She is gone and life might as well be over. Consumed by rage and self loathing Tom didn't see the latch on the garden gate begin to rise.

Tom did however hear the familiar squeal of hinges in need of oil. Desperately hopeful but also afraid, Tom's eyes swing and fixate upon the black gate. As if in slow motion the door makes a laborious arc and his precious Sofie is revealed unharmed and just a little muddy.

He would later feel ashamed at his immediate response but in the heat of the moment and driven half mad with worry he sprung upon his sweetest Sofie. Taking hold of her arm with excessive force he near enough screamed at her

"Where the fuck were you?"

Instantly Sofie collapsed into tears and pathetic whimpering. His insanely misplaced anger left him as suddenly as it had come. Realising he had gone too far he hugged the now limp and sobbing Sofie

"I'm sorry Sofie I'm so sorry I was just so worried, Please understand I'm sorry. I was angry"

Sofie had recovered her feet and tried explaining herself. She had woken early and gone to the woods expecting to see her squirrel friend. She didn't know why this had annoyed her dad because she remembered spending many mornings in similar ways.

"if I knew I shouldn't have gone Daddy I wouldn't have"

Sofie was still unsure as to what she had done wrong but was beginning to accept she was at fault anyway.

"I'm sorry I made you worry Daddy"

"It's ok Sofie" relented Tom "it's my fault. I didn't tell you about the new rules, come inside and help me with breakfast, we need to talk about some necessary precautions"

The Aga had been stoked up to temperature and Sofie helped her dad with the heavy pots and pans. Collecting oil, salt and pepper her assistance given gladly. The thick bacon began to fry as Tom realised he had forgotten the eggs while he was caught up in frantic paranoia.

"Sofie would you mind collecting the eggs today?"

Sofie's eyes light up and she was outside again before Tom had even handed her the little woven egg basket.

Sofie adored the funny looking chickens with their poofball heads and multicoloured feathers. Captain Flaps their rooster could be quite an aggressive little fellow at times. He would fluff up his feathers and rush anyone who dared to enter his domain. Protecting his harem with vim and vigour from any opponent big or small, beak, talons and spurs could deter even the most determined of predators.

Tom had made the coop in such a way that the nesting boxes were accessible from outside the run, legs could remain unscathed while collecting the eggs.

Sofie's favourite chicken was affectionately known as Henrietta. A most original name she thought. Sofie opened the heavy wooden flap, Henrietta was sitting in one of the straw lined nesting boxes. After a couple of strokes Sofie carefully lifted the fat bird to her feet and watched as she ruffled her feathers and went off to investigate the food situation. Four perfect eggs lay cushioned in the nest and Sofie carefully collected them before returning to the house.

She skipped happily along the uneven stone path with her

precious cargo clutched lovingly to her chest. She entered the kitchen with three remaining eggs and a freshly dirtied shoe. Fragments of shell, yolk stains and a copious amount of albumin telling their tale of baskets forgotten.

Tom looked at the mess and smirked to himself.

"forget this did we?" he said swinging the little basket back and forth.

The pair sat together demolishing breakfast. Tom knew he needed to have a proper chat with his little Sofie. Unsure how to begin he started

"OK Sofie I need you to understand how important this is."

She nodded slowly, eyes once more downward and fixed on her egg stained shoes.

-7-

Judith, driving Sofie and Caroline to the twenty four hour crisis centre had cut through Redhill and sped north along the single carriageway road that would get her to the A3M, a main road that joins Portsmouth's main transport artery, the M27.

Judith quickly navigated tight turns and hairpin bends before joining the three lane motorway near Horndean. She hit the slip road and her foot pushed the accelerator down hard. The three litre engine began to whine as the revs went towards the red. Once on the motorway she was able to safely push the car's engine and cover distance much faster than if she had taken the back roads. Countryside views gave way to concrete and eventually city lights were visible in the distance.

Passing an all night Macdonald's full of half cut students who were unaware of the horror that had taken place while they enjoyed over priced drinks in an over rated club. The local nightclubs had all closed around the time that Sofie was found. The party goers night was finishing up with a well practised drunken stumble towards hot food and soggy chips, while Sofie was being coaxed from behind the bin.

Judith was glad that these kids didn't have to deal with the problems she faced everyday but was aware that any of them might end up as her next case. The girls in glamorous dresses just a little too short to provide any real protection from the early morning temperatures and the boys with their alcohol fuelled posturing. Things could easily deteriorate into the type of situation that made up Judith's day to day.

The sun was starting to put in an appearance and first light was getting brighter

"How we doing back there?" Judith called while her eyes remained firmly on the road ahead.

Caroline had no idea how to respond. The visible wounds were only a minor problem compared to the psychological injuries Caroline imagined Sofie must be suffering from.

Looking up she said "I guess she's ok"

Sofie gave a small nod of agreement and her small hands clung even tighter to Caroline's small frame.

"Yeah we're good, Sofie is ok." Caroline confirmed over the noise of the performance engine.

Judith's car came to an abrupt halt outside a nondescript building, she slid off her seatbelt and got out to assist Caroline with Sofie. They had finally arrived at the sexual abuse centre. Greeted by two female doctors and a social worker the group made their way inside.

The request for a rape swab was serious enough but with a minor involved all the staff knew they were in for an emotionally draining admittance.

Judith and Caroline gently guided Sofie through the doors and into the well lit reception hall. These places try hard to be welcoming and appear safe, designed to mimic a normal living room. They unfortunately fall foul of the same design and decoration philosophy that allows you to recognise a doctors office anywhere in the world. The slight hints at a medical purpose and consistently beige colour scheme only broken up by noticeboards and chairs that both seem to be upholstered with the same blue felt material. Caroline was sure the NHS only had one catalogue of furniture to choose from and the layouts were repeated up and down the country. Caroline and Sofie took to finding a comfy seat while the others discussed the admittance.

Judith would liaise primarily with the Ellen Mackenna the social worker and brief her on the case while Sofie was examined by the two young doctors.

Both doctors were trained in forensic examinations these two had seen enough over the years to know this was a particularly violent crime even by their standards. The youngest of the pair approached Sofie

"Hey sweetie,"

It felt like the tenth time tonight that Sofie had been addressed in this way.

"would it be ok if we had a look at you in there" gesturing to a door marked private.

Sofie began to nod but tightened her grip on Caroline's arm.

Starting to wonder how strong this little girl was,

"It's ok hun I promise I will wait right here for you." Said Caroline.

Sofie shook her head so violently half dry tears and dirt flew from her face.

"Ok you want me to come with you that's fine"

Sofie stopped shaking and the beginning of a smile touched her lips. Feeling like she had got her own way, Sofie resigned herself to whatever fresh horrors lay behind the beige painted door.

"Aww poor girl" said the young lady doctor. Turning to Caroline she continued "I'm sorry miss but you do have to wait out here though. I'm sure you understand"

Caroline detected a patronising tone in the medics slow cadence but thought nothing more of it as the pressure on her arm shot up, to the point she was worried it might break.

The medic had taken hold of Sofie's shoulder and tried to lead her away from the still seated Caroline. Sofie was clinging on for dear life. Reflexively Caroline's free hand came up to claw at the painful crushing. The doctor was pulling harder on Sofie's body and her little feet left the white linoleum floor tiles.

Sofie could see the pain she was causing in Caroline's eyes and not meaning to hurt this kind lady she let go instantly. The doctor stumbled back with Sofie in hand and dragged her towards the forensic office.

"Can't you see she is scared you heartless bitch, let her go" shouted Caroline, in pain and already emotionally drained she couldn't deal with this as well.

Judith was restraining Caroline before she could get to her feet.

"They've got to do their job Caroline, let them get on with it. Ok?"

Evidence gathering and preservation is the most important thing at this point in an investigation. With a willing adult participant this process is invasive and embarrassing. Usually the victims need for justice can keep them going through the swabs, examinations and photos.

Trying to conduct the same tests with an uncooperative and screaming eleven year old would leave psychological wounds on both the doctors. Some physical ones too. Sofie had lashed out and broken the younger doctors nose when she tried to separate Sofie's legs. Realising what she had done, Sofie seemed to just switch off and she lay limp, completely unresponsive, allowing the medical team to conduct the required tests and procedures without any further hindrance.

Caroline could hear the little girl's screams, each one tearing at her heart. She would never forget the sounds coming from inside that room but when they stopped suddenly Caroline became even more worried and wished for their return.

Caroline was recounting how she had found the little girl to Judith and any other details she could remember about the scene. The two sat sipping tea and staring at the beige door with its black and white 'private' sign, waiting for news.

The forensic evidence was gathered and photographs taken, revealing the extent of Sofie's abuse. Sofie had been sodomized and raped multiple times. Her body was badly damaged all over with so much bruising that the doctors were surprised she was still alive. Five major head impacts had happened recently and her neck and arms had been forcefully restrained. It looked like Sofie had been subjected to a sustained and violent campaign of abuse. DNA had been retrieved and sent to the local lab for sequencing.

When the beige door opened, Sofie emerged subdued and compliant. Caroline stood up and ran to the girl, sliding on her knees she hugged Sofie who began regaining some animation. Caroline knew the doctors had an almost impossible job, she knew it was hard but necessary work. She knew they were the good guys and were on Sofie's side but Caroline had hated how they had dragged the distressed girl away. Caroline felt no sympathy when she saw the younger one's bloody and misshapen nose.

Sofie had been given a basket of luxury toiletries and a fresh set of expensive designer clothing. Sofie's unicorn tee shirt was now occupying a clearly labelled evidence bag. All of the gifts had been donated by the Dutchess of Cambridge. Her charity provides the best of the best to similar centres up and down the country.

. Caroline lead Sofie to the comforting showers. A completely different environment to the medical exam room. Sofie had reluctantly agreed to wash herself with a little nod. Caroline had promised to wait for her just outside the sweetly smelling cubicle. As the water washed the blood and dirt from her body Sofie slumped and her body began to shake. Her back slid down the white tiled wall while she hugged her knees in tight.

"Thank you." Said Sofie in a very small voice.

-8-

Sofie climbed out of the shower and wrapped herself in a bright pink towel. Warm and fluffy this was her favourite towel but it didn't improve her mood. 'How dare he' she thought to herself 'he could stuff his stupid rules'. Tom was downstairs listening to Sofie shower and cringing every time she slammed a door or dropped one of the plastic toiletry bottles on purpose.

They had finished breakfast while Tom laid out some of the things he felt needed to happen for her safety. They would be installing some cameras around the home and garden. Sofie was fine with this idea and had even offered to help with the installation. Sofie wasn't to leave the garden without supervision. This was a bit annoying but she had agreed and decided to work out the details later.

While they were out and about in public Sofie was to always stay within Tom's sight. She had agreed only after being threatened with constant hand holding. Lastly she was to have her internet usage monitored and restricted. Not knowing exactly what her dad meant by this she had asked. Tom told her that she would not be allowed onto any social media and a huge argument had begun.

Sofie had never actually set up any accounts but she was planning to. The photo sharing sites and video lip syncing apps looked like a lot of fun.

While at the Zoo she had made Tom take countless photos of her in front of each animal so that she could start her own page with lots of interesting pictures. She had even thought of uploading the video of her impromptu penguin assisted bath. Tom had no idea that was what she wanted the photos for, thinking he was just preserving the memories for later.

Tom's work with computers had made him distrustful of their more common and day to day uses. He knew exactly how vulnerable those social sites were and valued his privacy. He felt a certain amount of disdain for the people who post their most intimate information for all the world to abuse.

Tom felt even online shopping was too risky if you didn't want scammers having your credit card details. With this outlook firmly ingrained, Tom found it genuinely hard to see the same appeal that Sofie saw in social media.

She could whine and moan all she wanted there was no way she could get round the security measures he had already put in place to block all the well known sites. He figured the obscure sites would hold no interest for her, most having a limited or niche user base.

Tom had spent a productive afternoon installing the firewall that controlled all incoming and outgoing connections to the house's ethernet cable based network. Wifi was for idiots in his opinion 'if it has an Ethernet port you should use it', only his and Sofie's mobile devices were on the wireless network.

The off the shelf software was good enough for his purposes and was highly customizable. He had uploaded some amusing animations to the software but left most of the preconfigured settings alone.

Sofie stomped her way back into her bedroom now dry she began to dress.

"He never said anything about looking at the sites" she grumbled at Mr Ted.

Feeling rebellious, she opened up her bright pink laptop and powered it on. Sofie was struck by a wave of childish and pedantic genius. Grabbing her old digital camera she started taking pictures of the well loved teddy.

"He only said I couldn't have a profile Mr Ted, he never said you couldn't"

Pleased with her idea, Sofie opened the browser window and searched the name of a few sites she had heard of. No results.

"Strange" she said aloud.

Switching tactics she entered the well known address of the worlds largest social networking site. A blue stick figure ran onto her screen and began wagging its finger. She realised it was meant to be a police man and also that this was exactly the kind of thing her dad found amusing. In that moment she did the most naughty and rebellious thing she had ever done.

"Fuck you" she whispered at the floor above Tom's head.

Sofie instantly regretted it clapping her hands to her mouth. She hadn't meant it but she was just so mad. Having known the word for ages she had never thought it, let alone used it, before. It wasn't so much the word but the intent behind it that shook her. Never having wished anything bad for anyone before, she couldn't pin down exactly why she had in that moment. It felt natural to say though, even if the word itself was alien to her lips. Feeling guilty about saying it aloud she reasoned that she probably never would have said it but after all Daddy had said it to her an hour ago.

-9-

Caroline was surprised it was still only twenty past five in the morning after all that had happened, could it really have been just a couple of hours? Her colleges would be knocking on doors and asking a few uncomfortable questions soon.

The police could do nothing else without knowing Sofie's name. On call Judges had been petitioned and the slow grinding legal processes were in motion. These specialists only approve legal requests and make sure that the courts can operate twenty four hours a day to grant things like search warrants or emergency protection orders. Sofie would be safe she, would be protected by a seventy two hour holding order.

Fresh staff were due to arrive at the crisis centre and the smell of coffee was beginning to fill the air, the doctors, social workers and police all began to embark upon their next tasks. Reports needed to be written and evidence chains secured. Sofie's unknown abuser would be pursued from every conceivable angle.

This small group of investigators would do everything they could to find him . Each one of the women knew that the antagonist they imagined would be found eventually they just had to play their part and wait for results.

The evidence that had been diligently recovered would inevitably seal the attacker's fate. Forensics could not assist the investigators in their pursuit this time but it would provide the required proof to convict once the culprit was found.

There were no unusual clues to lead the detectives on their trail, nothing that could help find the perpetrator. The marks and bruising on Sofie were too confused and numerous to provide any helpful description. With Sofie still mute and the trail cold they needed a lead to follow. Something, anything, to point them in the right direction.

The sun was well on its way up when Caroline finally left the crisis centre. The mercury already hitting thirty degrees celsius. Avoiding the extreme daytime temperatures was just about the only positive feature of working the night patrol. She weighed up the different costs and benefits of private hire cars versus public buses. Deciding on the air conditioned electric bus she had no more than two minutes to wait.

This time of day saw most commuters on their way into the city and Caroline had her choice of seats. She boarded the driverless vehicle and her bank account was automatically debited by the public transport authority. Recognised by the myriad cameras and sensors, a civil servant would only pay a minimum fee for transport. The general public however, would be charged per kilometre once they departed the conveyance but for Caroline this was a cheap, easy option.

She stared out of the wide glass windows and began to asses her internal state. The bus rolled out of the city and north towards home. Never had she dealt with anything this traumatic. Replaying the events over in her mind like a short but tragic movie. She ran through her memories of the night up until the point where Sofie was taken by the social worker. Sofie had been lead away into protective custody by Ellen after having considerably warmed to her.

Ellen had brought out her laptop to type up some field notes, Sofie had marvelled at the sleek metallic construction. It was a dark shade of hot pink. Compared to Sofie's pink plastic computer at home this was a much more adult and professional device.

Sensing Sofie's interest in the laptop Ellen had sat Sofie on her lap and let the little girl run her hands over the wafer thin brushed aluminium surface. Delighted by the shifting tones and reflective coating Sofie was sure this was the best computer she had ever seen.

Caroline's mind contrasted the approach of the friendly and confident Ellen with that of the cold utilitarian approach of the doctors. She must have slipped into sleep, the bus ride seeming to take no more than a couple of minutes.

Caroline walked the familiar journey from town square to her little flat only stopping to pick up a few of her standard rations. The shopkeeper commenting that he only continued to stock the noodle cups for her benefit. Caroline was so shell shocked that the normality of life around her seemed foreign. She hadn't even acknowledged the daily joke about her woefully inadequate diet.

Caroline drifted home, past people going about their daily

business as if nothing had happened. The people didn't know what she had experienced, they couldn't imagine the extent of her grief. She walked, consumed by her thoughts and no longer a part of the civilised world that carried on around her.

Caroline entered her flat and with a remote, set her air-conditioning to run full blast as she sank into the depths of depression once more. DVD selected and pot noodle half eaten, she finally lapsed into a disturbed day's sleep. Racked by guilt laden dreams and uncomfortable positions she slept on her couch. The people outside worked and played, completely at ease unmolested, by the events her mind was so painfully replaying.

She woke just as the sun had started to dip behind houses. Caroline was freezing, having set her air con unit too high before falling asleep.

The diligent machine had continued to remove heat from the room. Nothing would stop its compressor from pushing the energy out through constricted pipes into the already scorchingly hot air outside. This marvellous device would fight a never ending thermodynamic battle until instructed to stop by either its captain the thermostat or commander in chief, Caroline's remote control. Communication lines with the thermostat severed by the control units instructions to cool regardless of ambient conditions.

This quiet war raged for hours with the forces of refrigeration causing a continuous attrition to the opposing side, while the defensive lines of insulation slowed the ingress of energetic reinforcements. As time passed the temperature steadily fell, eventually rousing Caroline from her sleep.

Feeling betrayed by its general, the machine was instructed to undo all of the good work it had achieved. The control unit was struck by the loss of endless watt hours sacrificed in the pursuit of cooling. The machine once again sent out a call to arms. Its mechanical parts employed this time to restock enemy positions. As the warmed air began to circulate Caroline got up off the couch and went to have a shower.

She felt keenly aware that her depression had been transformed into anger while she slept. The disturbing memories hardening her resolve to do something about Sofie's assault. Caroline's subconscious had worked to obfuscate the sadness and replace it with motivation. Standing in front of the bathroom mirror, clothes discarded she waited for the heating element in the shower unit to do it's work.

"Get up, push forward" she said to the reflection.

Caroline wasn't going to be a victim any more she wasn't going to let the greater world define who she was. The time had come for her to wrestle control of her life from the doctrines she had assimilated. Caroline stepped into the now warm shower. Collapsing to her knees, reminded of the little girl, once more Caroline screamed at the floor and beat the anti slip tiles with her fists. Tears lost in the cascade of water around her, she eventually found her feet and finished her shower.

Judith had provided her with contact details and asked Caroline to call if she remembered anything else about the case. Caroline knew that this was Judith's case but it bothered her that there was nothing she could do to help. Caroline wasn't even a real police officer let alone a detective. She felt that this incident was at least partly her responsibility as well, it was tough to let go. She had found the little girl in her hour of need. Caroline couldn't just walk away now, not after how much Sofie had clung to her for support. She had to at least find out what was happening.

Putting the kettle on to boil and switching the air conditioning settings to once again cool the now uncomfortably warm living room, Caroline dialled Judith's number. The connection went live as Judith's voice replaced the synthesised ringing tone.

"Hello?"

"Hi is that Judith? It's Caroline"

Judith had confirmed and their conversation continued past nicety on towards business.

"I'm sorry Caroline, I just can't discuss an open investigation with anyone." Judith really did sound sorry. "Look I know how you must feel about it but it's standard procedure, you know?"

Caroline resorted to thinly veiled begging and Judith's voice started to sound agitated, obviously concerned but held back from divulging any information. About to hang up Judith made a snap decision

"Hey Caroline I have to go but I can meet you for a coffee. Ok? How does that sound?" Taking any glimmer of hope she could get Caroline readily agreed.

"Sure Judith, that sounds great. I can send you a location pin on maps if you like?" Judith had thanked her and Caroline rushed to throw on her uniform.

Fifteen minutes later, Caroline sat in the Italian coffee shop near her house. She had taken a seat away from the glass fronted counter, facing the door so she could see when Judith arrived. Caroline ordered two long black coffees and her furtive glances alternated between watching the clock and the door, her coffee was all but forgotten. Another three minutes passed before Judith entered, to Caroline it had felt like hours.

In her black uniform and high visibility vest Judith presented a much more imposing figure than Caroline's. Caroline waved as if to an old friend and pointing, she indicated the two mugs in front of her, cutting short Judith's quest for service.

"Hey, thanks" said Judith lifting the coffee after taking her seat.

Judith knew she shouldn't have come but there was something about Caroline that made her feel comfortable and empathetic.

"Listen Caroline, I can't talk to you like that on the phone, they record all the calls to and from any police number, even our mobiles."

Caroline didn't know this but she should have as it had been mentioned during her training multiple times.

"Sorry" It was all Caroline could think of saying.

Judith nonchalantly waved away the apology while she took a sip of her coffee.

"Don't worry it's fine, no harm done, ok?"

Caroline nodded and Judith continued.

"Tough isn't it? Last night I mean, was that your first one?"

Caroline nodded again.

"Yeah I thought so" said Judith "I could see it in your eyes like they were open for the first time, or you know something like that anyway"

Caroline's head sagged a little.

"Was it that obvious?" She asked.

The affirmative reply came and Caroline's head drooped lower. Judith explained that she knew how it was and claimed that she could understand how Caroline must be feeling. Judith was wrong, she expected Caroline to be heartbroken and worried, when in fact she was angry and full of vengeful thoughts. Caroline kept those feelings to herself and started chipping away at Judith's guard for any information that might help her.

"So, what's the story? What's happened to the poor girl, is she ok? Have you got any leads on the suspect yet?" She asked Judith.

"No leads and that's not all" Judith said.

Caroline's interest was instantly peaked. Judith had dropped her professional secrecy a little too far and it all came spilling out. After they had left the crisis centre the police control room had received an emergency call from a guy claiming his daughter had gone missing and may have been kidnapped.

"He was some paranoid nut job, works for a government contractor or something" Judith said "he had cameras and electric locks everywhere".

Caroline listened intently to the story

"Anyway, the guy thinks someone cut power to his house and stole his kid, he said her name's Sofie and gave me a description that matches our little girl"

Caroline finished her coffee as her friend talked. Judith had been sent to his house and arrested him after a short interview. This was normal procedure in any case where a minor has been assaulted.

"We didn't even tell him she was safe just locked him up and started an investigation."

"That's horrible" said Caroline voicing her feelings "guy loses his kid and gets arrested because he's suspected of hurting her"

Judith just shook her head saying,

"Yeah, nah seems that way if the guy is innocent but in most cases it's always a family member or friend that's responsible. All we do is arrest them and send forensics through. If they're innocent then nothing to worry about right?"

Caroline was not sure she agreed, imagining how it would feel to be a suspect in your own child's case.

"Anyway" continued Judith "forensics hadn't even arrived at the guy's address when his boss walks into the custody unit with about four suited lawyers and a load of official looking paperwork."

Caroline was beckoning to the decidedly not Italian waitress

"What?" exclaimed Caroline in surprise.

"Yeah" said Judith "shocked us too. His boss must be in deep with some top boys over at number ten I guess. He had already secured the guy's release, hadn't even been inside for an hour and this Patrick dude managed to get an injunction stopping any and all investigations against him"

Caroline sat open mouthed.

"To be honest, Caroline that's not the most shocking thing. Sofie was on a seventy two hour holding order from the magistrate. Those things are air tight. No one can get past them, not even innocent parents with deep pockets."

"Was being?" interjected Caroline.

Taking the comment in her stride Judith answered

"Indeed, they had to let her go, this guy had some major

strings to pull somewhere up the chain. Our evidence even had to be recalled from the labs, sealed and sent over to the home office before any tests could be completed."

Judith paused for a sip of coffee.

"So what happened then?" asked Caroline.

"Well, he was released and some secret service type dudes took Sofie away. Haven't heard anything since and not even allowed to look into it any more"

The unfinished nature of the story bothered Caroline.

"So that's it?" she said "what about her father doesn't he want to know who did it?"

Judith sucked down more coffee before replying.

"Yeah, he was quiet anxious about it, kept saying he needed to know who took her. His boss though, that Pat guy, told him they had better people to deal with the situation"

Judith had put up air quotes when she said 'better', indicating her frustration at being passed over again.

"They even took all our notes and records" said Judith.

Accustomed as she was, to the glacially slow court system, Judith hadn't expected any developments for at least a few days. To have a suspect arrested and released in less than an hour was a new experience for everyone involved. The veil of secrecy that had been thrown over the affair had, in part, pushed her to the position she was in now, revealing details of an investigation to a community support officer. Technically it was no longer an open investigation but Judith was sure that was only a minor point that could be quickly over looked if any tribunal resulted from this clandestine meeting.

In general the proper police force view the community support officers as a jumped up neighbourhood watch group with no more power than the St. Johns Ambulance. They were only set apart from the populace by a neatly presented uniform and a sense of self entitlement.

Judith had instantly liked Caroline, sensing in her a similar soul, down trodden by the bureaucracy around them but with kindness still bright in her heart. They both wanted the best for little Sofie and they both felt shut out by the events of that day.

Caroline paid the bill and was horrified to learn that Judith had just now finished her shift. Judith had been at work all this time while Caroline slept. They said their goodbyes and promised to stay in touch.

It was unsaid between them but they both knew that neither was going to let this go easily. Judith would pursue every back channel she could and Caroline would help however she thought possible. Right now though, Caroline had to get to work if she didn't want to be late and miss the chance to tell Barry about her night.

-10-

Sofie half ran, half fell down the stairs into the kitchen.

"I'm sorry Daddy, I didn't mean it but I said a bad word" she said hugging her dad.

Taken aback by this out of the blue confession Tom replied without thinking.

"That's ok what did you say?"

Sofie refused to tell him, not wanting to say the actual word again. Tom happily left it at that and told her if she promised not to say it again then tomorrow they would have another treat.

"Zoo" was immediately shouted at the top of her little lungs.

Tom shook his head in dismay.

"We were just there yesterday surely you can't want to go again?"

Sofie assured him she could spend everyday at the zoo.

"No, Sofie we can't go to the Zoo again, I need to get a few things from the city tomorrow, how about you come with me and afterwards we can take you shopping or do something else together. How does that sound?"

Sofie hated shopping, she didn't like trailing round looking at things or even trying them on. Sofie had one overriding principle when it came to choosing anything, be it clothes, toys or even sweets. If it was pink it would do. This meant that the rest of it was all just a waste of time, she could locate a pink version of whatever items were needed and that was that, she didn't care what other offers there were or what other features items had, it was all the same to her as long as it was pink. This mantra made clothes shopping quick and toy shopping easy. Why waste the day? She would much rather visit the dockyard and HMS Victory. She knew it wasn't a pirate ship but she would be pretending it was.

Her mind was made up.

"What about the dockyard Daddy? That's near the city shops isn't it?"

It was, Tom readily agreed to the planned day's adventure. He enjoyed all things historic.

That night Sofie would reread Coral Island by R.M.Ballantyne, in her opinion a fantastically underrated story about three young boys shipwrecked on an island in the South Pacific. While her imagination was atop the high seas, Tom diligently worked on an email that had been promised many hours earlier.

The project was going better than expected and was yielding amazing results that Tom was now summarizing in his report to Patrick. Many years ago Patrick's first government job had been gifted to him by one of his many connections. This particular connection was inside an anti terror organisation. Tom's security clearance still didn't allow him to know the name of that shadowy organisation.

Patrick had been stuck and this was one of the reasons that he had sought out Tom to work with. The algorithm Tom had eventually written was to be aimed at sifting through mountains of surveillance data to ferret out the important information. Where that data was coming from Tom could only guess but he had his suspicions. Tom knew that the general public would be more than annoyed if they discovered how much of their day to day communication was being intercepted and how many of their civil liberties were just being ignored.

The problem Tom had faced when designing the software was one of volume and versatility. It's easy to skim files looking for key words or phrases but this simplistic solution will hit false positives more often than not. When applied to a population sized data set the resulting shortlist would take many man hours to check.

It's also true that anyone with nefarious intentions would probably be avoiding the selected words that were being searched for. Even criminals with below average intelligence can develop rudimentary codes to avoid detection. Tom's approach had to be a little bit more adaptable than Patrick's brute force approach.

In just six months of inspired and frantic work Tom had produced a program that could not only parse the gargantuan files quicker than before but also identify the most common and expected results. It was by looking for the normal and learning the everyday that his system would identify the unusual or extraordinary. If he had set about trying to identify the target words his system would have had much less data to learn from. Teaching it to recognise the mundane he had in effect reached the same result but with much greater accuracy than the current software could achieve.

Tom's work had saved lives, not just a few lives either. He knew that and it made keeping the work secret a much easier pill to swallow. The less than libertarian ideals of their clients bothered him but Tom reasoned that safety has a price and freedom in all its forms is only of use to the living.

On the flip side of this he worried that a lot of dangerous people were in jail or worse, dead because of his work. He knew that shouldn't matter to him, he was only an engineer but he was smart enough to know that no system is secure and not even his data would be safe if someone really wanted to get at it.

That was just the first success for their newly named company Accuracy Analytics. It wasn't until Patrick had heard the same joke for the hundredth time that he wished they had chosen a different name. His contacts in the intelligence agency would 'call the AA' every time they had a knotty or complicated computer problem. In the United Kingdom the AA is a roadside breakdown service. Although repetitive, this joke had worked in their favour. Brand recognition was important even in this underground marketplace.

Reminiscing aside, Tom finished his report and sent it. Tom was ready for bed he just had to check on one last important detail. Opening his unrestricted but secure web browser he navigated to the desired page.

Locating the information he needed quickly, before shutting down his computer. He was finally off to bed, armed with the knowledge that the historic dockyard attraction would, as with Marwell, not be opening until ten o'clock in the morning.

Tomorrow when Sofie tried dragging him impatiently towards the family car he could reassure her that they had plenty of time to complete his errands before the docks would even open their doors. Tom wondered if they were actually called 'doors' on a ship or if they had some other more nautical designation. He decided to ask one of the tour guides that were no doubt liberally spread around the ancient vessels of war.

It felt like his head had barely touched the pillow when the next morning came and an over excited Pirate Sofie boarded the good ship HMS Doublebed. She had chased the ship and its cowardly crew across carpeted and wooden seas alike onboard her own vessel the ever so fearsome WholesaleBox. Although not sea worthy in the traditional sense it served her current purposes.

Pirate Captain Sofie pulled up alongside the HMS Doublebed as the Sun's first rays made their way through Tom's net curtains. She had given them the full broadside with her paperclip cannon. When this onslaught had roused no response from the napping seamen she had boarded the vessel with gusto and abandon. Flogging the crew savagely with her cutlass and hook to wake them for battle.

Tom awoke to Sofie's game and quickly turned the tables on the black hearted pirate that disturbed his peaceful voyage. Disarming Sofie quickly he used her own cutlass to make the eye-patch wearing blaggard walk the plank. Disappearing over the side of HMS Doublebed the days of dread pirate Sofie came to an end.

The fine vessel WholesaleBox was returned to the cupboard

come shipyard and the seas once again knew peace. The pair went downstairs to enjoy another excellent breakfast and start their day. First to the shops for Tom and then on to the dockyard.

Over the last few years a curious situation has arisen surrounding the hardware stores of England. Once the purview of working class tradesmen who would at weekends turn their skills to improving their modest dwellings. The clientele of these warehouse sized establishments has dwindled as quickly as it has gentrified.

With house prices rising and an explosion in rental accommodation the once fine pursuit of DIY. is now an activity limited to the rich. Gardening has become an elitist club and is either enjoyed by the elderly land owners or confined to a poorly cultivated and lonely window box.

Tom and Sofie were strolling down isles of cameras and looking at the bright orange shelving full of locks and other security equipment. Sofie's impatience was growing as fast as the stack of goods in Tom's shopping cart. He had selected access control systems, CCTV, electromagnetic door locks and even an intruder alarm kit. Carefully weighing up the features and benefits of each model for himself.

Tom had dismissed two customer service representatives, one after the other, who tried to assist him. Tom was sure he knew more about these things than they did since everything was now computer controlled.

"Are we done yet Daddy? There won't be any tickets left if we don't go soon." Said Sofie.

Tom knew how Sofie's mind worked well enough to spot her over active fear of missing out routines. He tried to reassure her anyway

"They won't even open the doors for another twenty minutes Sofie and I think we have almost everything, don't worry, we'll see the ships today I promise."

It took a little more than twenty minutes to complete the sale. Tom having so much equipment to buy that the assistant had asked for his tradesman loyalty card after assuming he must be an installer. Learning that Tom was buying all this for his house the assistant whistled and said

"What you keeping safe? Just relocated Fort Knox did we?"

Tom smiled and patted Sofie's head while saying.

"Some things are worth a lot more than gold you know."

Their haul of security equipment now securely loaded into Tom's car they headed to Portsmouth's naval base and the astonishing selection of maritime firepower on display. They were going to spend may hours being wowed by the countless impressive vessels.

Inside the Mary Rose's viewing gallery Sofie had adored the way that scenes were projected onto the badly damaged hull. The museum was showing what it must have been like to serve aboard the ill fated vessel before it had sunk. Actors dressed in period clothing performing short little scenes that were highlighting the purpose of each room onboard.

The only thing Sofie felt was more impressive was the wealth of information and activities in the amazingly well designed museum built around the wrecked ship. Lifts and staircases taking her all over the exhibit. She pressed countless activity buttons and played with interactive exhibits all while learning by osmosis. Actively sucking in as much knowledge as she could.

Onboard HMS Victory Sofie had straddled cannons while

Tom bumped his head continuously. The low ceilings and lovingly preserved firing positions gave a real taste of war time conditions aboard Lord Nelson's famous flagship. Carrying one hundred and four heavy guns to the battle of Trafalgar. Sofie quite agreed with Victory's description as 'a first rate ship of the line'.

By the end of the day dread pirate Sofie had completely renounced her wicked ways in favour of adopting a far more wholesome persona. Admiral Sofie was the first female officer of Her Majesty's Royal Navy and the bravest lass to ever sail the seven seas.

With a head full of stories and a belly hungry for rations they headed home. Dinner was cooked and Tom set about organising his mornings purchases. Sofie was intrigued by the many boxes and endless rolls of cabling. Tomorrow Admiral Sofie was in for a serious demotion. Tomorrow Admiral Sofie would become apprentice tool holding Sofie.

-11-

The morning of September the first was going to be a harrowing one, Tom knew. Sofie had been due to start attending her high school today. They had purchased her a new school uniform last week along with a haul of pink stationery and various other writing instruments.

Tom had expected Sofie to be clawing at her bedroom door, she would be frantically hyperactive in her desire to attend the local comprehensive. Perhaps she was still sleeping? Tom finished his morning rituals, dressed and descended once again to his prized kitchen. As usual bacon and eggs were on the menu again. The copper kettle was deposited onto the Aga's heating surface. Tom would have to make do with instant coffee today.

He took pride in producing as much food as he could for himself, not trusting the commercially available offerings. He was sure 'they' even added chemicals and hormones to the birds that produce our country's eggs. Assured that his own chickens hadn't eaten anything other than the food he grew for them, plus the occasional slug of course. It made him feel safe to know where everything came from. Producing his own milk had been an idea that bounced around his mind almost daily, never to be solved. The problem being land usage. A dairy cow needs one acre of good grazing to support its insatiable appetite for the green stuff. Tom just didn't have that much space to spare.

A logical alternative being goats, Tom had toyed with this idea as well. Further research revealed that the much more manageable dairy producers would possibly prefer to eat his berry bushes and the lower branches of his fruit trees rather than subsisting on grass alone. With his garden in danger of being decimated by over eager goats he had tabled the idea for future deliberations. Quite unwilling to risk even ten percent of his small but perfectly manicured estate.

Tom added a generous amount of the commercially produced milk to his coffee. He had bought this bottle from the adorable village convenience store. Green label decorated with happy looking cows on rolling hills, he had the suspicion that this image portrayed a reality that was far from the truth. He happily paid the premium price hoping that it was at least a little less tainted than the regular bottles found in corporate supermarkets everywhere.

Depositing his teaspoon into the oversized white sink, it's job now done, he briefly surveyed his perfect vista. Something was tugging at the side of his mind. Something was wrong, he wasn't sure what but it was nagging at his subconscious the way a forgotten errand or partially remembered quote might. Feeling a cool draft around his legs, the various details suddenly crystallized into a horrible realisation. Coffee mug tumbling to smash upon the sink's wide edge, his mind brought forward the tiny indications that had gone unnoticed. The door. The door was open.

"She's gone Pat" screamed Tom at his phone. "yes I checked everywhere do you think I would be calling if I hadn't?"

Patrick's annoyingly posh voice tried to reassure Tom.

"It will be ok, don't worry old chap we will find her."

Tom was hysterical

"Someone's taken her, she could be anywhere, how in the name of hell do you think we're going to do that?"

Patrick cut off his tirade.

"Calm down man, Now stop and think, what about tracking just find her phone and you find Sofie right?"

Inspired to hope, Tom's anguish lifted for a moment only to descend once more into despair

"I, but, I disabled her data" he stammered.

Patrick's shock at the oversight evident in his voice as he asked

"Why in god's name did you do that?"

Tom realising he had made a mistake replied

"She kept trying to get onto social media so I locked out her mobile connection. The data only works on my home network now"

Trying to give him hope Patrick offered

"ok, ok don't worry give me the phone's number I will ask the boys to try and find it. Won't be as quick but if it's on and connected to a cell tower they can narrow down where she is ok?"

Breathing easier Tom passed the digits to Patrick.

"I never thought this would happen" bemoaned Tom "I built in so many safeguards,"

Patrick didn't think that any amount of cameras or electric locks would be able to deter someone who was truly motivated.

"How did it happen, what's the state of your system? Is there any footage that could help?" asked Patrick.

"I already checked" said Tom "but the power was cut before anything happened, the whole system was down, no cameras, no alarm even the god damn locks opened. It's a sodding safety feature in case of fire or something so you don't get trapped inside"

Patrick was getting frustrated at Tom's naive approach to security. Patrick had worked in some of the most secure sites across the country, dealing with the intelligence agencies and sometimes directly with the military. He had seen similar systems before but they always had at least two redundancy back ups.

Usually generators or steel bolts held back by the same power that activated the electric locks. In the event of an emergency or power outage and if the generators failed, steel bolts would drop into place sealing the doors shut until power could be restored. Health and safety concerns were negated by the fact that whatever these doors protected was worth far more than the expendable lives of those guarding them. It was a cold philosophy but a necessary one.

A police car arrived outside Tom's gate as he said

"Listen Pat thanks for the help but I have to go, I will call you again later the police are here"

Tom wasn't ready for the reaction this generated from Patrick.

"How in the name of god did those bloody idiots find out about this Tom?"

"I called them first before I called you" Tom answered.

"Why on earth would you do that?" Tom's answer made Patrick furious "We can't have that lot of half wits sniffing around there Tom. Think of the bloody project for god sake what about security?"

Annoyed that Patrick was thinking about op-sec at a time like this, Tom felt they needed all the help they could get to find Sofie.

"What else was I supposed to do Pat? Sofie is missing" said Tom angrily as he hung up the phone.

His friend was still irately questioning Tom's dedication to secrecy as the line went dead. Tom's phone was ringing again almost the second he had hung up. Seeing Patrick's name he sent the call to voicemail and opened the driveway gates by remote.

The police car swung into Tom's drive and Judith exited the vehicle accompanied by another uniformed constable. Waving at the kitchen window, Judith pointed to Tom's front door. Tom mouthed 'It's open' while making a beckoning gesture to indicate they could come straight in. He put more water into the kettle and placed it back onto the Aga once more.

Judith and her back up walked into Tom's kitchen while removing their hats and looking around the stately home.

"Wow" said Judith in an unprofessional manner "You have an amazing house" she said while offering a handshake "I'm Detective Judith Chaplin and this is PC Cooper." The big man just nodded at Tom without offering his hand.

"Hi, Thomas Anderson but just call me Tom"

"Ok Mr Anderson" Judith frowned as she replied "you reported a break in and kidnapping is that right?"

Tom talked them through his morning showing them the broken coffee mug and open door. He explained about his security system and how it worked.

"Looks like they must have cut the mains power and then stolen her." he said worriedly.

Judith tapped her pen to her lips.

"They, hmm, now who do you imagine they are?"

Tom looked at her as if she was a particularly stupid child.

"Who do you damn well think? Whoever took Sofie and what do you mean imagine?"

"Please Calm down Mr Anderson" Judith said, noting Tom's agitated mood "I merely meant who do you think might have done this? I mean no offence and apologise for my poor choice of words" Judith continued "Do you have any enemies, or maybe you have seen someone unusual hanging around?"

Tom realised why Patrick had said those things earlier. He couldn't exactly tell PC dipshit here the truth about anything. He couldn't tell her that he was a software engineer who had worked on top secret projects that possibly resulted in some terrorists becoming fertilizer. His mind grasped for something to say.

"No I have not seen anyone suspicious around" he finally said.

"and what about enemies?" Asked Judith.

"Nope, no enemies." Tom replied, with just a hint of nervousness in his voice.

Judith noticing the uncomfortable stance that Tom had adopted, changed tack.

"And what about you Tom, where were you when your little girl was kidnapped? Didn't wake up? Didn't hear anything I suppose?"

Getting angry now Tom realising where this was going.

"What do you mean suppose?"

Judith cut him off by raising her open hands.

"I am just trying to find out what happened here Tom, no one needs to get angry. If you are telling us the truth."

Tom's rage exploded.

"You stupid bitch. The truth? The truth is you need to go and find Sofie now. Don't you dare come into my home and start accusing me you stupid pi" Tom's rantings were cut short by the large hands of PC Cooper taking him down face first onto the kitchen table top. As the handcuffs went on Judith said

"Thomas Anderson you are under arrest" she badly wanted to add "my boy" but didn't.

Judith told him his rights as he kicked and screamed about

lawyers and government friends. He threatened both the officers job security and then resorted to pleading. As Tom calmed down his pleading turned to begging. By the time Judith and PC Cooper had him in the car Tom was subdued.

"Please, I'm sorry I just want my Sofie back, I'm just worried about her. Please you have to let me go you don't understand."

The door closed on Tom and the police car headed off towards Waterlooville and the police station's custody suite.

-12-

How the hell had he ended up here? 'I don't deserve this kind of treatment' thought Tom. Still in painfully tight handcuffs he sat in a tiny corner room. Not much bigger than a closet and with only enough room to stand or sit. The bench seemed to be extruded from the wall. Beige paint on every surface, thick and cracked in places. A solid door of plate steel between him and civilised life. Tom felt trapped, he was caged and Sofie was missing.

No phone call, no lawyer, just thrown in a cell and left to stew. They had taken his shoes and the contents of his pockets. He had been held in front of a plexiglass window while the police recorded his details and removed everything he had on him. They had bagged his personal belongings and squirrelled them away. Tom asked about a lawyer and about the phone call. The police had laughed at him.

"This ain't the movies son" the pompous desk sergeant had said. "you can have a lawyer when we interview you, if you ask for one"

With that he had been deposited in here and left to his

thoughts. His mind racing Tom started to look for any means of escape. The plate metal door had no handle on this side not even any key holes. The hinges were hidden and offered no hope. He knew even if he managed to get out of the tiny holding cell he would still be inside the police station but his mind wasn't thinking about that, he just had to get out. He looked for the ventilation grate or loose ceiling tile. It was all just smooth beige concrete though. Not a gap or loose brick anywhere. This really wasn't the movies.

After what seemed like hours, it had been five minutes, Tom heard the heavy bolt being drawn back, standing up he saw two of the roughest looking policemen he had ever seen. Both overweight, in just the white shirt and black pants, these were guards, not active duty officers. One had a set of keys on a retractable lanyard that he had used to open the lock. Tom's frightened brain instantly identified it and his eyes locked firmly on the keys as they swung back to be engulfed by the man's muffin top.

Noticing Tom's eyes the out of breath man said

"Come with us buddy."

Tom instantly launched into a garbled version of events protesting his innocence, convinced, that if he could make Mr Big here see that he was innocent he could be released.

"We're just here to search you and remove those cuffs buddy, save your stories for the interview ok."

Tom nodded and was lead away to another beige concrete room. This chamber being just as securely locked but with a lot more space.

Tom was stood in the middle of this concrete cage and the two police officers were in front of the only door stood on either side. They had released his hands and gestured to the centre of the room.

"Now Mr Anderson" began the senior guy "have you concealed any drugs, weapons or cigarettes anywhere on your person"

"No" Tom replied and Mr Big continued

"Ok well if you wouldn't mind removing your clothes so we can be sure"

Tom's mind was racing as he panicked.

"What, why, they already searched me twice."

The guard was used to this response.

"Well, were going to do it again and properly this time, Now take off your clothes Mr Anderson."

This was wrong, it felt inhumane, was it some sort of sick joke?

"If you need assistance Mr Anderson we can remove them for you."

This spurred Tom on and he began to pull his T shirt over his head. Next went his trousers and finally he took his socks off. Standing just in his boxers feeling small and self conscious.

"There happy?"

"Unfortunately not, Mr Anderson please remove your underwear as well."

'What the hell' thought Tom 'this is like some sort of Nazi organisation.'

"You can see I'm not hiding anything" said Tom "Is this necessary?"

"Underwear please Mr Anderson."

Disgusted and humiliated Tom obliged, cupping his genitals and feeling sick as he took the boxers down. Sure it was over, Tom stood there and lost a little piece from inside his psyche. Tom had always thought of the police as defenders of public order and felt that they had a tough job to do. Now though, he hoped every last one of them would suffer horribly. He felt an unexpected kinship with the criminals that appear on reality shows, who hurl abuse and violence at the police when being arrested. If they knew that this kind of dehumanising treatment awaited them at the station, then he could sympathise with their actions.

"Now Mr Anderson take the end of your penis in your left hand and raise it towards your belly button."

Tom was already feeling embarrassed by the ordeal.

"What's wrong with you?" Tom demanded

The guard just pointed to Tom's groin making an up gesture. Tom did as he was told while replacing the embarrassment he felt with a sick feeling in his stomach. The guards were examining him like a piece of art. Thoughtful and reflective they appraised his genitals

"Ok good, now with your right hand Mr Anderson raise your testicles first to the left and then push them over to the right."

Tom felt like he was going to actually vomit. After this indignity the guards made him turn round and bend over. Anticipating the worst he was relieved that they only needed to see between his cheeks. It felt like he spent an eternity bent double with his hands pulling open the crack waiting for the probing touch of latex covered fingers. Tom was so relieved when Mr Big said

"Thank you Mr Anderson you can get dressed now."

Tom was feeling better quickly as they walked him back to the tiny cell with his modesty restored. No longer exposed, his relief quickly made way for anger. Never again would he smile at police officer and if he ever saw one in trouble he would walk the other way and only look back out of interest and without pity.

The tiny cell door closed behind Tom, his mind full of hate, he was finished looking for a way to freedom, he was looking for a weapon. He quickly overcame this instinct and a strange sense of acceptance settled on him. 'He would survive this whatever happened.' Tom knew he was innocent but that was the worst thing.

Locked up and treated like a criminal, he reasoned, would be easier if he felt like he had done something wrong. If he knew there was a reason for this madness it would seem like Karma. As an innocent man though, subjected to this injustice, how else could he feel but hateful towards his captors?

Another eternity passed, this time ten minutes, and Mr Big returned to once again remove Tom from his sardine can. In those ten minutes Tom had experience every single human emotion again and again. His trapped mind wailed around the cold silent walls. He had relived good memories and time spent with long forgotten girlfriends. Trying to keep his spirits up so he wouldn't descend back into being that feral beast, ready to murder.

The only thing that could pull him back from the edge was Sofie. Her radiant brown eyes and loving smile pushing away his darker more homicidal thoughts. It caused him pain to think of her kidnapped and afraid. He would get out and he would find her even if that newly discovered dark side had to do some of the heavy lifting for him.

Tom was lead to Interview room two and placed on an empty seat. Left alone once more he put his head down on the cold steel table. Rolling it back and forth then side to side as if this alone could shake his thoughts into a coherent whole once more. The door opened and he shot back up to a seated position, hoping his crazy actions hadn't been observed. His thoughts coalescing finally as he greeted Judith once more.

"Ok it's September the First. Time is" Judith said looking at her watch " Zero seven thirty three hours."

'What the hell' thought Tom, had he only been awake for ninety three minutes? In such a short time he had discovered his Sofie missing and now he was stuck in a police interview room.

"Interview with Thomas Anderson conducted by Judith Chaplin Shoulder number four five seven six." Judith's posture changed and she homed in on Tom. "Right, why don't you start by telling me what happened this morning after you woke up?"

Tom looked at her with contempt and disdain.

"I plead the fifth." He said.

"So that would be the fifth amendment made to the constitution of the United States I take it? Ratified in 1791 as part of the bill of rights? That fifth amendment yeah?"

In disgust Tom looked at her, his anger starting to rise again

"Ok whatever get me my attorney."

Her smirk broke into a smile as she stifled a laugh.

"Watch a lot of American TV do we Tom? It might take a while to fly an attorney all the way over here."

It was at that exact moment the police station's public door swung open. Patrick, flanked by a member of the security service and three solicitors entered. One of the solicitors was a former attorney who had relocated to the UK fifteen years ago.

Six minutes later Tom and Patrick got into the back of a government owned SUV that had parked in the middle of Waterlooville's pedestrian precinct. They immediately headed for Tom's house, while Patrick explained that they had already found Sofie. She was ok and would be on her way home soon. Amazed at what his friend had achieved in such a short space of time he actually hugged Pat.

-13-

Caroline arrived at Waterlooville police station twelve hours after Tom had left it and five minutes after Barry and Rob had arrived. Their day on the quiet and quaint village streets had been unproductive as usual.

Barry, Rob and Caroline all worked the villages to the east of Waterlooville. There were four officers assigned to the western side in villages near Denmead and Hambledon, another team of six were assigned to cover everything north of Clanfield while the remaining team of twelve officers covered the larger suburban towns closer to Waterlooville. Places like Purbrook up to Horndean and through Cowplain.

These teams, although friendly with each other were like little cliques that tended to socialise within their geographical subdivisions. Today, the barriers had been discarded in favour of discussing last night's event. For these failed police officers it was the end of their day. They had been swapping the usual stories.

Littering prevented, youths tormented and minor fines presented.

This discontented, overrepresented group of lamented, demented people being cemented into society without any permissions consented.

Our Police force augmented and reinvented so laws could be segmented and circumvented.

Not repented but resented the population felt dented so they vented with sweetly scented solutions fermented.

--From the toilet door at Waterlooville police station. By WPC Anonymous--

Caroline walked in and the room erupted into half hearted applause. She was revolted by their celebration. Barry caught her eye.

"Here she is, the lady of the hour, everyone" his voice amplified to cut through the raised voices "Single handedly saved a girl's life."

It dawned on Caroline that her colleagues hadn't heard the whole story but they were desperate to recreate this cliche cop movie scene, no matter how prematurely. Not wanting to disappoint the sycophantic group or betray the trust that Judith had placed in her Caroline politely waved and shyly accepted the praise. Nodding and saying 'thank you' a lot she turned to Barry as the applause died away.

"Well" he said "how does it feel to be a hero"

She wanted to say 'rubbish' but didn't, opting instead for the so often used.

"I'm no hero, it wasn't just me there were lots of other people there."

"Nonsense you were first on scene," Barry said.

"You're not the only one who had an exciting shift" Rob said enviously "We caught a career thief this morning."

Barry looked at Rob sceptically.

"Not sure you can have a career by age twelve Rob. I think that even the thieves' guild has a child labour law."

Barry burst into laughter at his own lame joke before collecting his things and making for the door.

"I'm heading home now" said Barry "but seriously though Caroline well done excellent work. I need you to write up the incident report before you head over to Rowlands tonight and Rob before you leave I will need one on the milky bar kid ok?" Laughing again he turned to leave.

Fuming at Caroline, Rob sat at a computer directly opposite the one she was using. Both tapping away furiously adding data to their newly opened Incident reports. The office began to empty and Rob finished his report. Caroline's eloquent and concise account of last night's patrol was only half finished when Rob asked.

"Hey, so what was it like? It sounded awful I couldn't have dealt with that."

Remembering Sofie's reaction to the male police officers Caroline didn't think Rob would have been able to deal with it either.

"Yeah. It was bad" She said "I'm still not sure how I feel, Its like the world isn't real and all I can see is that poor girl's tears."

Rob looked stunned, he hadn't expected her to open up so much.

"I'm never going to forget it, Rob. It was horrible, the blood, the doctors, oh my god the screaming at the doctors office." She couldn't help the tone of her voice breaking as she fought back the terrible memories once more. Rob got up and walked to Caroline's side of the desk and patted her back.

"There, there" he said not knowing what else to do.

Rob had helped Caroline finish her report, thinking that, he could at least help with that and maybe it would cheer her up. Rob hated writing and having someone else do his paperwork would cheer him up no end, so why not Caroline right? If he couldn't fix her he could try to fix something else.

The logic might have been backwards but Caroline could recognise when a man was trying to help. Even if he got it spectacularly wrong, she appreciated the sentiment and it did actually cheer her up to know he cared enough to try.

Seeing her improved mood, Rob was sure he'd done the right thing. Helping her with the report made her feel better, it had worked.

"Ok Caroline, all done" he said "you got a crime reference to file this under or shall we just search for the police's incident report?"

Looking through the database they couldn't find anything to attach the report to.

"Why not try searching through it in timestamp order" asked Caroline.

Rob reorganised the data and began trawling.

"There, that's got to be it" she said pointing to '05:25JCHAPLIN4576'.

Rob opened the incident report and read the single line of contents 'Empty Record - Diplomatic Immunity Incident - Refer To Home Office Guidelines.'

"What the hell," said Rob "diplomatic immunity?"

Caroline had to tell him what happened to the case after she had left the crisis centre. She missed out a few names and told the story as if she had been there, to protect the promise she had made to Judith.

Rob realised why she had been so subdued at their impromptu celebration. He had imagined himself walking in, victorious, to rapturous applause many times but in his fantasy he was far more gracious and accepting of praise than Caroline had been. Now though with the rest of the story revealed he could sympathise with how she must have felt.

"Holy crap Cazza." was all he said.

Looking back at Rob's eyes, now full of pity, she said

"Please don't ever call me Cazza, it's Caroline ok?"

Rob nodded in agreement, the new nick name was banned. Caroline thought it sounded common or disrespectful, only briefly self aware at her constant use of 'Bazza'.

"So, I'll just attach this report to the file anyway I guess" inquired Rob.

Shrugging her shoulders Caroline looked once more at the sleek glass computer. Rob hit the attach button and the file was instantly uploaded to the database, the record now displaying a paperclip icon denoting the single attachment. As they watched the paperclip disappeared.

"What?" they said in unison.

Rob opened up the record once more, all that was there was the single line of text from before, the newly added data was missing already.

"Do it again" said Caroline.

"I can't, the file isn't saved here, it only exists on the database" Rob explained "the system moves the whole file to central records when you upload it. Stops these terminals getting clogged up with duplicated reports."

"So where did it go then?" asked Caroline.

"You saw it there the same as I did. The system definitely received it" said Rob.

"Maybe that diplomatic immunity thing?"

"Yeah," Rob nodded "best guess, its been classified, we have to leave it alone"

The thought of it being classified excited Caroline but with nothing more to be done the pair said their goodbyes and parted ways, not exactly friends but no longer enemies.

Caroline was heading for another night shift spent on the empty streets of quiet towns and sleepy villages while Rob headed home. Caroline realised she didn't know where he lived or if he was married, in fact she knew nothing about him. She knew nothing about any of her colleagues not even Barry, she hadn't ever bothered to ask. Selfishly, she realised that she hadn't even cared before. Content to tell her own stories and advertise her own achievements.

Caroline had never taken the time to listen to anyone else's point of view. She had always been sure that what she had to say was important and interesting to those around her.

For the first time she appreciated how that might make other people feel. Maybe that is why some acquaintances would seem hostile to her. She had never given them the chance to express their thoughts or feelings, hoping instead that the brilliance of her own narrative would attract and reassure anyone of her validity and importance. She wanted people to care about her and perhaps they would, if she could learn to care about them?

The silent streets of Rowlands Castle greeted her arrival once more, as a little black cat stirred from his bushy observation post. Last night's activity had given way to dawn and brought with it lots of strangely dressed people in white suits carrying about all manner of devices and containers.

Pickles had watched as they meticulously documented the car park scene while the sun began to rise and the elderly residents emerged from their homes only to congregate around the scene, held back from the action by blue and white plastic tape.

Pickles had returned to his home, belly rumblings drove him to the bowl of biscuits he knew would be awaiting his return. Sleeping for hours while his nice human doddered about their friendly little bungalow, he would awake, to find the streets devoid of excitement and returned to their regular lifeless state. Normality had been restored so he took up his position and awaited the night time lady and her delicious treats.

-14-

Yesterday, Sofie had been the first female admiral of Her Majesty's Royal Navy and now she was reduced to this. Cable after cable, camera after camera, her mind beset by boredom. It had started out as another fine day, she had visited her feathered friends and relieved Henrietta of her egg warming duty. Sofie retrieved five perfect eggs, this time remembering the all important basket. All of the eggs survived the trip back to become another excellent scrambled egg breakfast. Captain Flaps had been successfully shooed away while she distributed the chickens morning meal.

Sofie had gladly embarked upon her apprenticeship course in security system installation. They started by planning locations and Sofie had been overjoyed to be hoisted up by Tom so she could see what cameras would see from different locations. She had stood on his shoulders either side of the front door. The right side was the better choice as the branches of an ancient apple tree obscured the view on the left side. Tom had positioned Sofie on other tree branches and held her above gates. With their plan devised she had been asked to draw a map while Tom unpacked cameras and associated equipment.

Sofie loved to draw and gladly got on with her task. Her art supplies coming in handy. Pens, pencils and stickers all used to represent a birds eye view of the house and garden. Placing gold stars to show where the cameras would go, she was almost done.

"Here you go Dad." she said in a brightly confident voice handing Tom the finished masterpiece.

Tom took the map and squinting he turned it one way then the other making non committal noises and curious little sounds.

"What is it dad?" said Sofie, not happy with his lacklustre reaction at all.

Tom made a few false starts and not wanting to hurt her feelings.

"Its great I just have a couple questions."

Sofie nodded eagerly, ready to explain her slightly embellished portrayal.

"Well, what is this?" he said pointing to a furry looking butterfly.

Sofie couldn't believe he didn't recognise Henrietta, telling him it was the chicken coop. Tom continued.

"So that would make this?" he said, moving his finger to a bottle of ketchup.

"That's the tomato house" she said.

"Ah ok and this?" Tom indicted a unicorn's head at the edge of the map.

"That's a unicorn, silly" she said smiling wide.

Tom couldn't remember seeing a unicorn in the garden but allowed her some artistic licence.

Sofie had asked about the equipment and in return got a thankfully brief description of ethernet switches, digital video recorders and infrared sensors . Tom cut things short when he saw Sofie's eyes starting to glaze over during a tangent lecture about the benefits of a power over ethernet system. Later, she would remember that part and be pretty thankful that they were only running a single cable to each camera.

It was taking hours, lunch had come and gone, now dinnertime was approaching. The cameras had gone up easily enough as they followed Sofie's map. Tom still unable to find any unicorns even with their positions accurately recorded by his amateur cartographer. Cables had been connected in no time and Sofie was sure that the project was near completion. Then the boredom had come.

Tom handed Sofie a bag of nail in cable clips. These were to be handed up to Tom two at a time, he would hammer them into the underside or backside of wooden roofing trims, branches or fence posts. He would do two then move the ladder two feet. Sofie would have two more clips ready to hand him before he climbed up again, to repeat the process.

Thirty two times they conducted this dance around the garden. By the time it was finished, darkness was beginning creep across the sky towards golden tipped clouds.

"I think we can finish this tomorrow don't you?" said Tom.

Sofie was not overly eager to continue this mundane work ever again but she agreed, trying as she was to be especially good. Her birthday was the day after tomorrow. She was hoping that Daddy would remember what a good girl she had been and would have agreed to any tasks he set. Sofie had never asked for presents before but on this, her eleventh birthday she was going to make a special request.

Tonight's dinner was a true feast of home made slow roasted pork. The smell had been driving Sofie wild all day as it called from the Aga's wood fired interior. Tom had finished all of the prep work before Sofie had even finished her breakfast. It had only needed the occasional tending throughout the day, a basting here, a tasting there. At lunch time the combined smell of pork, potatoes, herbs and spices filled the kitchen, when the tools went down it was also filling the garden.

The pair had enjoyed the meal and Sofie remarked on its ranking as the new best meal ever. She offered to clear the table,

Tom was pleasantly surprised and also relieved. Tiredness had hit him like a brick wall. Spending most of his days sat at a computer Tom had not engaged in as much physical activity for many years. Yawning, he was ready for bed but first he had something to show Sofie.

"Hey Sofie, come here I have something cool to show you."

She bounced into the living room.

"What is it Daddy?"

Tom was starting up the television projector and as its bright light came to life it turned one of the walls into a giant screen. Sofie took his free hand and looked at the images splashed onto the white wall. Tom pointed a remote at his new security recorder and Sofie could see thirty two separate images. Most black but a few were monochrome night vision, showing things like blank walls, the edges of posts and a lot of the ground directly beneath cameras.

"Hmm" said Tom "I guess we need to change the angle for the cameras tomorrow but here look at this one" he pressed a few numbers and one of the small images expanded to fill the screen. Sofie shone with warmth and joy.

"It's Henrietta" she said, holding onto Tom's hand and bouncing a little "You put one in there to keep her safe. That's so cool dad"

Tom explained that he would make sure Sofie could check the camera from her phone whenever she liked and wherever she was. Slightly more excited about helping again tomorrow Sofie went to bed.

Tom watched her through the cameras as she went up the stairs and eventually he watched as she climbed into bed. He was comforted that he could watch all this on his own phone.

The idea to surveil the chicken coop had come to him while he tried to think how he could explain the camera he had installed in her room.

Unplanned but welcome were the words she had gifted him 'You put one in there to keep her safe. That's so cool'. He shut off the screen but left the system recording and went to bed. Tom needed to be up early, he had something else to sneak into Sofie's room.

-15-

"Come in agent Sofie, agent Sofie, this is Control calling agent Sofie."

On her bed side table was a new, pink walkie-talkie its gain turned up to ten, the rasping hissing tones woke her from sweet dreams. It hadn't been there last night, she had never seen it before.

"Agent Sofie are you there?"

She picked up the radio and depressed the push to talk button. Tom was amazed at her quick adaptability as she replied.

"This is agent Sofie send your message Control" a slight pause and then she remembered.

"over."

They had watched a spy movie the other night and she had assimilated the language that the agents used perfectly.

"Good to hear from you agent, we have a situation, it's serious. I need you to gear up, meet me in the briefing room ASAP." Tom took a moment to remember the sign off as well "over."

The radio static died a second later as the radios established a connection again.

"Roger that Control, instructions received and understood briefing room in five say again briefing room in five, over."

After a few seconds more the radios reconnected once more.

"Sofie to Control, over."

"Send your message agent, over."

"Where is the briefing room Dad, sorry I mean Control, over."

"It's in the kitchen, agent Sofie, repeat rendezvous in the kitchen, See you in five, over"

"Thanks, over."

The radios went dead and Tom finished making the breakfast.

Sofie sat, quickly inhaling her bacon and egg breakfast as Tom presented a military style briefing. He was dressed in army surplus clothing, usually worn to hunt, he had swapped the flat cap for a black beret. He had pinned the map Sofie had made yesterday to the notice board and was pointing to it with a wooden spoon. Indicating objectives and enemy positions. He occasionally bashed the spoon hard onto the work surface to emphasize the importance of their mission.

"I hope you realise how important this is agent" bang went the spoon "If we are going to save those chickens" bang "we need to get all of our surveillance systems operational and on target" bang "Lives depend on this agent" bang "once you have completed your mission exfiltrate to landing zone unicorn for extraction" Snap. The spoon had finally broken.

The rest of the morning was spent with Sofie running around from camera to camera as control issued instructions via the walkie-talkies. Tom was inside watching the cameras while doing the 'left a bit, up a bit' routine.

The game had enthused Sofie no end. Tom had seen how bored of installing cameras she had become yesterday but this take on the work had made the last part of their task far more enjoyable and exciting. The last camera to be aligned was above the garden gate.

"That's it agent, mission accomplished well done return to base. Over." Said Tom

The final device could now clearly see about fifty metres of the lane outside, instead of the branch it was pointed at before.

Sofie infiltrated the kitchen with finger gun raised, checking the corners she declared

"Clear." While holstering the imaginary gun.

Lunch today was a beautifully crafted sandwich with a few crisps, square cut lumps of cheese and a heap of Branston's best. Tom took huge pride in even the simplest of meals. Sofie had an appreciation for the presentation but was far more enthused by the taste. Plates now empty, lemonade glasses drained everything went into the dishwasher.

"I've got something else cool to show you Sofie," said Tom as he lead her once again into the comfy living room with its enormous display projection.

The image was a paused recording from one of the cameras. Monochrome hue indicating the footage was from last night's recordings.

"What is it Daddy?" enquired the now well fed little girl.

"Watch this." said Tom as he started the video playback.

The images began to move and he explained that the system would mark any footage that showed movement. This made it easy to review hours of archived video.

As she watched, a fox entered the shot and prowled around their garden. Sofie's fears for Henrietta's safety evaporated as the animal showed no interest in the coop. The fox had visited their garden many times before and had initially been intent on the coop but discovering the thick wire and tough construction had quickly realised it was impregnable. Attempts to dig under the wire revealed a concrete skirt sunk deeply into the ground. Tom had never actually seen the fox before but he had noticed the claw marks and knew that the animal was around.

Enthralled by the recording, Sofie was delighted to see two small fox cubs eventually venture out and join their mother. Their rough and tumble games made Sofie smile and bounce again. She watched with wide eyes as they jumped on each other, rolling around in the grass. She thought they were going to fight but the cubs would face off against each other only for a frantic game of chase to ensue. Tails pulled and ears molested the foxes had eventually left the garden to continue their night time exploration.

"Oh, they are so cute" she told Tom as he looked down at her.

"I thought you'd like that." he said "How about tonight we put out a little food for them?"

Sofie thought this was a fantastic idea. She had already planned on saving some dinner and smuggling it outside for the furry family. Glad that Tom had no objections she wondered if they would like broccoli. Reasoning that if they would eat the disgusting little trees she would happily sacrifice every portion that Tom insisted on serving her.

The morning's work complete, Tom sent Sofie to amuse herself with whatever she wanted while he set about installing the newly acquired electromagnetic door locks. These consist of two metal plates and a small box of electronics. When activated they would create a strong magnetic field that holds the two plates together. The magnetic field generated enough resistance that the door would break before the lock did.

Tom mounted one plate on the frame of each door and screwed the other plate into the doors themselves. He installed five in total. One on the large gate for cars at the entrance to his property and one on the small pedestrian door next to it. He added another to the front door and one on the kitchen door that opened out into the garden. The last one he installed on Sofie's bedroom door.

All the locks were connected to his network and could be controlled in any number of ways. He programmed the car gate to open if the camera system identified his car's number plate approaching, the front door would do much the same thing but operated by facial recognition software. He configured timed lockouts and set up routines for panic situations.

Tom had installed an emergency button discreetly in several rooms. One touch would activate all the locks and fortify their home. He could also control the locks from his phone with the same security app that monitored his cameras. With the addition of a few hidden keypad units that override the locks his work was complete.

The security system was starting to make him feel a little better but he was still nervous about the unseen forces that wanted to take everything he had worked so hard for over the years.

Sofie was not happy.

"Why it's like I am some sort of criminal" she moaned as he finished showing her how the lock on her door worked.

"Sofie, you are the most important thing in my life." he said "I need to know you are safe."

She had discarded a copy of Enid Blyton's Secret Seven onto her bed as soon as he began the work on her door.

"But Dad it's not fair." was her only angle on the argument.

"Look" said Tom "I'm not going to lock you up or anything like that, it's just there in case of an emergency."

Without being able to articulate her feelings she had grumpily given up on the conversation. That evening after another amazing meal Sofie employed her academic skills and with the internet's help learnt a lot about civil liberties and a concept know as human rights.

Sofie felt trapped in her room with no way to release the lock herself, she had stared at the shiny, oppressive addition to her door. She got up from her computer every ten minutes or so to check that the door had not become immovable. Reassured, she still had the option to leave her room she would return and continue with her research.

Sofie had all but forgotten that tomorrow was her birthday. Reminded by her subconscious about the impending celebration she resolved to finish building her arguments later. She went and said goodnight to Tom, who was having a heated discussion of his own. He was working in his office and talking to his friend Pat via the computer.

"Goodnight." he said to Sofie, looking up as he mimed brushing his teeth.

Sofie returned to her room and after finishing her nightly routine she climbed into the pink embrace of her duvet cover and went to sleep.

Five minutes later an interrupt request was received by the security systems control software. The camera in her room had detected no movement from Sofie and its facial recognition subroutines had identified that she was in bed. Satisfied that all requirements had been met by the peripheral devices and that the condition 'time is equal to or greater than nine' was now 'true' the software set the electronic locks instruction variable to 'on'. The current began flowing and Sofie was behind a securely locked door.

-16-

Tom's call to Patrick was not going to plan.

"Why not?" Tom said angrily, just after Sofie had gone to brush her teeth.

"You know why not Tom. Just hold your horses and finish testing things properly"

The project they were working on was ambitious but almost complete. Tom wanted to charge ahead, knowing it had the power to change the world for the better. Patrick wanted to take it slowly and make sure that everything was working properly before more rigorous or higher stress testing.

Tom had been instrumental in the creation of their new endeavour, he knew the workings of it much better than Patrick. Although both men were first rate engineers Patrick had the connections and business acumen that Tom lacked. It was natural that Patrick had a more managerial roll, while, Tom worked hands on with their projects. The arrangement suited both men well but the division had grown.

"Listen, Tom, old boy, I know you want to get cracking and see exactly how good it is but we need to get more data before proceeding any further." said Patrick while Tom began to nod "We both agreed on the schedule and for good reasons. If we want to convince the boys over here that it works I need real untainted data to show them."

"Ok" Tom sounded defeated

"We need to prove it operates under normal conditions before we get to testing the more exotic capabilities." Continued Patrick "This is about saving more than just lives, Tom, it's about doing it in the right way so that nobody knows what were up to."

Tom had heard this before and he understood the importance.

"Ok, Pat I know, you've got to trust me though it works perfectly." Hearing Patrick about to start up again Tom quickly continued.

"I promise I won't do anything yet though, I will stick to the schedule."

"Good man." Said Patrick "Now, isn't it Sofie's birthday tomorrow? Did you receive the present I sent over? Make sure she knows it's from both of us."

Their conversation drifted to the more domestic aspects of life. As they spoke, Tom had an idea that became the beginnings of great plan. He hadn't forgotten Sofie's birthday at all but she didn't know that.

The sun was already up when the camera in Sofie's room

registered her movement. It began to track the changing pixels but couldn't see her face. She had stood up and gone straight for her bedroom door. It was her birthday and pyjamas were perfectly acceptable attire today.

Foregoing the morning shower and bathroom rituals, she had instead decided on going straight down stairs to open the mountain of pink wrapped presents that she knew would be waiting for her on the kitchen table. She would shred paper and undo bows in a whirlwind of gratitude as each gift was exposed. She slammed head first into her securely locked bedroom door.

Unable to positively identify the person in Sofie's room, a chain of checksums and conditional logic gates that allowed the door to be unlocked had not been able to complete and the current stayed active.

Tom, hearing the bang realised something had gone wrong, he overrode the system and unlocked Sofie's door. Later, he would review the log files and discover the issue. A few tweaks here and there would mean that it would not happen again but the damage had already been done, both to his credibility and also to Sofie's mood.

She came downstairs in a rage, yelling about unjust freedom infringements and the inhuman treatment of prisoners. She was sure that Tom was being 'dragonian'. A statement that made him wonder why she thought of him as a fire breathing lizard, before realising the simple mistake in her language.

"It's draconian Sofie, dra, cone, ian"

"Yes it is." She replied smartly.

An apoplectic anger swelled inside her, she was going to explode. She had entered the kitchen ready to forgive her dad for the dictatorial, fascistic state she felt he was implementing. Expectations of presents could nullify even the most deep seated desire for liberty. As she entered the kitchen those thoughts evaporated.

Nothing. No cards, no presents not even a single small one. Even a small present would have tamed her rage but the table was bare.

Tom was hanging out, drinking his coffee as if it was any other normal day. He could see how mad she was but he knew she would be too polite to say anything. For a little while at least.

"Morning Sofie" he said in a happy tone "did you have a little problem with your door this morning?" before she could jump in with the objections he continued,

"Listen I have a lot of work to do today but I will see if I can fix it later, now go get the eggs please." he handed her the basket only to have it snatched from his hand.

Through severely gritted teeth she said

"Yes, Daddy, what a nice day it is Daddy, will be back in a minute Daddy, to enjoy a nice breakfast on this lovely day the twenty third of July Daddy." She had put emphasis on the date and every single 'Daddy'. Stomping angrily to the door shaking with fury she went to get the eggs.

As she lifted the well worn hatch her mood softened. Henrietta sat as usual blinking stupidly at her.

"Hey girl" Sofie cooed sweetly "how are you today?"

The fat bird bobbed its head a little as if in reply. Sofie stroked her back.

"It's my birthday," she told the hen "but Daddy forgot, I've been such a good girl and he forgot all about it"

Henrietta clucked in a most understanding way

"Thanks Henrietta it is unforgivable isn't it?"

The bird shifted uncomfortably,

"I don't even know how he forgot, Daddy even mentioned it the other day and I know he has lots of important work to do but it's my birthday."

Henrietta stood up to go, revealing a clutch of four eggs and a small but beautifully wrapped pink box.

Clutching her prize and feeling a little guilty about her earlier thoughts, Sofie ran back up to the house with a newly renewed attitude and a full force, super, jumbo hug, locked, loaded, ready to be unleashed on her dad. Flying through the kitchen door and closing the distance with Tom, in a flash, her arms wrapped tightly around him.

"Thank you Daddy thank you so much I thought you had forgotten."

With a massive smile Tom said,

"Don't be silly, I wouldn't ever forget your birthday Sofie," he picked her up and placed her on a chair

"A happy birthday to you Sofie" kissing her cheek, he placed the small box she had been holding on to the table.

"Now you open that in a minute after you've finished collecting the eggs."

She had completely forgotten the eggs and the basket in her excitement. Once again she went to fetch breakfast, this time in a completely different mood. 'I wonder what it is?' She thought 'it's small maybe its a necklace.'

Sofie was not a spoiled child at all and it wasn't the lack of gifts that had annoyed her so much as the thought that she had been forgotten. Whatever the gift was she felt assured it would be wonderful. Eggs finally collected and safely in the basket she skipped back to the kitchen and the mystery box that awaited her.

Sofie sat in silence looking at two pink rubber bands. She had carefully undone the satin bow and opened the metallic paper slowly, not wanting to damage the expensive looking wrappings. Inside was a plain white box and a tiny envelope. The envelope contained a birthday card, it was lovely, pink and clearly hand made. Tom was not an artist even by Sofie standards but she loved it. The thought really did matter to her. Once he had explained it was meant to be a unicorn she could kind of see it and loved it a little bit more.

The white box had a smooth surface that felt like the satin ribbon she had just removed. It had two halves that slid apart to reveal the pink rubber bands.

"What are they?" she asked.

Tom was smiling, clearly not upset by her puzzled reaction.

"They're amazing Sofie, latest thing, you will love it I promise." he was far more excited about this unusual gift than she was.

"Had to pull in a lot of favours to get these little babies, I can tell you. They're not even on the consumer market yet. No one else in England even has a pair."

Sofie still just looked at them.

"You know my friend Patrick? Well, he helped me get them

so you must say thank you to him next time you speak ok?"

Sofie nodded but was none the wiser as to what she was saying thank you for.

"Look closely," he said "see those little dots all over them?" Asked Tom

Sofie nodded, just able to see the microscopic marks.

"Those are cameras and some are laser arrays. They have red green and blue lasers all over them."

It sounded cool but Sofie had no idea what these were for.

"Ok, so the bracelets can sense each other right, and the cameras can track your face, that way they know exactly where your eyes are in relation to the bracelets. It uses trigonometry and makes a real time map of three dimensional space," realising he was losing her he said

"Ok don't worry about that, just trust me it's cool, anyway because they know where everything is, the lasers can draw images right onto your retinas."

Sofie still didn't get it.

"Isn't that dangerous Daddy?"

"No, no, it's fine, they are weak lasers, won't hurt you at all. So the computer inside moves the lasers really fast and with the three colours it can make you see things that are not really there."

Sofie had never been more sceptical in her life.

"Just put them on" said Tom gesturing to the box.

She took them out and slipped one over each hand, they

were too heavy to be just rubber she thought.

"Do they fit ok?" asked Tom.

Sofie nodded again and she looked around the room unsure of what she was meant to be seeing but sure that everything was exactly the same as it had been a moment ago. Tom was about to burst with excitement but Sofie just felt a little self conscious as he stared at her.

"Ok, now, Sofie give me a round of applause."

Confused but intrigued she began to clap. The second time her hands came together a phone appeared in her left hand. She couldn't feel it but it looked as real as her old glass fronted device. Her mouth literally fell open. She turned the phone over and looked at its silvery back. It was as if it was glued into her left hand, she couldn't drop it.

"What did I say its incredible isn't it?" said Tom, now almost laughing at her stunned face.

"It's a phone." Hhe said.

Tom had been ready for this response,

"Nope, it's an eye phone." He began to laugh and even Sofie appreciated the reference.

The bracelets really were amazing, she decided. Tom had told her to try and stretch the phone. As she did, it got bigger, then she pushed its edges back together and made it shrink again. This was just the start of what these bracelets could do.

The phone image was just the standard interface and could be customized to be anything she wanted but it worked really well and after a short experiment with some other preset interfaces had gone back to the phone. It worked just like a normal phone anyway. It had internet and games, you could watch movies and listen to songs.

The bracelets had tiny speakers in but you could wirelessly connect headphones or a speaker if you wanted. Some of the games were really good, using the bracelets to map her movements into the game world. The only problem with this was that when she got too enthusiastic with her movements the image would disappear completely.

At least one bracelet had to be able to see her eyes or the illusion vanished. Sofie had experimented with the limits of where exactly this would happen.

She could launch all of the games and apps from the simulated touchscreen interface. Any app would function normally appearing on the phone or she could move it off the phone and use it like a big screen in front of her.

A couple of the games were designed just for this new technology, allowing Sofie to catch falling droplets in a bucket or throw virtual paper planes through hoops that appeared wherever she looked. They were just fancy demos but showed what was possible. She had spent a whole hour chasing all manner of butterflies some clearly designed to look like ones from the real world and some completely alien. She spent another half an hour sorting coloured bricks and the fun went on and on.

-17-

Tom had some regrets about the present. First of all he hadn't spoken to Sofie for the last five hours she hadn't said a word since the enthusiastic 'thank you daddy'.

Patrick had only been able to get one set from the manufacturer. Tom was a little bit jealous, he knew he shouldn't be, but they really were awesome. He had tested them last night before wrapping them up for her to find this morning. It had been a late night. He just hoped that they would pass the required safety checks and become available to the public soon. He would be one of the people first in line once they were on sale.

Lunchtime brought Sofie back to reality briefly but he was destined not to hear from her again until dinner time rolled around. It was actually a good thing that Sofie was so distracted because he managed to get on with a good deal of work while preparing the evening meal.

Tom had been so busy with Sofie since she arrived after school almost a week ago now that he had missed deadlines, forgotten reports and updates. Patrick was understanding but Tom had resolved to get on with things after Sofie's birthday. The bracelets had given him back some time so he used it. Getting his work under control made him feel a lot better and by the time dinner was ready both Sofie and Tom would be in especially good moods.

Tom had found that he could configure the door locks he installed yesterday to recognise Sofie's new bracelets. This would prevent a repeat of Sofie's headlong dash into concussion town. It also meant that she would never realise when her door was locked. He could just as easily use the same system to stop her leaving. If he switched the settings then the doors would lock at her approach instead of opening. That could be useful for the outside gates and the main doors he thought. No more panicky mornings if she decided to go and tame half the woodland again.

The smell of roast chicken was permeating the house and Sofie began to feel hungry again. She gave the little double clap that made the phone display disappear and went in search of the aromatic wonders. A good roast dinner in Sofie's opinion is the greatest meal available anywhere on earth. Tom's choice for her birthday dinner had been an easy one.

The Table was laid, the gravy was hot and the bird was rested. Sofie took up her seat and sat clutching knife and fork. Tom looked over at her as she sat smiling and he happily began to plate up another of his carefully crafted meals. Sofie wasn't actually smiling though she was stretching her mouth hoping it would enable a higher flow rate and faster consumption.

Tom Brought over both their plates one stacked high with broccoli and one devoid of the hated greens. He offered her the plate with a mini broccoli mountain as she shook her head refusing to take the plate he held out to her. She was Pointing at the smaller but green free dish, he relented and gave over her meal.

Sofie gladly took her plate covering it in gravy she started heaping on Mint sauce for the potatoes, mustard onto the plates edge and finally strawberry jam onto the chicken.

"what are you doing Sofie?" said Tom with a horrified look on his face.

Looking puzzled and unable to answer with her face full of food she just pointed at her plate and gave a big thumbs up.

"Sofie that's Jam you just put on your chicken"

She looked at the red mess and gave the thumbs up again with an enthusiastic nod. Swallowing hard she had to come up for air.

"Its great you should try it. Honestly trust me" she said as her fork collected another slice of strawberry chicken, this time she added some mustard.

Tom blinked and her fork was empty again. She looked like a happy hamster at this point with cheeks bulging. Tom was curious. He had tried all manner of things in his life from possum to insects and one summer away from university while backpacking he had even tried a cat out of curiosity, but this? Well, it was Sofie's birthday after all.

He took the jam jar and spread a thin layer onto his next fork full. After a couple of chews he was adding a healthy lump of jam to his plate as well.

"its like cranberry sauce on turkey but better" he said.

Sofie tapped at her head to indicate that she thought she was clever.

The meal continued but not much more was said as Sofie could only grunt little noises in response to Toms small talk. When they had finished Sofie got up to take the plates to the dishwasher. Tom stopped her and told her to stay where she was he would do the dishes tonight. He deposited the plates and with much fanfare opened the fridge to retrieve a wonky chocolate cake.

"Sorry Sofie I know its not pretty but it will taste ok I have never been any good at cakes."

Sofie could not have cared less what it looked like it was an amazing cake. All eleven candles were lit and she made her wish. Tom allowing her to cut the cake herself. He glanced quizzically at her portion sizes and returned half of his own to the leftovers. She could try and eat a third if she wanted but Tom didn't fancy his chances of achieving the same goal.

Sofie had somehow managed to eat all of her gigantic portion. Covered in residue she sat exhausted from the effort.

"you have a little bit of face left on your cake" joked Tom.

She was so content and happy that she laughed along with

him.

"Hey Sofie did you play that puzzle game I installed for you?"

"Yeah it's ok but I like the butterflys one better."

"really" said Tom "why don't you open it up again for me quick"

She clapped her phone into existence and tapped the SoCo-Gaming logo.

The game awards stars for matching three or more coloured blocks together each block only able to move one space. You could collect the stars and when you had enough exchange them for flowers or decorations. These virtual flora could be planted in a garden and the more levels you cleared the bigger your garden got. It was a neat concept and Sofie had intended to play it later.

"Ok so are you on the menu" Asked Tom. He got a nod in answer.

"right ok do you see the little green person at the bottom right" another nod "click on him"

As she opened the submenu she saw four names. Tom and three of her friends from school. It was a multiplayer game. She could build a profile and even upload pictures to the chat window.

"Its not got as many features as those social networks but"

She cut him off with a hug

"Thank you Daddy it's great" She had left cake all over his shirt in her excitement.

For the next few hours she chatted with friends and sent pictures of lions. She had used the picture of Mr Ted as her profile pic still thinking that was a good idea. The little app had some neat features and she really did love being able to talk to other people. Only she could play the game in 3D but it worked perfectly well on any 2D screen. Sofie had been planning to ask Tom for permission to use a social network but this was good enough for now.

Before bed she had one last question

"Dad I'm just wondering what are these called" she asked while holding out her wrists as if ready to be cuffed

"ah" said Tom "those are Project two X four B five two three P a snappy little name huh?"

He went on to explain that they really were the latest thing and hadn't even been given a product name yet. It was something the marketing department in America still had to work on.

"How about we just call them your phone ok? off to bed now little lady"

As she sat in the back of another black 4x4 She remembered that birthday. Had that really only been five weeks ago she thought to herself, so much had changed. She had no idea where these men were taking her or why they had made her leave that nice social worker behind.

Ellen Mackenna had put up a hell of a fight calling everyone she knew to stop the men taking Sofie. They had the legal authority to do it but Ellen could not work out how they had secured such a judgement. Ellen even tried to physically stop them but they were big, well built security guard types and she was a tiny woman no matter how big her attitude. The paper work in order the two guys had removed Sofie from care and without another word put her into the truck that idled outside.

-18-

It was just after eleven p.m. when Caroline produced the first chunky treat for Pickles. He greedily set about chewing it. First with the left side then onto the right, teeth making short work of the fibrous protein strands. He sat up purring and raised a fur covered claw to grab at the next offered piece.

"gently there little buddy" said Caroline.

Pickles was continually confused by the noises she made but they had a sweet melodic nature these days and he didn't mind the way they reminded him of bird song. Unintelligible to the feline but both song and speech hinting at the prospect of a meal.

Tonight Caroline had a lot to tell her only friend. She recounted the story and feeling sure her words would not be repeated she told little Pickles everything. Caroline even offering her theory's and feelings on the matter.

"I'm sure that Judith is just jaded with the work she has to do. I know they have their procedures and stuff but arresting that poor girls father must have been awful for him."

Treat number three was disappearing

"Imagine Pickles, If someone took one of your kittens and then you got blamed for it, so wrong"

Number four was offered but pickles was still working on number three. Distracted by her thoughts Caroline was effectively force feeding the cat. Not that Pickles would complain but there is only so much food he could get down at once. Resolutely Caroline made a decision

"Ive got to find her and make sure she's ok. I can apologise to her dad and help catch whoever is responsible."

Caroline believed she was the only person who could solve this kidnapping and felt entitled to the case. After all she had found Sofie, She had rescued Sofie and now she would get justice for Sofie.

This idea had been circulating through her thoughts all day and was now firmly cemented into her objectives, she began to plan and strategise. Not the method of capture but how she would be gracious in victory. Imagination working double time she was already accepting another round of applause but this time it was well deserved. She was picturing a shiny medal and a firm handshake in front of adoring press photographers. Caroline was sure she would get a promotion to police detective, bypassing all the necessary training and experience that such a position requires. A little spark of reality intruded in on her fantasy.

"Where to start though Pickles?" She said to the cat and actually awaited an answer.

No answer was forthcoming so she continued to brief her friend hoping that the answers would present themselves.

"Ok so I need to find a clue, then follow that clue to the next and then to the kidnappers"

Caroline's understanding of detective work being completely informed by the likes of Holmes, Christie and Poirot she considered this a logical approach.

"Judith didn't tell me where Sofie and her dad live so, I'd have to start at the crime scene"

She felt inspired and expecting to find some torn note or unusual foot prints headed once again to the car park. Pickles sat licking his paws watching her swift retreat, safe in the knowledge that tomorrow would bring more meaty treats his way.

She had arrived at the pub just after the last few patrons had left and the heavy doors had closed. Starting at exactly where she found Sofie, just twenty hours ago, Caroline inspected the recycling bin and immediate area around it.

Nothing. How was there nothing she was sure there would be a clue here. Caroline turned on her torch and began walking a spiral away from the green sided clothing receptacle in an attempt to find her imagined lead. After a few ever increasing circles she began to think that maybe the forensic team hadn't inevitably missed the crucial clue that she now searched for.

Caroline had inspected cigarette butts and lottery scratch cards, discarded receipts and half chewed sweets in an ever more hopeless endeavour. After twenty more minutes the only place she hadn't searched was inside the bin itself.

"The Bin" She said aloud.

Why hadn't she thought of it earlier? 'It must be in the bin'. Assured that she had finally cracked the case and positive now that the bin contained the all important first clue she ran once more to where Sofie had lain.

The recycling bin was a large square sided metal one. Designed to hold clothes that people donated to charity shops, ostensibly, to help the impoverished. Most people believing that the clothing itself would be sent to whichever third world country that they currently worried about. The charitable souls would bring plastic bags, full of forgotten closet contents and put them into the bin through a large swinging flap on the receptacles front side.

Some of these bins employ an airlock type design so that the clothes cannot be removed once gifted. The manufacturer of this particular design felt that if someone needed to steal clothes from a charity bin then those people were the ones that needed the charity in the first place.

The flap was at head height for Caroline but with some arm strength and a few scrabbling kicks she had managed to fit her torso into the bins interior. Legs still outside and flailing to maintain a careful balance in hopes of preventing her from disappearing as if swallowed by the bin's green mouth. Caroline heard a door swing open, the sound muffled by her new surroundings she could still make out a angry lady shouting at her now skyward rear end.

"get out of there you disgusting little thief. Those are for starving children. What sort of person would steal from a charity." screamed Marge.

After all the excitement of last night the pub had done a roaring trade during the day. Chef and barman alike under a pressure that almost rivalled the busy Saturday afternoon bingo hour. As locals who normally only visit on special occasions poured into the pub with hopes of hearing the gossip. 'what happened?' 'had they really found a girl?' 'was there any news?' and on it went.

The tills might be full but Marge and her husband were happy when the crowds began to disperse. A news crew had arrived and while trying to interview the bar staff were less than politely asked to remove themselves. The reporter had set up over the road and recorded a short piece about the mystery girl. With no real information about the incident it had only run on the local news channel. Patrons gone and staff sent home, the doors were locked and Marge went upstairs to relax and unwind. She was about to get into her brightly coloured bubble bath when she saw a most unusual sight indeed.

The light was going round and round in circles. 'What was happening in their car park now' she thought. The bathroom window being mottled Marge could only see the light making its circular journey. She put her clothes back on and went to see if the little window at the top of the stairs would offer a better vantage point. With her view now unobstructed she could see it was a person holding the light. Marge watched as they gave up circling and then tried to get into the clothes bank.

As Caroline wiggled her way out of the bin she raised her hands

"Its ok I'm a police officer" thinking 'sort of' to herself. "I'm just investigating the kidnapping"

Marge realising her mistake and relieved she wasn't going to be fighting off a teenage vagrant she noticed who's bin diving she had interrupted.

"Oh Its you, you're the one who found that poor little child last night. Would you like a cup of tea dear"

Caroline had seen enough of the bins completely vacant interior to know it was a dead end so she readily agreed. The women went inside and upstairs to swap war stories and rumours.

-19-

"There you go dear" said Marge placing a milky cup of tea in front of Caroline.

She thanked Marge and looking at her thick walled red coffee mug wondered how much Marge's gold gilded bone china cup had cost. Matching the teapot and Saucers Marge's cup spoke of serious investment into the finer tea drinking arts. The whole living room was like that, it looked like the centrefold in a country living magazine. Doilies and taxidermy cluttered the surfaces. Decorative plates and horse brasses were hanging from black painted beams. Cute floral print curtains bordering all the windows. The furniture was either solid wood or upholstered in similar vintage patterns. A few more seats plus the addition of a till could have transformed this space into one of England's most stereotypical tea rooms.

Marge's husband worked diligently in the corner checking credit card receipts and counting spare change, he added up the days takings. Before Caroline arrived Marge had voiced her displeasure at him taking so long to complete the task. He had be flabbergasted at his wife's short sightedness.

"Dear" he had said with a patronising tone "the longer it takes the better. Would you prefer me to have less to count"

Marge had seen the logic but still had a schedule to keep. On a Tuesday night they would watch an episode of Heartbeat then she would have a bath and go to bed. Unwilling to wait any longer she had decided to skip their TV ritual and go straight for her bath. Only for that plan to be interrupted by the mysterious light.

Caroline took a sip of tea, her taste buds instantly alerting her to the mistake she was making. Caroline enjoyed strong black coffee without sugar. The bitterness and the warmth making her feel comforted. This tea on the other hand was half milk, almost stone cold and full of sugar. Grimacing she said.

"mmm that's good, bit hot though, might have to save that for later" she put the cheap mug down as far away as possible.

Marge smiled and took a sip of her own tea.

"Good I am glad it's ok, I don't take sugar or milk myself but I know you youngsters like it sweet"

Nodding in response Caroline was to polite to tell Marge she had tasted less sweet sugar lumps.

"So why were you trying to get in to that bin then" Asked Marge.

Caroline was slightly worried about hyperglycaemia but explained her actions and moaned about the lack of results. Marge had been working on her tea listening all the while. Marge decided to help fill in the events after Caroline and Judith had left with Sofie.

"Well dear the police dogs turned up just after you left and they went running off through the village but were back not long after it started raining. Then another lot of your friends showed up with cameras and evidence bags. It was like something off the telly you know. They went over everything in the car park and they even had a look in that bin"

Caroline's heart sank they had checked the bin her clue was gone. Marge noticing her dismay asked Caroline

"Everything alright dear hows that tea doing?"

Caroline reluctantly retrieved the red mug.

"Right where was I? Oh yeah, then we opened up the pub and what a palaver that was I can tell you. Every man and his dog wanted a pint. Busiest we've been in ages, had some reporters show up but I told them where to go."

Marge paused for a sip of tea.

"Then the second barman came in early at twelve and I came up here for a nap."

That seemed to be the end of Marge's story for now. Caroline couldn't tell Marge what had happened to Sofie but Marge seemed to accept her explanation that it was normal police procedures.

The conversation was faltering as both had told all they could. Marge seemed ready to ask about Caroline's tea again.

"So Marge any theories any ideas?" Asked Caroline in an attempted deflection.

This had opened the flood gates of racist and bigoted conspiracy theory. Shocked by the amount of different culprits that Marge had imagined committing the crime. Caroline sat in silence and enjoyed another twenty rambling minutes of tea free time. Eventually Caroline's avoidance efforts had been pushed beyond the polite and she was forced to dance with diabetes once more. Swallowing the tea flavoured syrup Caroline was eager to stop Marge's wild accusations. They were only one paranoid step away from lizard men being the reason that Sofie had been kidnapped.

"Ok Marge, Hold on you said some terrorist types had moved into Finchdean a couple of months ago. Is that right?"

Only to eager to expand on this point Marge had said some things that Caroline was afraid to write down in her little notebook she settled on. 'Newly arrived immigrants possibly religious'.

"Ok thanks and you also said something about sex offenders being moved here in secret?"

Marge looked taken aback.

"Oh no dear not here god no, not in this village we wouldn't have that sort here. No the government has been putting them up in Forestside and West Marden out that way. You see the people out that way are a little funny anyway and I guess they think a few more weirdos won't be noticed."

Caroline had also patrolled these villages, they were well inside the eastern teams catchment area. She knew some of the people and none of them were 'weirdos' the truth was that Marge was just so xenophobic that even the next village over was a world away to her.

The tea was finished and Marge had been checking her clock with sideways glances. Taking the hint Caroline stood up to leave.

"Thank you so much for all your help Marge but I have to be going now."

Feigning sorrow Marge had weakly protested while ushering Caroline towards the door. As she walked back towards her car Caroline heard the first bars of Heartbeat's opening credits coming from the pubs upstairs windows. Marge and her husband would watch tonight's re-run it seemed. Caroline hummed the familiar tune and almost stepped on Pickles.

"Hey little buddy"

She dropped a treat and as it started to disappear she picked up her furry little cat friend.

"So we have two options Pickles its either option A the secret government is putting paedophiles into Marden or option B Terrorists have set up a new cell in Finchdean"

Caroline shook her head believing both leads to be ridiculous

"not much to go on is it little chap?"

Pickles couldn't understand a word of what she said and in

this case that was a good thing. If he had understood Pickles would have chosen option B. because he didn't even like cats who had different coloured fur. Pickles was a massive racist.

Oblivious to her feline friends beliefs, Caroline happily carried Pickles all the way back to his garden wall. Leaving two more treats behind she climbed into her car. With no other leads and nothing of importance to do she drove for West Marden.

Arriving fifteen minutes later at twenty past twelve the date had rolled on and it was now Wednesday morning the second of September. These date changes in the middle of her shift were a constant source of annoyance for Caroline. Whenever she filled out her time sheet for work she would have to remember to split the shifts into two parts.

On any particular day Caroline had to note two different times from two different shifts. Her times were firstly the end of one shift that ran from midnight to finishing time and then secondly the start time of her next days shift until midnight. It was a most tedious and confusing task to fill this out correctly. She would become confused by dates and knew well that any mistakes would result in a delay to her pay.

She had driven slowly through Forestside's main street before reaching West Marden, she had been mulling the time sheet problem over while looking for any signs of, well, anything. The street looked the same to her as it had every other night, beautiful and alluring with its gracefully elegant houses.

Suddenly she had it, she knew what to do. Each day she would write her hours onto a calendar. Pleased with this idea she continued on to West Marden.

As Caroline came round a sharp bend she saw the village sign against a flint wall. They were pretty big on flint in these old villages. It made a fantastic building material looking pretty and being reasonably strong.

Villages all over the south of England feature flint construction, mostly due to the lack of any better or stronger rocks to be quarried. This sedimentary form of quartz had formed in the chalk downs over millions of years. It has a crystalline structure so small that it is even hard to see under a microscope but it is this structure that gives the rock its other useful properties.

Being formed in soft chalk, the harder flint rocks had been exposed easily by weathering. When the early settlers had discovered its ability to cut through thick hides many villages had been seeded along the chalk downs.

Centred around the production of sharp tools these prehistoric communities had prospered and thrived. Flint arrowheads and blades are still found to this day all over the South of England.

As the march of time has rolled on it is conceivable that at least some of the stones now used to build so many garden walls and attractive little houses were once employed in a similar fashion but by a much older people.

West Marden is dotted with flint cottages and has a lovely bed and breakfast built with a mix of flint and brick construction. Not that anyone who looks upon this beautiful building would know what it was built from. It's completely covered by attractive vines with only the windows and doors free from leaves. In one of these windows Caroline sees a friendly looking man tending the front desk for this mini hotel.

She entered through the white panelled front door as a tiny

bell announced her ingress. The greying man looked up smiling broadly.

"Hello and a warm welcome to Home Farm, I'm John and I'm sorry but all our rooms are full tonight. Anything else I can help you with?"

Caroline extended her hand and they awkwardly shook over the counter.

"Hi I'm officer May, I'm not looking for a room though, I'm on duty. I was just passing and saw you were open. I didn't expect to see anyone awake at this time"

The man gave a big smile

"Ah right well Its the secret to a happy marriage you see" tapping his nose conspiratorially.

"I run this place with my wife and she works the day shift while I work the night" now laughing "haven't seen her for thirty years"

Caroline gave a polite acknowledgement of the attempted humour.

"I'm just joking I love my wife and we see plenty of each other. I'm what you call a night owl and the guests appreciate the service if they need it." John gestured to the stairs behind him

"So thanks for checking up but everything is fine here"

Caroline gave a big grin.

"No problems just making sure the community is safe." deciding she had nothing to loose said "You might be able to help me actually"

Caroline asked if he had seen anything unusual . He hadn't and he wasn't the sort to engage in village gossip anyway. He had heard about the little girl who had been found in Rowlands Castle and told Caroline all about it. The version John had heard was slightly more embellished, having travelled further to get here. He told her how people suspected the new Russians who had moved into Finchdean.

"Hold on what was that? Russians?" said Caroline.

"Oh yes that's what everyone is saying. Nice chaps though its totally not true of course but you know how these village women talk."

Caroline was intrigued and asked.

"You know them, these Russians?"

"Oh yes dear three of them. They stayed here before they got the house in Finchdean."

John began reminiscing.

"Not been as drunk as that since I finished uni."

He proceeded to tell a story of nights spent playing cards and drinking hard alcohol. The friendly men had been the perfect guests in Johns opinion clean, well mannered and best of all fun. His usual clientele being comprised of elderly hikers or worst of all middle aged cyclists. John felt that Lycra and manners were seldom possessed by the same individual.

Caroline had realised now that the rumour mill had swapped a lot of details by the time Marge had heard of these new arrivals. Maybe Marge had even added some details from her own prejudices before passing the tip on to Caroline.

"John, do you know what these guys do for work?" Asked

Caroline

"Oh not too sure but its something with computers they had all that equipment set up in their rooms, screens and stuff. My wife thinks they're hackers but I think they're working on that new power station"

"Why do you think that John?" asked Caroline

"Cause that's what they told me dear. Well, I think they did it was pretty late."

Caroline almost couldn't believe that her plan was working but she pushed these thoughts aside with her usual overconfidence. It was perfectly logical after all. Everything had gone exactly as planned. She had gone to the crime scene where through Marge she had found a clue. She had followed that information to this village where she had picked up her next lead.

The fact she had come looking for sex offenders ensconced into the town by a shadowy government organisation had been forgotten. This second connection to the formerly 'Religious Terrorists' now 'Russian Hackers' having been placed in her lap, she was convinced of the significance.

The convenience that she had been lucky enough to bump into the one person who could advance her investigation seemed like fate to her. It confirmed everything she believed about her skills as a detective. Truth was, she could have spoken to any resident in West Marden and she would have been directed to the Bed and breakfast. Every single person in the village had noticed their foreign guests and although the villagers are friendly and welcoming to all they are also prone to gossip and fantasy.

Caroline had to track these men down somehow. Thinking that John might know where exactly they had moved to she asked him. John, assuming he was talking to a police woman, handed over their address without a second thought. The men had left it in case there was any mail to be forwarded or if John had fancied loosing even more money to the proficient poker players.

Caroline had said her goodbyes and left John to tending his beautiful establishment. She walked through the villages main street while mulling things over. The pub was shut and in the rest of the houses she didn't spy any more lights, all having been extinguished many hours ago. Caroline came to a junction with another main road. This road was where flint built housing stopped and green fields took over. She retraced her steps back to the bed and breakfast's car park.

Climbing into her car once more Caroline headed for a little well in a village square that offered her the perfect place to enjoy her midnight meal. Just between a delightful cafe and a handsome pub Caroline would sit in the same spot every night to eat her packed lunch. As she ate her food and drank her coffee Caroline was completely unaware that she was so close to where Sofie had lived all this time.

After lunch Caroline's journey to Finchdean would take her within two hundred meters of the country lane that lead to Sofie's house. For now though she just sat and enjoyed the moonlit scene before her.

Back in her car Caroline was full of coffee, the caffeine adding a jittery edge to the adrenaline that began to circulate around her veins. She was hot on their tail. She was going to finally catch them. She was going to confront the three Russians.

What the hell was she thinking these could be seriously dangerous men on the run and afraid of the police. They could be armed. If they could do such horrible things to Sofie then they wouldn't think twice about hurting Caroline.

She almost didn't see the turning. Stopping just in time she took the left into Idsworth and headed south, on towards Finchdean. She passed an eleventh century church, she knew it was famous for being the oldest church in existence and being built buy the arrow in the eye guy from Hastings. She was wrong on both accounts. It was actually built by king Harold's father and there are many older churches in England, for example St Martins in Canterbury, constructed in the sixth century is the oldest parish church which has been in continuous use.

Starting to really worry as she got closer to the Ashcroft Lane address Caroline decided to do a quick reconnaissance tonight and then come back in the daytime to have a proper look around.

She drove past the property on a poorly maintained road. She had turned off her headlights and slowly crept past with just the cars sidelights on, barely providing enough light to drive safely. She couldn't see a thing and having no idea which house was which was forced to drive away.

She Told herself it would be better in the daytime and she would be able to see the house numbers at least. In reality she had bottled it but drove away thinking that she had made a sensible choice. They could be dangerous and she was a single officer alone at night. Caroline didn't think anyone else would have done any differently. A little part of her ashamedly remembered the look on Sofie's face.

-21-

"Hello my dear may I help you with something" A heavily accented voice said.

Caroline spun already reaching for her pepper spray. A heavy set but powerful looking man stood before her. He was wearing a track suit and was already raising his hands in a display of non violence.

Caroline hadn't noticed him standing behind the hedge she had just walked past. Hidden from the street by the green wall he was out of her sight line as she concentrated hard on the now familiar two tone building, inspecting it for the fourth time.

She didn't draw the pressurised canister of capsaicin from its black pouch but she did keep her hand on it ready to use it if he made one wrong move.

After her retreat from Ashcroft Lane earlier that morning Caroline had finished her shift and attended the briefing as usual. Barry and Rob met her, both looking fresh faced and ready to go about their day. She hadn't told them of her investigations, instead relaying a report she was now used to giving. This report consisted of a repetitive structure built by joining village names with the words 'nothing of interest'. They had listened to the report with feigned attention.

The Police lead briefing hadn't lasted long and she was free to go home. Instead she had chosen to make her way once more to the Village of Finchdean. Sun now up, cockerels were informing everyone of this fact, just in case they couldn't see it for themselves. In the light of day the lane seemed much less oppressive.

Caroline began conducting a walk past. She would casually walk along the lane past the houses and without appearing too interested she looked for any signs of criminal activity.

"I am sorry if I have scare you" The thick accent continued "I mean no harm"

Caroline relaxed a little but kept her hand on the defensive device.

"Oh" She said "that's ok don't worry about it" She turned to beat a hasty retreat.

"Excuse me young lady may I be knowing why you have interest in my home"

She denied it and tried to leave again.

"Don't be thinking I am stupid you have been up and down five times now each time you watch my house. I grow the roses to be beautiful but it is not them you are looking for I think"

Caroline felt caught she had been stupid all she could do was say sorry. The man tried to smile.

"Do not be misunderstanding little police woman I am a good law abiding person and if you are interested in my house I just hope to know why? We do not want any trouble and if there is some problem I would rather fix than ignore this"

He spoke in a confident way and reminded Caroline of her father and his dislike of subterfuge. Taking her hand off her pepper spray she put it out to be enveloped by the man's huge hand. As they Shook she introduced herself and he returned the greeting

"and I am Frank you would not be able to say my real name I think" he chuckled "Caroline may we go inside my home we can talk in there as you may have noticed my neighbours are already twitching at the window cloth"

Feeling like she had no option and not sensing any threat from this man she had agreed and she came through the garden gate.

Now sat in a perfectly normal living room she waited for frank to make her a cup of coffee. In the kitchen he called out

"Milk Caroline and do you take Zakhar sorry sugar do you eat the sugar?"

She called out her refusal and noticed the black sub machine gun sat casually on a small dinning table. She was on her feet and drew the pepper spray. As Frank entered carrying two mugs he had a confused look on his face.

"What the fuck is that" she shouted indicating the German built weapon with a twitch of her head. Frank broke out into a relieved grin

"This is just toy Caroline do not be worry. My friend likes to play soldiers on Sundays. It is like paint ball thing you know here I will show"

"Don't fucking move" Caroline said cutting him off.

Frank stopped moving towards the table.

"Ok for little girl you scary, how about you check it for yourself I stay here"

She kept the spray pointed at his face and inspected the weapon. Pulling the bolt back exposed a plastic cylinder instead of a brass filled chamber. 'It was a toy.' She lowered the spray.

"Sorry but it looks so real"

Frank went to sit on the couch sensing her relaxed stance

"Yes looks real but shoots plastic ball, very legal, I tell my friend to keep in room but he does not listen to me. Other friend Clousarr he listen ok but Plamen no listen me"

Frank indicated the opposite couch

"Come Caroline sit and tell me why you are here."

As she was sitting Frank shouted to the other room in a language that sounded like a donkey being run over with a soviet tank. She did catch the name Plamen though.

Another tracksuit wearing man appeared at the door and began collecting his toy.

"I tell him to away this and put safe. Ok?"

"Thank you Frank" Said Caroline.

"He say name Frank?" said Plamen "Him name not call Frank him call Francis is girl name"

After a short burst of expletive laden tank sounds Plamen was running back upstairs to escape Francis's tirade.

"I am sorry Plamen is no good English speaking I am Frank ok no Francis I Frank"

She nodded in agreement.

Caroline was stuck she had no idea how to begin her story. What could she tell Francis as to why she was here? She had no cover story, she had no way of asking the questions she needed to ask. Why hadn't she thought about this before? She hadn't exactly planned on meeting these men let alone ending up sharing a coffee with them.

Francis could see she was struggling to explain her self and wanting genuinely to help.

"It is ok Caroline, Frank knows what these little village people are like they are the same everywhere in Bulgaria we have this to. I will not be offend you can tell me what they think we Bulgarians are doing in their little village."

"Bulgarian I thought you were Russian?" Said Caroline without thinking.

Francis was obviously upset by this faux pa.

"No Caroline no we are proud Bulgarian people. You English think all Eastern Europe is Rusiya but we make alphabet in Bulgaria and it is the Russian who steal this and sound like us"

"Sorry Frank I didn't Know" said Caroline apologetically

"This is ok we forget this no problem, please why are you here?"

Feeling now that she agreed with John's opinion and that they were indeed a friendly people she decided to explain herself. She didn't get very far.

"Ok so two nights ago I found this little girl"

"Ah" Francis cut in "it is you who is rescue our friends little Sofie."

"How in the hell do you know Sofie?'

"Caroline this is no secret we work for her father Mr Tom and his friend Mr Pat. Everyone in company has hear of little girl. Is very sad story. Although we didn't know Mr Tom even had little girl before yesterday."

She couldn't believe it these men worked with Sofie's Father.

"Yes yes Mr Tom although we do not see Mr Tom in long time. He help us with software issue before though Mr Tom is super genius with computer, he works on secret projects for Mr Pat not with us on simple things"

Francis went on to explain that they had been hired by Patrick to work on a the control software for a new power reactor.

"It is Williamsburg reactor we help design this in Bulgaria, made by very clever Bulgarian physicist much cleaner than dirty American designs. Mr Pat is very clever man to use Williamsburg design"

Francis had continued explaining how they had come over and stayed at the Bed and breakfast.

"Ah you are also meeting Mr John he looses a lot of money when he drinks, good friend"

They had stayed there until Patrick had found them this house.

"Mr Pat has just buy this house and he say we can live here while we work for him. Mr Pat pay us very good moneys"

Francis was a little concerned

"So Miss Caroline do the village grandmothers think we are hurting little Sofie?"

She had tried to avoid answering but Francis could tell they did by her evasion. Caroline could see how upset this had made him and she tried to change the subject.

They had continued chatting about the three friends time in England. Francis had said how he and Clousarr had been friends for years, both working as software designers on many of the same projects. They didn't know Plamen that well but all three had come over on the same flight and had lived together since arriving.

"Clousarr Is joking but he says Plamen is assassin for Mr Pat is funny yes? But is true Plamen does not know how to use computer. He is also enjoying the shooting game here very much."

Francis unlike Clousarr thought Plamen might be a security

guard or something

"He is always out at the night time and in day he will sleep. He is quiet friend but no trouble so is ok"

Looking at his phone Francis realised the time.

"Oh Miss Caroline I am very sorry I would like spend all day talk with pretty girl like you but I must be going work now."

She looked at his tracksuit

"No no I work here in my room on computer can wear what I like."

With this another dead end she got up and thanked Francis.

"Thanks for your time Frank listen if I wanted to check up on Sofie do you know where she and her dad live?"

"Yes" said Francis "they live very near just up road in outside of different village. I will Send your phone message with address ok?"

Ecstatic that she had at least managed to track down Sofie she happily handed over her contact details. Caroline had left with a friendly wave while Francis was blowing kisses at her. She felt weak, realising that she was in need of food and her bed she decided to go home and continue her investigation later. If she didn't look after herself she knew she would be no good to anyone else.

Three marriage proposals later the address finally arrived on her phone.

-22-

The sound of fireworks exploding all around her Sofie opened her eyes in horror. Trumpets blaring as a medieval looking scroll was carried into her room through the window by two little blue birds. A knight in shinning armour took the scroll and as it was unrolled fairies flew from the page revealing "Friday 24th July. Good Morning"

Sofie would definitely be changing this new alarm feature. Named 'Fantasy' and described as 'being awoken in a fantasy world of wonder and delight' she had selected this mode from a long list of possible alarms before going to sleep full of birthday cake.

She stretched herself and rubbing at her eyes fell into the shower. She didn't feel any different today she had imagined that being eleven would make her feel more grown up. It Hadn't. Heading downstairs and into the kitchen Sofie was greeted by silence and a distinct lack of coffee smell. Where was dad? Perhaps it was just another of those days where he was still in bed. They didn't happen often but she always had fun waking him up when they did.

Remembering the ship battle and the adventures of dread pirate Sofie, she would plan a new game for now. Today she would be a proud lioness, apex predator on the African savannah and Tom would be a sleepy wildebeest unaware of the danger creeping towards him. She quietly opened his door ready to pounce but his bed was empty. The wildebeest was safe for now.

Sofie was prowling on all fours hunting her prey. The game not over yet she had tracked the sleepy animal to its den. The door to Tom's office was open wide enough for her to slip inside. She observed the animal in its natural surroundings. Her keen hunter's ears could detect the sounds of its hooves tapping at a keyboard. The Wildebeest was distracted and for this, it would pay the ultimate price.

She froze, the beast had stirred, perhaps its senses detected the danger. No, she was undetected the hooves had begun their tapping again. The time was now, she sprung, her lightning fast approach startling the creature. She had it. Her teeth would bring down this oversized pray.

"Owe that hurts Sofie why are you biting my arm" Said a confused Tom.

"I'm a lion and you are in my grasp now silly wildebeest"

She had been dismissed. It had upset her far more than was reasonable she knew that but it had just been so abrupt. Tom had been too busy to play with Sofie. It didn't matter to her how important his stupid work was she didn't care that his friend Patrick had deadlines to meet. She wanted to play and daddy didn't.

Sofie hadn't had breakfast and perhaps that was the problem. Well she was a big girl she could get her own breakfast. One trip to the hen house later and after a good chat with her friend Henrietta, she had come to the conclusion that Tom was grumpy because he hadn't had his coffee.

Sofie loved the smell of coffee and it would forever remind her of her dad she knew. She had watched him many times, fiddling with his machine, all knobs and buttons she was sure she knew what to do. Sofie stood in front of the black and chrome device tilting her head from one side to another. She had expected pictures or instructions.

Confident as she was in her memory still she wanted some reassurance or at least an indication of what the controls did.

The wavy little lines and random pictures of cups were as incomprehensible as if they had been Hieroglyphics.

'Ok, Step one' she thought ' take off this silver cup with the handle and put coffee inside' She could do that. If she got stuck then she could get Tom and hopefully he would help.

The portafilter holds the coffee but unaware of its name, Sofie thought of it as the silver cup. Pulling on the handle hadn't worked but pushing it to the left the portafilter had come free. Spurred on by this victory she had become more confident with the idea.

'Now to add the coffee' She took down a copper coloured tin that contained toms 'Lazy Coffee' these pre-ground beans being reserved for the morning when the noise of his grinder would disturb Sofie or when he was just feeling lazy. Not Instant coffee lazy though those days were rare indeed.

She added the Coffee grounds to the portafilter and feeling creative added some of her instant chocolate drink powder to the mix. She would make Tom a mocha. Having heard about the chocolate coffee blends she assumed they must be superior because the addition of chocolate made anything superior. Tapping down the coffee and chocolate mix she was ready to begin.

Noticing the little protrusions on the top of the portafilter and realising how they must engage she returned the cup to its caddy. Turning the handle she saw it sliding upwards and into place.

'Ok the next thing was the mug' She knew everyone had a favourite mug. For this special brew she wanted her dad to really enjoy it. She would find his best mug. Tom's most prized coffee mug was adorned with characters from an eighties cartoon. The imposing robots forever in the midst of a frenzied battle to save planet earth. Sofie located this antique mug on a hook, retrieved it and placed it under the portafilter. She knew the hot coffee would slowly pour from the bottom of that silver cup.

Now the Button. Tom had let her press the 'go' button before and she reached up once more to activate the great machine now.

As she left the kitchen in search of help the machine was making unusual noises. The water heater inside had built up a head of steam and began to exert almost two hundred and twenty pounds of force per square inch into the portafilter. The cup's diameter measures in at two inches. The seal held back over one thousand pounds of force.

It is this incredible pressure that pushes the flavour from the grounds into the cup. Even these powerful forces are safely contained and used by people every day. That is of course as long as the pressure can escape.

As the first water drops had made their way through the coffee grounds they had encountered chocolate powder. The sticky substance melted and began to cement the coffee grains together, forming an impenetrable barrier that prevented the ingress of any further water. The heating element continued to pump more energy into the system and the pressure built. The coffee grounds became more and more compacted.

Toms machine had been made cheaply but the people who sold it had boasted about the high pressure brewing. The machine had been marketed as a premium piece of equipment. Thinking he had purchased the best Tom had gladly made a bad decision. This unit used steam pressure alone, where as a quality unit will operate at a much lower pressure and employ a pump to do the work.

The factory that made Tom's machine had also over looked the cost, benefit analysis that would have urged them to install a pressure relief valve or cut off device. It is in this perfect storm of false advertising, poor design philosophy and an inexperienced user that we find Sofie asking her dad for attention once more.

Tom reluctantly got to his feet as he could see the worried look on Sofie's face.

"What is it? What's making funny noises Sofie?"

The seal gives way, releasing three times the amount of pressure that the sloppy designers had ever envisaged it experiencing. The resulting bang they hear, was interestingly, in part produced by the portafilter as it briefly broke the sound barrier. Producing a sonic boom on its way downwards to end the robots battle that they had been fighting all these years.

-23-

The black and chrome machine lay in ruins. Toms mug was scattered through a badly damaged kitchen in small pieces. Pieces so small that most people would refer to it as dust. The portafilter or silver cup as Sofie thought of it, had after passing through Tom's mug slammed into the drip tray and impacted the marble work surface with enough force to crack the great stone slab. It had ricocheted into the ceiling where it still stuck as a testament to its supersonic flight of destruction. The escaping pressure had sent fragments of steel shrapnel forwards in an arc that had caused more devastation and the demise of a window.

Tom stood in the doorway too shocked to speak, Sofie behind him also stood in stunned petrified silence. The spell seemed to lift as condensing water dripped from the hanging rack above the once perfect marble topped island.

"What did you do? What the hell did you do?" Asked Tom sounding defeated.

It was a terrible row and no amount of protest had tamed Tom's anger. When Sofie had reached the point in her story about his prize mug she had thought he was going to cry those angry frustrated tears we all know too well.

Sofie had forgotten about the chocolate powder that had catalysed this catastrophe and in this moment it was better for that detail to go unsaid. Banished to her locked room she would remember the addition of chocolate to coffee. She would wisely decide on keeping one small secret from her dad.

Tom was calming down and had even begun to realise what would have happened if his Sofie had been stood next to the unit when its group head had failed so spectacularly. This scenario making him equal parts angry and relieved. Tom was already planning a lawsuit as his anger redirected from Sofie to the manufacturer. He would research the company only to find out its UK office was just a mailing address. The owners and those ultimately responsible for this dangerous device were well outside his ability to bring legal proceedings against them.

She would stay in her room though, Tom had decided that she needed to learn a lesson about not messing with dangerous things. He had set the door to lock her in and there she would stay until dinner time. He had taken the new phone bracelets off of her but did offer the olive branch of a promised return.

The buzzing was driving her mad. Just on the edge of hearing but definitely there. A high pitched whine that oscillated constantly. At first Sofie hadn't noticed the noise as it was drowned out by even the tiniest of sounds. Easily obscured by the cooling fan in her laptop it was only when she shut down the pink plastic computer and picked up her copy of Robert Westall's, The Machine Gunners, that she could hear the continuous auditory annoyance.

'What is that?' she thought to herself. She tore her concentration away from the exciting events that were happening to Nicky and his gang. Garmouth, Fort Caporetto with its machine gun and world war two would have to wait. Sofie had her own battle to fight. She checked everything in her room and finally tracked the source of her annoyance to the bedroom door.

Pushing on the door to open it and find whatever was making the buzz, she realised it was stuck. Pushing harder she discovered that she had been locked into her room. The buzzing was the electromagnetic components of the lock. Rage, anger, injustice and captivity all hit her at once. Sofie braced her shoulder into the wood and pushed with all her might.

Sofie was made of strong stuff, having been raised the way she was. She hadn't sat wasting her life on a comfy cushion consuming chemical concoctions, passed off as nourishment while soaking up the dopamine release of virtual entertainment.

All of her strength couldn't move the door an inch. In her rage she punched the unyielding wooden prison. Her little hand now hurting she sat on the floor. 'Its my fault' she was accepting her punishment. The thoughts chased each other one logical assumption leading to another. One acceptable denial followed by a reasoned self admission.

It was her fault the kitchen was ruined. She hadn't meant to do it, but it was her fault that the machine had exploded. She hadn't known the powder would cause a problem but she hadn't asked for permission. All she wanted was to help her dad but he didn't know that. It went on and on like that. Sofie finally understood that no matter what her intentions had been the results were her fault. She knew daddy loved his kitchen and he was mad because of her.

The buzzing stopped a few hours later and Sofie fell backwards. She had been sat against the door reading when Tom had sent instructions to release the lock. Now free from her prison she felt pangs of guilt, her sentence had concluded but perhaps she deserved worse.

"Sofie dinners ready"

Came the call from downstairs, rising to her feet she went to face the music once more.

She had been amazed at the transformation in the kitchen. Broken window was boarded, shrapnel had been removed, cup dust was gone and the water had been mopped up. The cause of all her troubles had been removed, the devastated machine conspicuous in its absence. The cracked marble island and ceiling hole were now the only obvious signs still visible.

Sofie stood in the doorway ashamed of herself she began to make apologetic noises. Tom's anger had now been redirected and he wouldn't hear Sofie's apologies, he insisted it wasn't her fault. This made Sofie feel worse, her guilt and self loathing building, until Tom opened the oven.

"WOW that smells so good" said Sofie

The prospect of food once more pushed all other concerns out of focus.

Tom really is an excellent cook having dabbled as a kitchen hand during his days spent at university. His primary goal, to earn beer money, had quickly become an interest in the culinary trade. He was eager to learn and a friendly chef was more than happy to pass on her extensive knowledge. Bridget gladly took her time explaining to Tom how the right techniques and skills could be used to craft art. Not mere food to dull hunger but art to feed the soul as well.

The plates he had assembled tonight were once more laden with roasted wonders. Potatoes, Yorkshire pudding, carrots and peas all surrounding whole mini roast chickens darker in colour than the bone stock gravy. Sofie had never seen such small chickens on her plate but began work at once. The mustard, Mint sauce and jam came out once more.

'Potato first' Sofie thought as this one item alone will inform the consumer as to the quality of the meal as a whole. 'Excellent as always'.

Next came the pudding raised to perfection, covered in gravy and a mustard selection. Onto the chicken she pulled free a leg. So small and so dainty with teeth she now fed. A flavour unusual and gamy in nature confused by its species her question would quaver.

"Mmm what's this dad its not chicken is it?" She asked

"No its those Pheasants I shot last Friday" came Toms answer.

On the last day of Sofie's middle school education he had a few hours to kill before she would be delivered to his home. Tom had been so excited to start their holiday together he couldn't concentrate on work. To pass the time and entertain himself he had strode out across the downs in search of some shooting. On the edge of the woods he found two fine looking pheasants. The shot from his gun caught both birds together. Tom had no choice in the matter driven by sheer necessity

"Two birds one stone" he said.

These unlucky fellows had hung for five flavour developing days before Tom had plucked and dressed them. Another two days in the fridge soaking in even more flavour from the salt, pepper and herbs rubbed onto their skins. This morning had seen them stuffed with an onion and placed in the oven for a long and low temperature roasting. Over that week Tom had forgotten about Sofie's views on eating pheasant. Unfortunately for Tom as she now sat there with a mouth full of one, she had not.

Without thinking she spat the mouthful of flesh onto her plate and dropped the tiny leg. She started to wipe her fingers and mouth clean of the bird.

"Sofie that's disgusting don't spit your food." admonished Tom his shock replaced by anger.

She wailed her reply while trying to clean her tongue with now dirty napkin.

"But dad you know I didn't want to eat pheasant"

"Why ever not what's wrong with pheasant?" He asked.

She explained about the road kill and how it had made her feel.

Tom didn't understand why this had affected her at all let alone so much.

"Its just a bird Sofie, They are food to be eaten. Same as chickens or turkeys"

She couldn't understand her own feelings well enough and lacked the vocabulary to articulate her thoughts properly. Tom wouldn't listen and she would not eat.

Tom's phone made a little chiming sound. Tom took out the device and seeing an alert he jumped to his feet.

"Get to your room"

Tom hadn't meant to shout but the words still sounded

angry to Sofie. Sure he was upset with her reaction to dinner she began protesting.

Tom didn't have time to deal with this he needed to get her safe and quickly.

"I don't care about dinner Sofie someone is coming now get to your room now." He shouted the last word.

Sofie saw that it was panic not anger that agitated her fathers words. She was instantly scared, Who was coming? what did they want and were Sofie and her dad in danger?

As she went for the stairs she saw Tom grabbing the shotgun he had used to procure tonight's meal all those days ago. She was more scared now than when the ill fated coffee machine had started with its protest song.

Reaching her room she was comforted as the lock's buzzing noise started once more. She had time to reflect on the change in attitude towards the hated lock. Once jailer now protector, were safety and freedom always at odds?

The deafening roar of a shotguns thunderous report just one moment later would see a terrified Sofie hiding under her bed in freshly wet knickers. She very bravely ventured out from cover quickly to save Mr Ted. She lay there with her teddy friend curled up and shaking. It was all she could do to reassure Mr Ted in a whisper.

"It will be ok, It will be ok, It will be."

The pre programmed alert on Tom's phone had been the final action of his security system. Activated by movement that the gate camera had detected, clever sub routines had sprung into action. These software packages were called on by the operating system to identify what was moving. They searched libraries of image files and compared the results at a fantastic rate. Just today they had been able to correctly identify crows, badgers and even a deer that had passed unnoticed by the human occupants that these cameras guarded.

In the event that they find a human or car the images would be passed to a different set of routines. These specialists would work on further identification in an attempt to discover what level of access would be granted to the subject. For example, if it was Tom approaching, the system would open the gates. In this case even after consultation with the facial recognition database the individual had remained unknown. The Gates locked shut and as instructed the system sent a live camera feed to the phone in Toms pocket.

He could see a shape dressed in black it was sneaking towards his front gate and shining a torch about looking for a way into the garden. When the intruder had tried to climb onto the garden wall Tom had pulled the trigger and split the night with explosive lightning. The Shot aimed skyward sending an obvious message.

-24-

Caroline had made it to her bed. That was a nice surprise. She had slept exceptionally well not sticking to plastic furniture but cradled comfortingly by cloth. It was Thursday the third 'no, it's still Wednesday the second' she thought to herself. Checking her phone she remembered she could see Sofie today and with that happy but sad thought she got ready for work. Kissing her dads photograph on the way out of her flat she felt for the first time that he would actually be proud of her.

She had called Judith and once again waited for her arrival. The Italian coffee shop was deserted once more but today its lone staff member was a young man. Caroline thought he was probably working this job to earn some extra cash on the side. She would have been shocked to know that he was in fact working this job after his dreams of a career had come to a screeching halt.

He had completed his degree and was ready to take up a position working for any of the biggest and best media companies. CVs sent and promptly ignored the value of his combined media and gender theory qualification was starting to dawn. A harsh reality that confronts many in today's marketplace. Caroline's abandonment of higher education had on the other hand been a more successful path to employment. No crippling debts behind her she was already beginning a career that had potential. She may be overestimating that potential but it definitely would take her further than the business end of an espresso machine.

Judith had been happy to meet Caroline, she had very few friends and none she could discuss work with. It also didn't hurt that Caroline was nice to look at. Feeling a little flush when she had entered the coffee shop Judith quickly stowed those thoughts and approached Caroline as a friend not wanting to telegraph any desire for more. 'Well not yet anyway' she thought to herself.

The conversation had started pleasantly enough, the waiter assuming the pair were old friends. They talked easily and soon Caroline was telling Judith everything that had happened.

"Are you crazy" Judith said "You could have been walking into anything. Oh my god you can't do this you are just a PCSO you could have been killed"

The concern Judith was showing for Caroline's safety was well deserved but Caroline dismissed it as overblown she was especially annoyed by being referred to as 'just a PCSO'.

"Hey Judith that's not fair I'm not a complete moron I knew they were friendly, even that John chap in West Marden said they were good people." Caroline was being defensive and Judith knew that wouldn't help.

"I know he did Caroline but what if he had been wrong, What if they had been hiding something you could have been in real danger." As she said this Judith took Caroline's hand.

"Look I know how much this must bother you, It got to me too. The fact that they have put this down as a diplomatic incident though, that should tell you something. Right? powerful people are involved possibly dangerous ones to"

Caroline nodded and withdrew her hand.

"look I got to get to work ok" said Caroline "but I promise to be careful, I will watch my back"

Judith was already agreeing when she realised what Caroline had said.

"What do you mean you will be careful? Tell me you haven't got any more investigating to do." Said Judith.

Caroline lied and didn't tell Judith about her planned visit to Sofie's home. The pair finished their coffee with tension in the air. They went their separate ways after a polite but guarded goodbye. Judith wasn't convinced that everything had been said, she was worried for her new friends safety.

Caroline walked to the police station through Waterlooville's pedestrianised precinct. As she past the budget retailers and chain cafes she thought about everything tossing around all of the information and ideas she had. Deciding that a visit to Sofie couldn't be dangerous, it may even help her draw a line underneath all of this and walk away. Perhaps seeing the girl safe and at home would mean that she didn't feel the need to pursue the unknown person behind Sofie's abduction.

Caroline arrived and changed into uniform quickly. Her handover briefing from Barry and Rob completed moments later, Caroline had set out on her way to Compton and to Sofie. Barry had for once given her real instructions though.

During her previous nights investigation a teenage visitor to Rowlands Castle had decorated the train station waiting room with a pictographic representation of male genitalia. Lacking the nuanced genius of a renaissance masterpiece the crude artwork made up for a lack of skill with its sheer size, measuring in at nineteen feet.

In an attempt to stop the art piece being recreated tonight, Caroline was to spend her shift in or near the freshly repainted waiting room. Assuming that the fledgling artist wouldn't strike until after dark Caroline had told Barry that she would complete her rounds of the other villages before setting up shop at the train station. The sun would still be up for at least two hours so she was on her way to a pretty country lane outside Compton.

Not trusting the ability of her police car to navigate this unpaved surface she had parked two hundred meters east of the address. The lane went steeply up over a small hill and then descended just as quickly on the other side. Flanked by fields and watched by sheep Caroline made her way round puddles and over deep ruts left by the 4x4's that enjoyed this type of terrain. Between the roadway and field was a wooded bank that gave the lane the feeling of being tree lined.

From the summit she could see Tom and Sofie's house. Surrounded by a wall and protected by heavy gates the Edwardian building inside was clearly a farmhouse but reminded Caroline of Portchester castle. The charming building looked beautiful nonetheless.

Even from this distance she could see the interior was also exquisite in its taste. Living room looked comfy and warm. Two plates beautifully decorated with a feast, sat on a giant oaken dinning table. Then she saw the kitchen and was honestly impressed. The upstairs windows showing sills decorated with flowers and bordered by country print curtains. Caroline couldn't see much but everything she could see spoke of a bank account the size of which few could dream of.

Caroline approached the walled in garden as the front door opened and a man appeared. He matched the description that Judith had given her, this must be Tom. He knew exactly where she was, he had come out looking for her.

Caroline was still at least ten meters from the edge of his walls. Looking around she quickly saw the cameras trained on her approach. They were made of white plastic and stood out against the natural backdrop, their main purpose was not covert surveillance, instead acting as a visible deterrent.

She gave a friendly wave but Tom made to return inside. Caroline called to him.

"Hello, sorry excuse me"

Tom stopped his retreat.

"Hi could I just have a quick word?"

Tom nodding his agreement he turned and began the walk to heavy perimeter gates. The black wooden door opened and Caroline was greeted by a very angry face.

"What the hell do you lot want now?" he said with hatred etched into both voice and eyes.

"Hi I'm so sorry for how you were treated"

"How I was treated" Tom cut her off "are you joking? You lot just threw me in a cell because my Sofie was missing"

Caroline had not been expecting this attitude but in retrospect should have been prepared for it.

"Look I'm not really with that lot I'm not even a real police woman" This was the first time Caroline had ever admitted that fact even to herself, she continued "I found Sofie I'm Caroline"

If she thought that this revelation would result in a change of Toms attitude she was wrong

"I don't care who you are, unless you are here to arrest me again, for no sodding reason you can go and hang yourself"

"Look I'm really sorry about that." Apologised Caroline "but I only came to see if little Sofie was ok, I'm sorry"

Toms face changed slightly at the mention of Sofie

"She is fine now are we done can I get back to my dinner please?"

Caroline was glad that Toms temper seemed to be cooling a little.

"Could I please see her I just wanted to say hello"

Again Tom's expression changed this time to a more worried look.

"No sorry I'm afraid she isn't here right now." He said

"Oh where is she?" Asked Caroline automatically.

"How in the hell should I know? Now please leave us alone" Tom was already closing the heavy gate when he said "sorry what was your name again?"

"Caroline May"

"Right and shoulder number"

"Oh one zero seven seven" the request catching her off guard as the gate slammed.

She stood there in disbelief staring at the abruptly closed gate for a moment before making the muddy return trip to her car. Shoulders slumped as she avoided the puddles. Caroline looked back at the house one last time before cresting the summit.

Caroline arrived at the train station still replaying the encounter in her head. It was over what else could she do? All of her detective work had ended up in nothing. No leads no clues no nothing. What would she do now? It wasn't the loss of the medal and the promotion that bothered her so much although that was a bitter pill to swallow. She still didn't know what had happened to Sofie. It was a case unsolved and it was her only case. Well apart from the dick diagram bandit.

Pickles had found his friend and he could smell the fish flavoured treats in her pocket. Jumping onto the bench she occupied, Pickles attempted to retrieve a treat from her pocket. Having no luck he began to purr loudly and rub his body against the friendly human.

The sound woke her and she attended to her friend's hunger. Caroline realised she must have fallen asleep while she sat on the station platform. She had sat and thought for hours. Something about her visit to Tom was nagging at her mind. It wasn't right he had said 'leave us alone' why had he said 'us' if he was by himself.

Caroline had remembered his words around midnight but by one o'clock she had convinced herself that it was just a slip of the tongue. An easy mistake to make while so angry. By two o'clock she was again racked by the same feeling that she had missed something important. Tom had said he didn't know where Sofie was, that seemed unusual for a protective parent.

Caroline looked at her watch 'crap' it was already four o'clock. She had been asleep for two hours. Reaching into her pocket she produced another meal for pickles. Her hand held out two of the little treats. Two meals 'Oh my god' there were two meals on the dining room table. Her thoughts erupted with possibilities, at the front of them was her belief that he had lied, she was there. Why had Tom lied to her about Sofie being there? Perhaps he just wanted Caroline to go away? Why hadn't he just said that she couldn't see her. Why lie? This thought became her world in that moment.

She sat there starring across the tracks and supplying her little friend with more treats thinking over and over 'why would he lie?' It made no sense. Pickles had left Caroline's side just as the first commuters began arriving. In their heavy coats and bobble hats the early workers shuffled onto the platform.

It wasn't freezingly cold yet but early in the morning, September temperatures still require an extra layer of protection until the sun puts in an appearance. Stamping her feet and bouncing herself up and down on the seat to get a little more circulation going Caroline let out an audible groan as she stretched her arms.

The first travellers were laughing at her. 'Perhaps she was amusing to them' Caroline thought. Well it was about time to go anyway. she would leave these braying idiots to their morning coffee and long trips. As she stood up and turned to leave she saw that the ticket hall, waiting room and toilets had been transformed into a canvas, decorated with one bright blue twenty six foot long spray painted penis.

-25-

The shotgun blast rolled away across the downs. In its wake a silence that was only broken by a terrified voice.

"What the hell man don't shoot, Don't shoot" coming from outside toms garden the voice sounded angry but heavily tinged with fear.

Tom had moved quickly he was through the gate and had come out with his gun trained on a black shape against his wall. As Tom sidled an arc away from his gate keeping the Barrell pointing at the crouched figure. The man who was the centre of toms circular walk had his arms wrapped around the top of his head. Tom didn't close the distance keeping the barrel well out of reach.

"Get up" Tom ordered.

"Are you crazy man? stop pointing that thing at me." Hands now raised in surrender the unannounced visitor got to his feet "please man stop pointing that at me. Ok?"

Tom lowered the barrel but kept it pointing at the ground near the man's feet ready to bring it back to the aim if he moved.

"Who sent you why are you sneaking around my house" Barked Tom.

"My wife sent me she lost her Husky again. I'm not sneaking round anything mate honest" The man was clearly scared and didn't seem to be a threat.

Tom relaxed his stance and lowered his weapon completely. Tom knew he was still far enough away from the man to shoulder the gun and get it on target in time if he had to.

"If you are looking for a dog why climb my wall then?" Said Tom.

"Like I said I'm looking for her dog its a great big black and white husky called Beefnburger or just Beef. I thought I would just stick my head over and see if he was in there."

Tom looked at his white wall with its tiled top.

"My wall is seven feet high?"

"Ha you think that would stop him. He is a bloody escape artist mate. fence round his kennel, easily over seven foot, can't figure out how the hell he's getting out. It's like the thing can climb chain link or something."

Tom questioned the man further but sent him on his way with an apology for the warning shot and a promise to keep an eye out for the Houdini Dog.

"Thanks Tom that would be great" Handing Tom a lost dog flyer he pointed to the phone number "Call us if you see him ok? Or if these do." The man gave a nod while pointing at Tom's gate camera. "They any good mate? Been thinking about getting some of my own"

Tom replied as eagerly as any man does when questioned about his purchase choices.

"Yeah they are great. Good image, night vision and motion detection. That's how I knew you were outside before you jumped my wall."

The man was leaving to continue the search for the wayward Beefnburger but he had one last question.

"You put em all round your wall or just out the front here?"

Tom thought he heard a slightly suspicious tone in the question.

"Yep all round three hundred sixty degree vision" He hadn't installed cameras all round the perimeter just concentrating on the front of his property and the gates. As Tom went back inside he decided to rectify that oversight. Tom would be going shopping again tomorrow morning.

The front door slammed shut behind Tom as the man carried on his search.

"Its Ok Sofie just some guy looking for his dog"

Tom reloaded the shotgun and placed it back on its wall hanging. He used his phone to unlock Sofie's door. Lifting the emergency protocol he had written for situations like this. When Tom had seen the video alert he had hit the panic button. This initiated a complete lock down and all doors would seal shut only to open if Tom approached them. The one exception was Sofie approaching her bedroom from the landing. In that situation her door would also unlock. It would not unlock to allow her out but it would let her in.

Security levels now reset to normal he had expected to hear Sofie running downstairs in relief. He called her again. Still no reply. Toms heart was beating fast as he stormed into Sofie's room, bed empty and en suite vacant he called

"Sofie!"

Panic once again making his thoughts race. Had the guy at the gate been a diversion? Had some unseen accomplice infiltrated the house and taken Sofie? Where was she? Tom heard a very frightened little voice from under the bed.

"Daddy?"

He had helped Sofie calm down and waited patiently as she washed herself. Her sodden clothes had been put into the washing machine and he now sat on her pink bedsheets cradling her teddy, talking to her through the bathroom door

"I'm sorry Sofie I didn't think the gun would scare you like that but everything is ok I promise"

"I hate it" she shouted above the noise of the shower "Daddy why don't you get rid of that thing?"

Tom didn't want to scare her but he felt that his shotgun was a necessary security measure.

"What about the chickens though? What if a fox tried to get in the hen house?".

"You can't shoot those foxes." Said Sofie Remembering the little fox cubs "Daddy they were only little"

Tom had underestimated Sofie's love of all creatures once again

"So should we just let them kill Captain flaps and all his girls then? Sometimes we have to do things to protect the things we love ok?"

She had become quite concerned about the danger to the cubs now

"Don't shoot them daddy please just scare them away"

Tom had promised not to shoot the foxes and after one more concession that would help preserve the local pheasant population she had relented in her efforts to disarm their household. Tom made the point that the gun was a good way of scaring things. Sofie who was proof of this fact was now clean and getting ready for bed.

Tom brushed the hair from her eyes as she rested her head on the pink pillow. Placing her bear shaped friend under the covers with her he tucked them both in.

"Now lets hope tomorrow isn't as eventful as today was."

She smiled and nodded an agreement.

"I'm sorry about your coffee machine Daddy."

To Tom that calamity felt like it had happened ages ago, instead of occurring just this morning.

"That's ok Sofie it really wasn't your fault. Here you can have these back now"

He placed her birthday bracelets under her lamp and kissing her forehead he turned of the bedside light.

"goodnight Sofie"

He left her room and She was already unconscious before the door closed behind him. The buzzing resumed once more.

Tom still had work to finish and made the journey to his study. Sitting down he powered up his work computer and the screens came to life. Typing in his overly long and complicated password activated the facial recognition and thumbprint scanning that was the next layer of security to protect his system.

The desktop loaded and Tom navigated to find his games folder. Opening this he selected a old retro role playing game and started the program running. Familiar epic music played as the menu appeared. He could spend hours in this game waving a sword at Dadroth or shooting arrows at Dremora but instead he opened the options menu and changed the display resolution to its lowest quality setting.

This convoluted sequence of actions opened up the real operating system and allowed Tom access to his work. If he hadn't completed all of these steps correctly and in the proper order he would have to restart the computer and try again to access the heavily encrypted files he now worked on. Try too many times and his life's work would be replaced by a library of cat pictures.

-26-

Tom had worked late into the night every evening for the last two weeks. He had become increasingly annoyed at Patrick who was holding back testing of Tom's project while pushing him to help out with the control systems for the new Williamsburg reactor. The Bulgarian engineers having been unable to make the individual systems work together fast enough to control the reactions.

Designed almost twenty years ago. No one had actually ever built the revolutionary fusion generator until the design had been selected by the British government. Driven by political pressure for cleaner energy a comity had been set up to asses the benefits of three competing designs. Williamsburg's design had been selected primarily because of budget constraints.

The government had learned a tough lesson about subsidising renewable energy after many schemes had failed. The free market wouldn't invest in green energy without a guaranteed rate of return.

Huge swathes of countryside had been disfigured by companies cashing in on the chancellor's generous offer to set a fixed price for wholesale electricity. Cheap solar and wind farms had sprung up everywhere assisted by an easing of planning restrictions. Poorly maintained and quickly built the generators had been a disaster.

Taking matters into their own hands had been the governments only option. The upfront investment required to build fusion reactors was beyond anything reasonable for a private company. With the backing of a country sized economy the energy commission had started their first reactor.

It wasn't just one reactor but in fact three. The first two were older molten salt designs and produced energy by fissioning material to heat water that would turn to steam and drive turbines. These turbines spun huge magnets inside miles of copper wire to generate electricity. Simple enough really.

That power was then used to drive an electromagnetic containment system as ambitious in scale as it was in accuracy of control resolution. The field could be moved and shaped by its controlling software. If you wanted to it was accurate enough that you could use this magnetic field to split the shaft of a needle from top to bottom and into ten equal parts. But at the same time it was large enough to contain a passenger jet. This incredible device was however dwarfed, in terms of energy consumption, by the array of pumped pulse lasers that surrounded this magnetic monster.

These lasers had a combined point temperature that was an astonishing thirty nine million degrees celsius. At these temperatures mummy Tritium and daddy Deuterium will happily get together to produce little baby Helium. With every single elemental birthday producing over seventeen million electron volts of energy.

From an interview with J.G. Williamsburg Featured in the March Issue of Physics Today.

"Well as you know in a traditional fission reaction we take an element, most commonly isotope two thirty five of uranium and split it with neutron bombardment into its daughter isotopes and that *process releases energy. One pitfall of this process being the highly toxic and radioactive daughter products. Well I thought it was about time we finally cleaned up this whole mess and since the nuclear industry has produced more than enough daughters I felt it was high time we finally had a sun."*

The Williamsburg design also incorporated a Dyson sphere to capture all of that lovely energy. This sphere was not made of garden variety solar panels but instead employed carefully tuned silicon sheets that could capture not just photons but a wide spectrum of radiation as well.

Cooling this sphere of solar energy siphons was a water jacket with a litres per second flow rate that makes Niagara falls look like a leaky tap. Along with stopping the whole sphere simply melting away it also has the added benefit of producing high pressure steam that in turn captures and converts the thermal output via more turbines.

It was this unquenchable thirst for water that meant the plant was being built by the coast. The sea being the only viable option as even the largest lakes in Britain would quickly be drained by the unstoppable water pumps long before the resulting steam had time to condense and replenish the levels.

Once running this fusion reaction could produce more than enough energy to feed back into the lasers and magnets to sustain itself. The left over energy powering half of England's national grid. One problem being the unpredictable energy requirements of the population and the constant need for adjustments to power output.

The sun would be brought into existence and snuffed out again many times a day each time requiring a huge amount of energy to kick of the inferno. Storing those kind of energies is dangerous even in perfect conditions so the slaved molten salts were an obvious choice. The whole system when seen as one unit could actually be used to burn up waste from older reactors. It would one day solve a lot of problems.

But the problem Tom had to solve was the communication latency between so many separate control systems. The reaction had so many individual parameters being monitored and adjusted on the picosecond scale that even the speed of light was becoming an issue.

The control software would blink down one end of a fibre optic and by the time the signal had been received and processed the condition in the magnetic fields may have already changed. The best solution lay in quantum entanglement he was sure but answering that curious question would be the job of scientists like Rutherford and Fry.

Tom had found an inspired solution and it was this he now worked on. Each individual system would control everything. Well, basically each individual control unit would have a virtual reactor to work on. Modelled from reality only the controls of the system that the particular program worked on in the real world would be accessible to them. He explained how this would work using one of his favourite subjects.

"Ok so think of a line cook right. He is working on making a burger. Now once the meat is ready he passes it to the bun guy who has just cut the bun and adds the salad. What if they couldn't talk to each other or see each other? How would bun guy know when to cut? Well bun guy could fry his own virtual burger. Ok? Then when that burger is almost ready he cuts the bun just as the real burger arrives. Its just that the bun is a terrifyingly strong magnetic field and the burger is a two hundred trillion watt laser array"

It was a solution that would require a monumental amount of computational processing power but It could work. So until the physicists could figure out faster than light communication Tom was stuck working on programming telepathic fusion chefs and it was making him hungry for breakfast.

Tonight Tom was going to craft another marvellous meal for Sofie. She was still asleep but he could get the messy bits done before she woke. He headed to the chicken coop basket in hand while Sofie was dreaming about rabbits and seagulls after her lonely evening with Watership Down. Tom had been so busy these last weeks he had barely seen her.

Tom opened the hatch and collected the eggs.

"Hi Henrietta old girl" He said "I'm afraid its not going to be a good day for you."

The bird was past her egg laying best and the new generation was now starting to lay. He picked up the fat bird and cradling her under his left arm he took hold of her neck with his right hand.

"Good girl. Good chicken now shh everything is going to be ok"

Flicking the chicken like a bull whip separated her vertebrae and she hung limp at his side. Tom felt this method was both more humane and a lot less messy that the cone of silence.

By the time Sofie was awake the bird was dressed stuffed and in the oven. Egg sandwiches were ready and on the table for breakfast. When she arrived to consume the bread egg combo Tom was already making his excuses and heading to his study for another long day in front of his screens.

Sofie was so bored of this. In the last two weeks she had got up finished her chores, played by herself, seen her dad for meals and been confined to the garden or house. No trips, no days out, no nothing. She had argued about playing in the woods and Tom had sent her to bed early. She had complained about a lack of freedom and he had just ignored her. Tom had explained about his work being important but to her she may as well have been a prisoner in some totalitarian state.

She had bored of the bracelet games and the device was now just a fancy phone to her. In her thirst for excitement and exploration she had taken to reading her books. She had ordered the complete works of Tolkien, with Toms permission of course, but it was as yet undelivered. Sofie liked real books. There was just something about holding them and turning pages that made her feel warm and fuzzy.

She felt is was worth waiting for a physical copy but with no new pages to turn she lay on her bed playing once more with the bracelets and their settings. Messing around she disconnected from the home network and loaded an app to see what would happen.

She sat up straight. Deprived of their mainline data feed the bracelets had resorted to a mobile phone connection. Establishing communication with a local cell tower had opened up a route to the internet. A route that did not go through her dads impenetrable firewall.

Holding her breath and too rational to hope that her dad had overlooked this feature she opened up a window browser. Typing in the address that had always resulted in stick figure police wagging fingers at her she was instead greeted by a prompt asking her to log in or create an account.

Had she been more entertained these last weeks or even less contained she would have probably backed away from the forbidden social network and been content. But she wasn't content, she was filling out the registration form. She should stop, no need to go any further. It was wrong to disobey Daddy.

She lied about her birthday being too young for the site. She almost stopped herself and now she had her profile and was uploading photos and videos to it. Ok it was done she had a profile and as long as she didn't start looking for friends or adding people her profile would remain private and hidden. She scrolled through the suggested friends.

Her dad was calling. Fearing she had been caught clapped the phone out of existence and shouted.

"I'm not doing anything Dad"

"I didn't ask what you're doing I said dinner is ready." Shouted Tom.

She glided into the kitchen with her hands behind her back eyes ablaze at the roasted dish laying on the still cracked but usable kitchen island.

"ooh chicken my favourite" she said

The last time he had cooked her chicken was her birthday but that had been a shop bought bird. He was far more proud of this dinner having raised the feast himself. He was starting to feel guilty about the time he couldn't spend on her. This would make up for it he thought as Sofie began covering one of her best friends in strawberry jam.

The potatoes were perfect as usual but she could see some little green trees on her plate. She would deal with those later, disgusting things. The chicken was fantastic and as she chewed each juicy mouthful a pure sense of enjoyment tickled her brain.

To deal with the broccoli Sofie cut each tree into slices and sandwiched them between a slice of chicken and a lump of potato. With enough mint, strawberry and mustard she could ignore the insipid bitterness that she tried so hard to disguise.

Broccoli gone, breast meet digesting and potatoes finished she had just one succulent leg left to chew. Holding the bone like a medieval lord she tore at the skin with her teeth. 'Wow' this tasted so good. 'Better than usual' she thought happily.

"Mmm the people at the shop did a great job on this one dad"

She would be sure to tell the store owner in Compton how good this batch was. Tom was so glad she was enjoying the bird he had grown.

"Oh yeah I forgot to tell you. She's not from the shop it's Henrietta"

-27-

Two weeks ago in this very room a coffee machine had exploded with enough force to break marble and glass alike. The explosion that now took place, although metaphorical, dwarfed the earlier literal one in both intensity and duration. Tom had no idea that Sofie would react this way.

To him all the chickens were the same he didn't realise she had formed a special liking for this bird in particular. Sofie's rage and disgust were making her feel sick and in pain this culminated in a fit of screaming and swearing the like of which had never left her mouth before. Sofie had thrown her plate and banged her fists on toms chest.

Everything stopped instantly and abruptly.

They stood there, Tom and Sofie looking at each other a ringing silence in the air.

Her cheek on fire and Toms hand stinging. The silence dragged on, disbelief in both sets of eyes. What had just happened had he really just hit her. The pain growing quickly the truth dawning he hadn't just tapped her he had really hit her. More pain more burning. Sofie opened her mouth and screwed up her eyes she stood their crying and shaking. The red mark on her cheek was four fingers wide.

The apologies came thick and fast but made no difference he promised things he could never deliver with no effect. The screaming continued he couldn't stop her crying

"Sofie stop crying" amazingly she stopped crying.

She carried on whimpering and trying to suck in badly needed air but the bawling had stopped. Tom realised she wouldn't respond to his niceties but she wasn't prepared to risk disobeying him.

"Sofie I am sorry I had to hit you but you need to understand you left me no choice?" She gave a pathetic little nod,

"Good girl."

Sofie reached out to hug him. Sofie was craving reassurance and protection, Tom was the only source available to her.

He happily returned the hug explaining

"You were out of control saying such naughty things and you hit me Sofie you must never hit me ok"

She never would again

"I'm sorry Daddy" She said "I didn't mean to I was just upset about Henrietta".

"Ok I understand and I can forgive you this time if you promise never to say or do such wicked things again"

"I promise Daddy," she would have agreed to anything. "I

promise I will be a good girl."

Tom was now sure it had all been her fault the earlier guilt at striking Sofie gone.

"I think you should clean up all this mess and then go to your room and think about what a naughty little girl you've been" He had work to do anyway.

By morning the physical mark was gone but the phycological one remained. At breakfast there was a new quietness between them. Tom had collected the eggs this morning not wanting Sofie to be upset further by the loss of Henrietta he really didn't think it would have upset her as much as it had. She knew what chicken was and where it came from but he should have realised she liked that one in particular. Still what's done is done. On Sofie's side of things she was trying to behave not wanting to do anything else wrong.

Tom decided to cheer her up.

"Hey I know we have been cooped up for a couple days how would you like a trip out?"

Sofie seemed eager to get out of the house.

"Where are we going Daddy?"

Tom liked surprising her and this would be a good one.

"Oh nowhere special just for a walk it will be a surprise ok?"

Sofie loved surprises.

"Sounds fantastic after breakfast I will get ready what do I need to bring"

"Just bring your little backpack" looking out the window Tom added "and put a raincoat and a bottle of water in it, wear your boots"

"Are we going hiking Dad I love hiking."

They would be going hiking but first Tom had to be sure of a few things.

He started by asking Sofie if she knew what foster care was and then he asked if she knew what jail was. She had a rudimentary understanding of both.

"And would you like to live in foster care never able to see me again Sofie?"

She was horrified what was he saying was he sending her away because she had been bad?

"look" continued Tom "you know it was your fault when you made me hit you last night yes Sofie?"

She was still ashamed that she had made him do it and agreed.

"Good well you mustn't ever tell anyone what you made me do ok. Not even my friend Patrick ok? If you ever tell anyone they will take you away from me and put me into jail with lots of nasty men. I might even be killed in jail and that would be your fault if you had ever told anyone."

Sofie was getting upset again but she promised and she really meant it. She would never tell a soul what she had made Daddy do to her.

"Good girl now give me a hug and finish your food" Said a relieved Tom.

They had finished breakfast and Sofie loaded the dishwasher. She went upstairs to pack while dark clouds turned black and rain began to fall. It had quickly developed into a thunderous storm.

Tom and Sofie stood in the front porch looking at the sky then the car then each other and back to the sky.

"raincheck?" They said together before heading back inside.

"So what do you want to do now then watch a movie or something?" Tom asked Sofie.

Sofie was happy to watch a movie with Tom but soon figured out she would be watching alone. Tom didn't want to watch it with her he wanted her to be entertained while he got on with some more work.

A week. A whole week of rain. Sofie had raged at the near continual deluge. She had spent the last week waking up excited for their mystery trip and every day her heart broke a little to see the curtains of water still falling outside her window. It had been a most dull and boring week.

Her permitted domain had shrunk even more although no rules prevented her from exploring the garden it may as well have been the surface of Venus. No laws or rules preventing a trip to the green planet either just the atmosphere of sulphuric acid and pressure that could crush a car.

Sofie was well aware that Venus isn't green but her mental picture had been informed by the adventures of Dan Dare and the excellent radio dramas of Charles Chilton. Nothing could now shift that mental image. Just as acid clouds would prevent the exploration of Venus these terrestrial cousins made of water were preventing her exploration of Earth.

Mr Ted had become somewhat of a hit with her new social media friends. Sofie's avatar had joined a few groups and added a couple of people to her friends list, here and there. Sofie's outlook and naive optimism had been a breath of fresh air to a lot of the people that she interacted with online. Especially as it appeared to be the musings of a little pink bear. He, or in reality She, had been reposted and followed many times now as Mr Ted's fame grew.

One source of amusement had been Sofie's failed attempts to find any of her school friends online. It seemed that not one of those kids had actually been able to convince their parents to allow access to this site either. Every single one of them had been lying. All the time she had heard them talking about what they had seen or what they had posted was a complete lie. The age limit was thirteen for a reason but Sofie had believed all the stories they told during the breaks between lessons.

This was how she had spent her free time for the last week, alternating between social media and the newly delivered Tolkien book bundle. Thankfully the book seller had wrapped the box of books in a waterproof bag. It had been a fantastic morning. The books were presented in a lovely sleeve and each hard back tome had gold gilding on the edge of each page.

It was the most amazing collection she had in her library. One annoyance was that the presentation box was about two millimetres to tall to sit neatly in her shelving unit. So it now took pride of place on her little dresser table. She was just too short to place the books on top of the book shelves.

She did wish for more free time despite the lack of entertainment options because her chore schedule had been filling up fast. Tom had been delegating more and more household duties to her.

She would empty the stoves ash box then clean and stoke the Aga, clean both of the en-suites, do all the dishes, including hand washing the expensive pots and pans. Tom would not risk the high quality cookware in the dishwasher. She also had to collect and launder all the clothes, iron and fold them once clean, mop the kitchens stone floor, vacuum all carpets and finally empty the bins.

Those were just the daily tasks, weekly tasks included things like dusting of shelves and washing of windows. The lists went on. This cleaning regime had two benefits as far as Tom saw it Sofie was occupied so he could work in peace and secondly he had less domestic chores in the first place to keep him from the all important project.

-28-

For all of its intriguing problems and potential Tom did not give a single damn about the Williamsburg reactor software. It was a job he had to complete, a hurdle that must be jumped so he could continue work on his pet project. The quicker it was over the quicker he could go back to normal and do some real work and of course that also meant he could be spending a lot more time with Sofie. It was for her that he now worked so feverishly and he hoped she would understand that.

After its inception Accuracy Analytics had gone from strength to strength working on every imaginable problem. They would intersperse their more exotic and theoretical work for military types with high paying civil engineering projects like the one they now worked on. The financing they received for these high tech projects like fusion reactors was funnelled back into what Tom considered as their 'legacy' projects. Projects that could operate in secret and would render certain evils harmless or at least reduce their capacity to bring misery into the world.

Tom had been there for Sofie's birth and witnessed a life come into existence at that moment he had really understood why these things were far more important than his earlier sense of morally right actions had allowed him to experience. He had always known the work was good and righteous but only as a parent did he experience the deep seated desire that now drove him to protect all the children of the world.

This was why he now argued with Patrick.

"Honestly Patrick they will never know the software is even in there. Its completely undetectable. Look man I've tried to find it myself and I wrote it. If I cant find it once it has buried itself into the system then how the hell does anyone else stand a chance. If they cant find the software then they will never know its there its totally safe we can move to the next stage."

Patrick was not happy about Tom's willingness to sacrifice the testing schedule but more so he was unhappy that he was once again asking about the personal project and not thinking about his work to help Francis and Clousarr with the reactor systems.

"What about those damn reactor controls man. Get a grip for Christ sake. Once we have finished those and proved that they are working as advertised we will have all the money we need to do all the good in the world ok? It's not like the Bulgarians are going to get it up and running by themselves they need your help"

Tom was sure that the excellent computer engineers were in fact perfectly capable.

"You hired them Pat. They are excellent coders I'm sure they can finish the programs now that I have figured out how to solve the communication problem, Come on Pat please let me get back to normal work I haven't had any time with Sofie lately"

"For the last time No you will do as you are told man. Look

Tom think about it logically please, how long would it take you to explain your code to the Bulgarians and get them up to speed on how to finish from where you are now? Probably just as long as its going to take you to finish the damn things yourself right?"

Tom sheepishly agreed before Patrick continued.

"I do not expect to hear another word about your damn bleeding heart project until they are finished. Your project's system is up and running and it seems to be operating exceptionally well under normal conditions lets just leave it running and see what results turn up, think of it as an extended beta test ok. Under no circumstances are you to proceed any further with it. Do you understand Tom?"

"Yeah, sure whatever you say Pat."

"Good man. I mean once you start the final testing phase I doubt you will have any time to do anything else and I need you working on the reactor. We can't do both at the same time. So just concentrate on the job at hand please. I do understand that you want to be spending this time with Sofie but she will be there once the reactor is working won't she?"

She would but if she would ever forgive Tom for the neglect and domestic labour he was heaping on her Tom didn't know.

"Ok Pat ok. But I want a promise that once this reactor business is finished I will have all the time I want to spend on Sofie ok."

Patrick decided it was only fair

"Of course Tom you can do whatever you want I promise. You have definitely earned it my friend. Accuracy Analytics wouldn't be here without you Tom but that is a double edged sword now crack on and send me a report when you can I have a meeting with the energy minister tomorrow. The woman is an idiot and couldn't tell the difference between an integer and a string but she wants a technical briefing"

Tom didn't feel too sorry for Patrick

"And that's what you are good at Pat, Accuracy Analytics wouldn't be here without your ability to sell people dreams in a way they understand. We both have crosses to carry and yours is communicating with the uneducated."

Becky Lang Minister for Green Energy was not an idiot but she knew that's how both Tom and Patrick thought of her. She had met them both when they had won the contract to provide software for the Williamsburg reactor. She was in fact a genius of the political sciences and had a very strong grasp on civil engineering including both the technical and budgetary aspects.

She was however a complete dunce when it came to computers. Even using them made her groan with loathing. She had dabbled with psychology as a bright eyed university student. Becky had formed some interesting opinions about, why we seem to think that anyone who is not proficient in our field of expertise, should be considered a fool. This effect, she noted, was prevalent within the IT community.

A group of people who would dismiss with a wave the multiple doctorates she had as if they were meaningless and all because she had forgotten how to find a simple power switch or the like. She could still hear the spotty young boy laughing.

"Did you try plugging it in?"

How was she supposed to know it had been unplugged.

Patrick was from the same profession as that kid, she hated Patrick. She only had two very simple questions that she needed two very simple answers for.

"Why isn't it working and when will it be fixed"

These simple questions would be answered with streams of technobabble and she was sure some of the things he told her were made up completely.

Patrick would try to simplify things and she would get angry. He would start using analogy instead of explanation and that's when her temper would rise further. She would furiously beg to have the answers she needed and he would politely tell her that's what he had been giving her for the last hour.

He felt that, if she couldn't understand the answer she should either ask better questions or find an advisor that could understand the finer points of computer engineering. She felt that, he should be able to explain in a way she would understand and also give exact dates.

Both were to blame for the break down in communication but neither could understand the others position. However right or wrong either of them were only one would get angry enough to show it and only one of them was in a democratically elected position. All the votes in the world wouldn't put Patrick out of a job.

During that meeting Tom should have been at home checking the mathematical modelling of magnetic field fluctuations. Instead he was with Sofie navigating some rather more mundane fluctuations in a grassy field north of Winchester and just south of Ecchinswell.

-29-

Surrounded by fireworks exploding, Sofie opened her eyes in dismay, trumpets were still blaring. A now well known medieval looking scroll was carried into her room through the window by two easily recognised little blue birds. The knight in still shinning armour took the scroll and as it was unrolled as familiar fairies flew from the page revealing "Wednesday 12th August Good Morning".

If she didn't remember to change this stupid alarm today she would scream. Every single morning it was the same. She now hated those little birds with a passion. She would wake swear to change the alarm get washed and be about to go into settings when.

"Breakfasts ready Sofie" Yelled Tom

Forgetting to change the alarm, Sofie trotted downstairs once more, to enjoy the couple minutes with her dad before he would disappear and she would be trapped in the mundaneness of domestic maintenance. She knew that today, Pat, her dad's friend was meeting some politician and Tom had been up late writing a report.

Sofie paused on the stairs, sunlight hitting her face as she looked through the little window. She couldn't believe it. A miracle had happened she was finally free. Jumping the steps three at a time she slid across the stone floor in her socks and erupted into the kitchen

"It's not raining." Said Sofie excitedly.

She had been so happy at the thought of spending some time outside that she had forgotten everything else. Breakfast disappeared in a flash and she got up to run out into the garden. Tom decided he had to halt this before it got started.

"Where do you think you are going Sofie?"

She stopped dead in her tracks and her head slumped forward eyes now pointing at the stone floor.

"Aw dad I was only going to play for a bit I can do my chores later. What if the rain comes back? I don't"

"Sofie" Tom tried to cut her off but she ploughed on.

"I don't want to miss out and I have been such a good girl you will just be working anyway"

"Sofie" He tried again with no success she continued.

"What does it matter when I do my chores? You are too busy to notice anyway its not fair its so not fair please let me go outside Daddy please"

"Sofie" He tried one last time

She spun around now quite angry at the injustice

"What Daddy?"

Tom stood holding her walking boots and backpack.

"Wouldn't you rather go on an adventure?"

They had driven to Winchester but it was still too early to see the round table. Tom promised that they would stop on the way home if they had enough time. From Winchester it took another half hour of driving north to get to Ecchinswell. Tom found a spot to park the car and they were off hiking through fields and along winding country roads.

Sofie loves hiking but she was confused about what was so special about this walk. Maybe they were going to a castle or perhaps something Roman.

She really enjoyed visiting historical sites, feeling that the ruins of past cultures give a better understanding, of the people that had lived there, than the pages of any book no matter how eloquently written. This was despite the fact that when she would visit a castle, for example, she would spend most of her time there imagining battles between elves and orcs as opposed to the daily lives of human peasants.

Sofie was interested by how similar to Compton this area was. If you had placed her at random in either area she would be completely unable to tell you which area she was in. Short of seeing a familiar landmark or place name the environments were completely interchangeable.

They left the country lane and walked along a footpath, field on one side and forest on the other, as the forest fell away the path became steep. The landscape was identical to the hill near their house and this is why Sofie felt somewhat bored by the time they reached the summit of a perfectly normal looking hill to stop for food.

They had only covered about three miles but the climb had still tired her out. The views were spectacular and Tom decided that by a little copse of beech trees was the perfect spot for lunch. He had explained this type of wind break is called a hanger as it hangs to the hill. Factually right or wrong Sofie didn't know but she accepted his explanation of the term.

Lunch consisted of sandwiches. Sofie had her choice of Cheese with Marmite or cheese with Branston pickle.

"Its quite the impossible decision daddy" she had explained. "on the one hand Marmite is fantastic and on the other pickle is amazing. You cannot expect me to make such a difficult decision."

"How about we have half of each" suggested Tom

They had opened their cling film wrapped sandwiches taken out half and then swapped the reaming halves. Tom sat eating his happily but Sofie just stared at hers.

"What's wrong now Sofie?"

"well you see dad which ever I eat first I wont have to enjoy second and whichever I eat second will have to wait until I am done with the first"

It was a most vexatious of problems but before Tom could suggest a simple coin flip to decide she put both halves on top of each other and took one mighty bite out of both. As she began to chew she first looked puzzled then a bit shocked and then as if she was going to be sick.

Any English person will attest that there is a constant war between Marmite and Branston fans. Both side's of this never ending debate will claim that their preferred spread is the best. They can both produce scientific research to back up their claims and market statistics to make their case.

Many people do enjoy both to a lesser or greater degree and the 'love it or hate it' reputation of Marmite is very well known. Some people think Branston to be the victor for its inclusion in a ploughman's lunch. The opposition will fire back, about the undoubted superiority of Marmite, able to transform a toasted cheese sandwich into god's own ambrosia.

There is however, one thing that both sides will whole heartedly agree upon. You do not mix them under any circumstances, ever for any reason, it is one or the other never, ever both. Sofie has just learned this lesson for herself.

"Yuk that's disgusting its worse than broccoli."

Tom laughed as Sofie bemoaned her poor lunchtime choice.

"I would rather eat Henrietta again" She said.

Tom fell over backwards laughing at her screwed up face. He was relieved to hear her joke about the awful incident. He knew that once she was able to joke about it, she had honestly forgiven him. Tom made a joke of his own.

"Maybe some Worcestershire sauce would help the flavour"

"Really you think that would make it work?" She hadn't heard the sarcasm.

"Gods no, don't ever try that it would be so much worse."

Sofie stopped eyeing the packet of Worcestershire sauce flavoured crisps in the lunch bag accepting Tom's wise words.

The coin landed heads and the Marmite went first. They finished their sandwiches, crisp packets were emptied and chocolate bars consumed. They collected all of their wrappings and packets and carefully put them into Sofie's backpack. They both knew that some people are far too stupid to take home their rubbish and believe it is acceptable to leave things like coke cans or sweet wrappers on fields or in hedgerows. Sofie wondered what sort of horrible monster would do such evil things.

"Right ready to go home then?" Said Tom

"What? But I thought we were going to see something special Dad?" Sofie was sure there was a surprise or adventure waiting for them somewhere.

"Well, yes we have, it's here, isn't this special enough?" Tom said as he gestured to the view.

It is a lovely view but by no means unique, many similar views exist all over the south and many much better views are all over the north. Sofie was not sure why they had driven an hour to get here and then walked for another. This was a regular looking hill with a steep northern face and a gently sloping southern one.

"Its very pretty but what is so special am I missing something?" She asked

Tom was enjoying this a bit too much

"What Sofie don't you know where we are this is a very famous hill"

She looked at him with questioning eyes.

"Why is it famous?"

"I don't believe you don't know why this is such a famous hill," Tom was grinning "why its name alone is known by everyone around" he gave a sweeping gesture to indicate the world

"Ok dad so what's its name then?"

Tom feigned hurt shock like a fainting lady from old movies.

"How could you not know its name? oh my"

Sofie had had enough of this silly behaviour how was she supposed to know what this stupid hill was called. She clapped her phone into existence and opened up the maps app. After a second a blue dot showed where she was and right next to her satellite accurate position was the name of the hill.

"Oh my god this is Watership Down" Sofie hadn't even known that it was a real place. She had assumed it was a made up name for the book.

Tom had two blissfully peaceful hours lying in the middle of a field watching the blue sky with fluffy clouds slowly rolling past. Sofie had two excited and frantic hours of searching hedges and fence lines. When she finally found some rabbit holes she took endless pictures of them. Not the most interesting pictures in the world but to her they were priceless. She was convinced she had seen Kehaar flying above them and wanted to stay until the rabbits came out for silflay.

"Its up to you Sofie we can go now and see the round table in Winchester or stay and wait for more rabbits" Offered Tom.

She had seen lots of rabbits today and had even seen one or two on the Down itself. She really did want to see the round table as well. She wasn't sure if it was another of Tom's poor jokes and would end up being just a round table or if it was the actual round table.

Two hours later as she stood inside the cathedral sized hall reading the famous names of legendary knights, from the edge of the table, her whole world view had changed.

On their way home after a long and exciting day she had been discussing things with her dad.

"It's quite remarkable really, that all those stories are real Daddy. I mean I know not all stories are true but to find out the round table exists and being stood on Watership Down makes you wonder doesn't it? Wouldn't it be amazing if all those places like Nottingham Forest or Green Gables or Paddington Station all existed? You could just visit them any time you liked. Ha."

Tom decided it was best to let Sofie discover the truth behind these locations at her own pace rather than all at once.

"Yeah that would be like finding out there really was a Uther Pendragon and you could visit his castle if you wanted." Sofie gave a sweet little laugh of agreement and Tom drove them the rest of the way home.

-30-

Caroline had waited in front of the blue phallic art for two long and embarrassing hours. The police had finally arrived to take her statement and the councils graffiti removal team were getting to work with the high pressure hoses.

"Shall we step inside the ticket hall Caroline? So I can get your version of events" Said the patronising male officer.

As she told her story the guy would interject with questions.

"So you were sleeping you say?" or "uh huh so it was a cat that woke you up?"

Caroline was sure that she could hear the two officers laughing as she went to the car for her return trip to the morning briefing. She drove steadily towards Waterlooville and the police station. Her phone started to beep, pretty regularly, with notifications from various apps. Caroline hated the hands free system so ignored the little noises until she had pulled into the car park. Forty six private message and post notifications. She would check what all the fuss was about after the briefing she was almost late already.

Caroline entered through the staff door into a hallway. Separated from the public entrance which is basically just a waiting room and a pair of service windows. The glass in these windows is bulletproof and the police use a speaker system to communicate with the general public. There are a couple of desks with computer terminals for the police to use behind the glass.

Also on the ground floor is the control room where there are many more desks and computer screens. The telephone systems are all run through VOIP software and managed by a call handling program. Long gone are the days of analogue phone lines and blackboards. Lastly the ground floor also contains a custody suit.

Heavily isolated and only accessible through secure doors with electronic access control it is sound proofed just in case they are holding a 'screamer'. Caroline doesn't have access to the secure area and heads upstairs to the briefing room. Along with the briefing room on the first floor are the changing rooms, lockers, administration offices and break room.

As she entered the briefing room it erupted into applause again, but this time there was nothing halfhearted about it. The officers were spread around the room, some sat at the communal use computer terminals and some were stood by the windows or just sat on the chairs dotted about. All had stood as one to give her a resounding standing ovation. Some police that had been in the break room and seeing her pass had followed her so that she was now surrounded by adoring fans.

For the first time Caroline realised how much this room resembled a school class room, with its whiteboard as a central focus point and in the way that the free-form seating was always arranged. Sometimes the room was actually used to host classes but was far more often used as a briefing room or over spill for the break room. The classroom idea had settled on her now because not since her school days had she been so confused and embarrassed at the same time in front of a group of her peers.

Caroline went bright red as she realised they had heard about the graffiti incident. In the past she had enjoyed the camaraderie and comfort found in this room. Joining in laughing at other peoples misfortunes when they had been on the other end of a joke or some low level pranks.

In that moment though she was acutely aware of how there is a certain balance and order to these things. Currently there were twenty PCSOs and five actual police officers in the room, each having a small amount of fun at her expense. She felt that their combined enjoyment was balanced by her feelings on the opposite end of that spectrum. But where their enjoyment was spread out her displeasure was concentrated.

Waterlooville has twenty five PCSOs in total two were off sick twenty were laughing at her and the last two Caroline was glad to see them coming to her rescue. Barry and Rob waded in between Caroline and the wall of onlookers that revelled in her failure. With stereotypical threats and shouting Barry and Rob had dispersed the crowd and rescued their team mate. She was so grateful to the two men who had saved her that it didn't leave much room in her emotions to be upset any more. The act of kindness had helped her in many ways.

"how did they find out so fast" Caroline was asking "I just left the scene and came straight here"

In the police force and PCSO teams alike there is a sense of professionalism and it actually takes a fair while for work rumours to propagate through a station. Carried on whispers and between good friends. Even something like this should not have spread as quickly as it obviously had. The officers will not sit around and openly share the news of an individuals failings.

Rob hated having to be the bearer of bad news.

"Caroline have you not checked your phone? I sent you a message when it went viral"

Caroline's heart fell through the bottom of her stomach she knew what had happened but asked anyway

"What went viral rob?"

It was like watching someone else on the video sharing site. Unfortunately it was a good quality phone that had captured the now famous video of an officer sat on a bench in front of a graffiti phallus The officer Stamping her feet and bouncing herself up and down the woman on the screen lets out a moan as she stretches her arms. Then she stands up and turns to see the big blue artwork. The video was called 'cock up cop caught napping' it had been viewed more times in the last couple of hours than any other video on the site. It was at the current number one spot having pushed the video 'Buttons da Wonderdog' into second place.

"Oh crap everyone has seen this haven't they?" Said Caroline remembering all those notifications.

Both Barry and Rob were nodding when the briefing started. The room came to order much the same way a classroom does when a teacher walks in. Conversations ending and attention being diverted to the police sergeant. Caroline was expecting some sort of acknowledgement but the briefing progressed as normal without any mention of the incident.

Everyone was dismissed and started to file out of the room. As she went to leave the sergeant stopped her.

"If I give you ten minutes Caroline we can meet in here or would you like to use one of the private offices?" Said the officer.

Caroline was completely lost

"I am sorry sir what do you mean?"

"You should have received the email and text notification this morning." The sergeant did look sorry as he said "We have a meeting with the chief inspector and some human resource types for your disciplinary"

Her worst fears having been realised, she set about readying herself. Ten minutes later she had taken a seat in front of five people, three uniformed officers and two wearing office attire. The briefing room had been slightly reorganised with a long table for the tribunal to sit at. One chair in front of the table and far enough away that she would feel isolated, as if she was on trial.

Caroline waved her right to representation by any representative or trade union. The video evidence against her was as damning as it was public. Caroline knew they were going to fire her for bringing the force into disrepute. She had known it was over as soon as she had seen the chair all by itself.

It had started out as a dryly administrative and official process, the procedure for disciplinary action was explained and Caroline finally got a chance to speak.

"I know the video looks bad and reflects poorly on the force so I am prepared to accept the full consequences of my actions. Will I have to work a notice period or am I being fired immediately"

Caroline didn't expect the chief inspectors response.

"Miss May, If I had to fire every officer who disgraced us in some viral video, I wouldn't have anyone in uniform left to work the streets. The video is not why you are here Miss May and you're not here to be fired."

She couldn't believe it and listened intently

"We are giving you an official verbal warning for sleeping on the Job"

At his words Caroline's features brightened and colour returned to her face the relief she felt was obvious to all.

The meeting concluded quickly after that and she signed a single page document to acknowledge her acceptance of the warning. She was warned about further action if the infraction happened again and then she was sent away. The door closed behind her and she looked down at her uniform with pride, still able to call herself an officer of the law. Caroline headed to the changing room and swapped her uniform for her baggy and comfortable civilian outfit. She put her work things into her locker and was so glad that it was still her locker.

Leaving the station Caroline checked through her messages, seeing the disciplinary notification and Rob's worried texts along with many messages from old acquaintances asking if that was her in the video. She put in a call to Judith but it went to voicemail. So she sent a short message asking about a coffee tonight before her shift.

Despite everything that had happened in the last few hours she was really happy, mostly from relief but she was also looking forward to tonight's shift. It would be her last night shift before it was Rob's turn to take over for two nights. She was going to get to do some day work and she hoped to show Barry how competent and useful a member of the force she could be. But first, it was noodle time.

-31-

Sofie opened her tired eyes with hatred at the cursed Fireworks and annoying trumpets. Detested fairies revealing "Tuesday 25th August Good Morning". She still hadn't remembered to change the alarm.

Just one week till summer ended and high school would begin. Today they would be shopping for her uniform and Sofie wasn't looking forward to a tedious day. It was a sad day in many ways for Sofie it was the start of the end for her summer. She had been living such a lousy Cinderella existence that going back to school felt like the ball she had been waiting for.

The start of her holidays had been outstanding with zoos, shipyards and birthdays. Then Tom had started having to work more and more. Their visit to Watership Down, almost two weeks ago, had been a pleasant change in their daily schedule. Since then though Tom had sunk himself even deeper into work. He had explained that the sooner he got done with the work the sooner he could spend time with her. Sofie wasn't even allowed out of the garden unsupervised because Tom was afraid of what might happen.

The arguments were getting more frequent. Sofie knew her dad's stressful job was getting to him and no matter what she did to help with the house work and no matter how well behaved she was she was still sometimes in the way. Like the unfortunate coffee machine incident, refreshed in her mind every time her dad took a sip of instant coffee. Tom still hadn't purchased a new espresso machine, no longer confident in his buying choices.

With the end of summer close and the start of another school year on the horizon Sofie anticipated more freedom and new friends. She was looking forward to adding real life friends to her social media. She would be attending Compton Comprehensive but knew little about it. Sofie was sure that it couldn't possibly be worse than her daily chore regimen. Tom had organised everything and Sofie hadn't visited the school yet.

Sofie collected the eggs for breakfast and felt a pang of sorrow when she opened the flap. Not being greeted by her fat old friend still hurt, just a little bit. The other chickens were nice enough but were not quite Henrietta nice. None of the birds were broody so were all outside scratching for seeds and bugs. Having left their eggs untended they were cold to the touch and lacking the reassuring warmth of a chicken warmed egg.

Sofie sat alone at the cracked marble island to finish her breakfast while Tom, in his office, took another work call.

"Ok Pat I'm almost finished on my end" he said to a relieved Patrick.

"That is great news, good man, good man indeed. I knew you would sort it. So what do you need from me to finish up?"

Tom was always a little surprised by how Patrick would always know what he was thinking.

"How do you know I need anything Pat."

"Tom. First you have not finished, secondly you're using that tone of voice you use when you want something."

He did want something

"I need access to the power reactors. I need to install everything and check it all works fine. I also need the engineers to run the system without it actually operating."

Patrick agreed that it was best to test the system worked without actually running the reaction.

"Ok Tom how long until you will be ready to install the system?"

"Two days maybe three actually" Tom wanted to get this over and done with as soon as possible. "I have to take Sofie to get her school uniform today" This subject always annoyed Patrick.

"You can't still be serious about letting her attend that bloody two bit comprehensive Tom, think about the choices you are making for her please"

"No Pat" Tom had made up his mind "it's perfect, it'll be good for her and I've checked the school it's fine."

Exasperated Patrick tried once more to make Tom see reason.

"Tom we have much better options available for Sofie."

"No Pat." Tom had had enough. "She is going to a real school with real kids I am not sending her off to some institution she is going to the local school" In truth Tom had been worrying about Sofie being out of his control but it had to be done. "Listen I got to go Pat its a long drive to the city"

The tiny shop seemed like it hadn't changed in at least the last fifty years. Cloth covered mannequins and heavy oak display stands were scattered between wooden shelving that formed a tight warren of twists and turns. The stock was to the ceiling and some seemed to lean from overhanging storage at impossible angles ready to tumble from shelves. With an entire wall of school shoes the shop smelled of leather, old paper and nostalgia. Sofie loved it.

The ancient shopkeeper had a friendly face and a welcoming voice.

"Hello my dear" he spoke directly to Sofie "I guess you are here to order a gown for university?"

"I'm not that old" giggled Sofie "I'm only elven. I'm going to high school in September. It's my first year at Secondary school"

"Oh I'm sorry my dear" The old keep feigned surprise "it's just, you look so grown up next to your grandfather."

"He's not my grampy that's my dad, he's not that old." Said an amused Sofie.

Tom had shaken the shopkeepers hand and introduced himself. He was impressed by the man's easy nature and clever way of making Sofie feel at home instantly. It was probably these simple jokes that had kept this dinosaur of a shop open all these years.

Children who had visited every year during their school journey would remember the experience and as parents bring their own children back many years later. This kind of intergenerational brand loyalty being the shop's saving grace. Despite the advent of mass market products and next day delivery, it was customer service that had proofed this establishment from the 'cheap and now' economy.

The shopkeeper put on a pair of gold rimmed glasses and produced a large well worn leather bound book of embroidery samples from under the counter.

"Right my dear, which fine halls of learning will be graced with your attendance this year?" He asked Sofie.

"I will be receiving my lessons at Compton Comprehensive." Sofie said proudly emulating the keepers cadence

The shopkeeper hummed and flicked through his book

"No not there? Is that a boarding school? Maybe part of another school?"

"No" Tom cut in "it's just our local school"

The shopkeeper looked over the top of his glasses raised an eyebrow

"Right I see, well, I'm sorry but I haven't done any work for them before. I don't appear to have their crest in my collection."

Tom was not surprised as the Compton school only catered for the local children, he doubted that their farmer parents would be paying for tailored school uniforms.

"That is ok." Tom said "We can do without the crest."

The shopkeeper had spent his years tailoring the finest uniforms, for the finest schools and he charged a hefty fee. Not having the school crest on file meant that his regular clientele would probably not choose to send their kids there.

"Ah, you are going to a proper school," He said "not some stuffy institution. Good, best education if you ask me. You will have the best uniform to go with it my dear. Now up you get."

He gestured to a bench that had seen so many little feet over the years the varnish had rubbed away in two, roughly shoe shaped, spots.

Sofie was measured and Tom selected the appropriate materials and patterns. This process was bothering Sofie. She saw a lot of grey some black a bit of white even some tartan material being chosen but there was not one pink item in the store. Not even a single stitch of pink anywhere.

"Is nothing going to be pink at all? Is it just black and white."

The tailor looked at her with a gleam of mischievousness.

"Hmm, like pink do we. Well, the skirt has some red?" he looked at Sofie for a reaction she didn't look too impressed "No no not good enough. You know the uniform rules of most schools only mention the Blazers outside colour." Tapping his chin with the a little white pencil "How about, a pink silk lining if Dad agrees?"

Sofie had begged and Tom had agreed. The Inside of her school jacket would be pink.

Two hours later and Sofie was getting bored. After the excitement of pink linings the rest of the afternoon had descended into a monotonous search for shoes, sports clothing and other equally dull attire. It was the shoes that Sofie hated most of all. None of them pretty and all of them either pinching or floppy. The perfect pair eluded her and she was ready to give up.

"Can we just go I hate this" She asked in a whinny voice.

Tom insisted that they stay until everything was purchased. She kicked her feet in a childish display of displeasure. Tom grabbed her foot and tried to force on another sample

"You will do as you are told." Said Tom "I don't have time to be messing around with this"

Sofie had come to fear anytime her dad got upset. As the shopkeeper returned with yet more boxes he could sense that the mood had changed. The bright friendly girl was now meek and the seemingly perfect father had adopted a fierce expression.

"Everything ok here" he said.

"Oh yeah no problem, Sofie, just hates choosing shoes"

The kindly shopkeeper wanted to defuse this tense scene.

"Well not to worry," he said "I have found the perfect pair"

He offered a box to Sofie, as soon as the shoes touched her feet she said they were fine. Tom had agreed and they would take this pair. Sofie didn't seem too happy about it though.

Tom paid the bill, having been assured that the completed garments would be delivered to them the day before school. Term would start on Tuesday the first of September and the tailored uniform would arrive on the Monday. The shopkeeper offered reassurances that if there were any problems, then alterations could be made at weekends. He was also confident that none would be needed.

As the pair had left his shop the old man was upset with the rough way that Sofie's hand had been grabbed before she was led out and away from the shop.

-32-

The trip home was turning into an argument before Tom had even left the Island of Portsmouth.

"Why couldn't you just behave for ten minutes Sofie?"

She had no answer, not feeling that she had been particularly bad anyway. She had offered platitudes about boredom and painful shoes but Tom didn't care.

"That is not the point Sofie. How do you think your little outburst made that shopkeeper feel? He was being so nice to you and then you made him uncomfortable"

Sofie was sure it wasn't her that had made the tailor uncomfortable but she had learned not to disagree with her father.

"I'm Sorry daddy I didn't mean to. I Promise I will be better in future."

"That is not good enough" Tom had heard these lies before "you are always saying you will be better behaved and then something like this happens"

This argument would continue all the way home. During a lull in hostilities Sofie had seen a sign for a fast food restaurant that was ahead. They would be passing it in two miles and she felt hungry.

"Ooh Dad can we go there for lunch please"

Tom could see her pointing at the red and yellow sign

"Why do you want to eat that trash? Is the food I make not good enough for you?"

By the time they had passed the restaurant Tom was threatening to fill her food with sugar and salt if that is what she wanted

"Or perhaps I could just buy the cheap food in the supermarket and boil it to death that way it will taste like that crap. You want to eat that rubbish Sofie I can make it for you, do you want bad food Sofie? Do you?"

She did not.

"I'm sorry I just thought it would be easier to get lunch now. That way you would have more time when we get home and we could play a game maybe?"

Tom was already being unreasonable but it got worse

"Game? Sofie I don't have time to play stupid games. I have work to do when we get home. You know I have to finish the project. You know that, come on Sofie. Once it's done we can any games you want. I will get to you once I am finished"

This hurt Sofie, she hated being secondary to the project. If Tom had been saving the world she didn't feel like she should have to wait until after he was done. Sofie was learning how to be a good girl though and didn't tell Tom how that last comment had made her feel. She was wicked for feeling that way in the first place and she knew it. She was being selfish and good little girls are never selfish.

Tom's car pulled into the driveway and he told Sofie to go to her room and think about how badly she had behaved today. He could see a few letters had ben delivered while they were out. Tom collected the mail and went inside to continue work. Tom dropped the mail onto his desk as he powered up his machine.

They would skip lunch today but Tom had decided to make an effort for dinner. He wanted to show Sofie that she didn't need to want the pretend burgers at that place they had past. He couldn't bring himself to think of it as a restaurant. Taking out a pack of black Angus beef mince to defrost he went to get on with his work.

Tom had worked like a man possessed, being so close to the finish line he was motivated to work fast and hard. Having skipped lunch hunger caught up with him. Saving his work he left his office on a mission to make the best burgers Sofie would ever eat.

He started with a lump of the best steak mince available and added a pinch of salt and ground black pepper. The secret to the Tom's burgers is stock. He would reduce down some beef stock or add powdered stock. Tom began to combine all of these ingredients in a large bowl and kneaded it like bread dough until thoroughly mixed. After it looked like raw burger in both appearance and consistency he used his hands form the mix into evenly sized balls. Tom pressed the balls into the desired shape both the simple circle and the ever impressive dinosaur shape. Sofie would love the dinosaur shapes.

Cooking on a hot charcoal barbecue he turned the burgers every thirty seconds. After the meat had browned but before it was cooked through he began to baste them with maple syrup on every rotation. As soon as he saw the first speck of black he removed the cooked meat and placed each one in a bun with red onions finely diced, two rashers of bacon and a single slice of a cheese.

Sofie could smell the barbecue and was near enough clawing at the locked door to her room when Tom finally opened it. She flew downstairs and through the kitchen into the garden. She looked like a child possessed as she stood next to the hot barbecue inhaling deeply.

"Wow they smell great dad" She said between nosefuls of

burger smoke.

"You wont get better burgers anywhere Sofie"

The point of his statement wasn't lost on her and Sofie became annoyed that he still hadn't dropped the argument from earlier. Tom had gone to a lot of trouble to make an excellent dinner and her wicked little mind was being petty. She knew she was a bad little girl and she hated herself for having such incorrect thoughts. Despite all of these conflicting emotions and rationalisations the burgers still smelled amazing and she distracted herself from the internal conflict.

They had carefully brought the plate inside, Sofie bearing it aloft as if it were some gaudy trophy awarded for a trivial game. The imagery made Toms mind divert on a tangent it ended with the conclusion that football really is a stupid game. This prize plate of food worth so much more than some trophy especially if you needed to eat.

Sofie's world exploded in a shower of sensory ecstasy. Flavours combined to overwhelm her brains ability to function properly and all of her bad thoughts floated away on a cloud made of meat. She thought that even if she was to choke on the last bite of this burger it would have been a fair trade and she would have died happily.

There is only one drawback to knowing the secrets of food this amazing and that is finishing any meal becomes a sad farewell to a friend that you wish could stay longer. Despite Sofie's best efforts her dad finished first. While she was still working on the last of her meal Tom said.

"I hope you are enjoying that"

He could see she was but the fervent nodding was still a welcome sight.

"Listen I am very close to finishing the work Sofie I should finish tonight. I told Patrick that it will take me three days though. Once I finish it I will have to spend a lot of time away installing and testing so I wanted a little break to spend with you first. How does that sound"

The thought of having her dad back made her extremely happy she showed this with a big thumbs up and while covering her full mouth.

"Great that is amazing." She said through her mouthful.

She got back to eating. Thinking that maybe if he wasn't stressed about work he would go back to being a nice dad and not angry all the time. Stopping herself thinking these bad thoughts was hard. She mentally chastised herself once more for being such a horrible little girl. She must not think of her dad that way it was her fault he was angry.

Tom had one more surprise for Sofie.

"I hear that Marwell zoo is sending the lions back soon I guess we should go see them before they leave"

She was so excited that she did almost begin to choke and tom had to slap her hard on the back while offering water. Once the meal was concluded and Sofie wasn't in danger of any food related injury it would be her job to clean up the dinner mess and she would complete her task with pleasure.

That night she would go to bed early and leave Tom to work. She didn't feel the need to mention that she was more interested in the penguins now. She would still love to see the lions again but it had been a long time since she had read Narnia and the penguins had been the more memorable exhibit from their last visit.

Sofie went to sleep with a head full of flippers and fish. For a moment she thought it was a flipper that had slapped her awake in the middle of the night. It wasn't it was Daddy and he was beating her.

-33-

As Sofie had put the dinner plates into the dishwasher tom made himself a coffee he had a long night ahead. He would be finishing the code tonight and he was glad he had lied to Patrick about it. A little time with Sofie was just what he needed and he deserved it. There is no way Patrick should begrudge him this. Rather than risk telling Patrick the truth though he had decided to take matters into his own hands.

He knew Patrick would want Tom to come into the reactor facility the moment he finished and he would probably be stuck there for a few days. This was the better plan of action. A little rest and relaxation a little treat for him and Sofie and then he could go to work once she had started school it was only a week away after all.

Taking his coffee upstairs while Sofie completed the rest of her day's chores he began work. The longest part of any software development cycle is or at least should be bug fixing and testing. Tom had finished the bulk of the system code but was ironing out a few little bugs here and there.

Tom remembered one simple program he had written for an energy sales company. He had finished the system in thirty hours, despite the fact it used a language he had never learnt. It took him the best part of two full days to fix it though.

The software would be used to calculate a potential clients energy usage and costs. It could then be used to project the kinds of savings the client could make by improving their efficiency or installing various energy solutions like battery storage and solar panels. The sales representative would fill in a form with the customer's details and current setup. Things like gas and electricity bills. The representative could then add potential upgrades and the software would model the savings based on real world data.

When Tom used it everything worked fine but as soon as a sales representative used it the system would crash or spit out garbage results. The problem had been Toms lack of experience with the language he used. If one of the boxes was left blank on the form, say gas usage, because the customer was only using electricity then the system recorded that as a 'null' value. When Tom tested the form if there was no gas he would type a 'zero'. Tom also made the mistake of thinking any field left blank would be automatically set to zero. With the system recording blanks as 'null' this made the mathematical algorithm crash. It would for example try to multiply cost of gas at 'null' by amount used at 'null' not being numbers this made the calculation impossible for the computer to understand.

That had been a frustrating two days for Tom. When he discovered this quirk of the language he almost cried from relief, having been working for almost seventy eight hours straight at that point. He wasn't the sort of person who could leave a problem unsolved. As he had matured and aged he had started taking regular rest breaks and not working such stupidly long hours. He probably would have found the issue much sooner if his blood hadn't been half caffeine at the time. He had fixed the issue with a single line of code that set all values to 'zero' when the program was opened now if a box was left blank it would be a 'zero' already.

He marvelled at how such simple mistakes could have such a huge impact. He stopped typing and took another sip of his coffee. Instant coffee might lack the subtle flavour profile of the proper stuff but it does the job and is a lot safer than its potentially explosive counter part.

Noticing the pile of mail still unopened on his desk he began to leaf through it. Two bills, three takeaway menus and a political pamphlet. Opening the first bill he logged into his banking software to get them paid and out of the way then he could throw all of this trash away.

'How much' his brain screamed he was looking at a phone bill that had one to many zeros after the amount owed. 'This is ridiculous' he thought to himself as he began looking for a mistake. No mistake, the data usage on his phone plan was astronomical. How had he used so much data he and Sofie had barely left the house everything should be running through his unmetered fibre connection.

Tom checked the usage statistics on his phone, the numbers were tiny. It must be Sofie's bracelets perhaps they had fallen off the network and were using the cellular network instead. It was an easy fix and the money didn't really matter.

Tom crept into Sofie's room and collected the bracelets from her bedside table. Heading back to his office he would reset their connection and change her alarm. Sofie had been complaining about it for weeks every morning. How she kept forgetting to change it he couldn't understand.

Tom sat down in his chair and slipped on the thick rubber bracelets. They reminded him of those charity bands that people buy in a misguided attempt to feel better about themselves. Trying to show the world how much they care for the pygmy stoat or whatever other sort of nonsense they believed.

On Tom they were a little tight but were perfectly usable. He clapped the phone into existence and checked its connection. Strange they were connected to the home network. He connected them wirelessly to his computer and downloaded the connection logs and history.

The Logs showed that almost every day the devices were disconnected and reconnected to the home system. While they were connected they used little data but while off the home system they were transmitting and receiving a huge amount. Tom was cold he could feel the familiar sense of panic rising again. As he opened the history file to see what the system had been doing panic turned to rage as his worst fears were confirmed.

"What do you think you were doing?" Tom hit her again "Did you think I wouldn't find out?" Another slap to the face "Do you know how dangerous those sites are?"

He grabbed Sofie and dragged her out of bed dropping her onto the floor.

"Well what have you got to say for yourself you stupid little girl" Tom spat the last word.

She was so shocked and although the slaps had woken her up she definitely didn't know what was going on or what she had done wrong

"What Daddy? I'm sorry whatever it is Ive done I am sorry"

"Don't you dare fib to me you sneaky little liar" Tom screamed his face close to hers

She didn't know what else to say so she just kept repeating

"I'm sorry Daddy"

She was sure it must be something bad she was always doing bad things lately. She looked up to see Tom holding out the pink bracelets. Oh no he knew about her and Mr Ted's Profile. How had he found out? Why hadn't she deleted it? She wasn't sure about all the other bad things she kept doing by mistake but this she knew had been wrong.

After she admitted it, Tom had calmed down then he had explained what she had done wrong and why it was dangerous. She hadn't realised how unsecure those sites were and she loved that her daddy wanted to keep her safe. She knew he only hit her out of concern and it just showed how much Daddy loved her. She was such a wicked and evil girl she didn't deserve a daddy that cared so much about her. He had even hurt his hand teaching her this lesson. She would have to be extra specially nice from now on. She hadn't even protested when the zoo trip was cancelled. Sofie doesn't deserve nice things or special trips she told herself. She hated herself so much for being such a bad little girl.

Tom had returned to his office and he told Patrick that he was finished with the programs. Tom would be spending the next few days away from home, except for meals and sleeping.

Sofie had been locked in her room and was only allowed out for meals. She knew it was good of Tom to be feeding her she didn't feel like she deserved the nice meals he cooked.

After a couple of days Tom had returned her bracelets, he had disabled the cellular connection by removing the chip that connected to his account. Sofie hadn't even checked if the connection still worked she had no interest in any rebellious acts no matter how small they seemed at the time. No matter what it took she would behave properly. She was going to be a good girl.

"Sofie is a good girl. Sofie is a good girl. Sofie is a good girl." She said to her mirror.

-34-

A well behaved Sofie opened her eyes in expectation. She accepted the Fireworks exploding all around her and greeted the trumpets blaring. She waited politely for the medieval scroll to be carried into her room. She welcomed the little blue birds. She thanked the knight and the fairies for revealing "Monday 31st August Good Morning"

Sofie washed herself quickly and ran to make Toms coffee. She would collect the eggs feed the chickens and be ready waiting quietly for Tom to descend. After breakfast's she would clean the house and lock herself away in her room. Sofie was a good girl, now she knew how to behave properly.

She was also a very scared little girl terrified of angering her father. But those were the bad thoughts. She knew that and was learning to squash her bad self away. Every terrible thought she had or impulse to misbehave was being expunged from her. It was hard work to be a good girl but she was trying so hard. It must be working because she hadn't made Daddy hit her again.

She stood in the kitchen in silence waiting for the door to open her heart was racing faster and faster with the anticipation. She finally heard her dad's door open and he descended.

Tom had had a very good night sleep and he was in a good mood. The work at the reactor was coming along very well and he had been given some truly amazing kit to work with. Stuff that made even his powerful home system look like a pocket calculator. He was a bit worried about leaving Sofie alone for all these days but he could use the cameras to see her sitting in her room and reading.

Tom had let her resume her household duties as long as she had promised to lock herself away once she had finished. Sofie was behaving very well lately she had had a huge change in her attitude. She had been too naive and impulsive before. This new

Sofie was much easier to deal with. Tom reasoned that If she were upset or unhappy that's when she would act out. Sofie responded to boundaries and now she knew where hers were, she was obviously a lot happier. She was always smiling and being helpful. She was being a fantastic asset to his house and he was very glad he had her here to help out.

"Good morning Sofie" he said as he entered the room giving a little nod to indicate it was ok for her to talk.

"Morning Daddy I love you and I hope your day is wonderful. Is there anything extra you need me to do today?"

There wasn't he would be happy if she completed her chores and then went to her bedroom. The nod to talk feature was new. She had noticed that Tom would subconsciously indicate when he wanted a response from her. She had learned only to talk when these were given. Be it looks, waves or little nods like the one she had just received it made him a lot happier if she looked for these cues instead of just speaking whenever she felt like it. It was little things like this that kept her safe from his anger. 'No bad Sofie' that was wrong thinking again. It was little things like this that kept Daddy happy and she loved daddy and wanted to maximise his happiness.

After breakfast Tom left for work and Sofie had cleaned and cleaned. She went to her room and the door closed behind her. It wasn't locked any more because she was a good girl now and Tom could trust her not to leave her room. She had been very glad that she had this freedom. If she wanted to she could even open her door for fresh air or to look out of. She was very happy about not being locked in during the day.

Today she would read The Hobbit. She sat in her room silently crying. Sofie didn't even realise she was doing it these days the tears would just fall off of her cheeks, she had no idea why it happened she wasn't sad or anything, she was a happy girl, a good girl, but it did make reading a book harder. The door bell rang. Someone was at the gate it looked like a delivery van outside.

She tried calling Tom but he wasn't answering, his phone didn't even ring it went to voicemail. What should she do? She knew she was going to make a mistake somehow. If she ignored it Daddy would be mad because he missed a delivery, if she answered it he would be mad that she left her room. Ok She knew what to do. Opening her window she shouted

"Who Is it"

"I have a delivery for T Anderson." The shouted reply came "can you come sign for it please?"

Sofie wasn't allowed to leave her room what could she do now

"What is it" She asked.

"Looks like a load of clothes." The guy shouted back.

Oh no. She knew what it was, her school uniform had arrived. She was going tomorrow and she needed that uniform. She couldn't show up on her first day without it.

"Ok coming"

The words had left her mouth before she thought about what she was saying. Then she was stood behind the front gate.

"I cant open the gate its locked and my dad is out."

"No worries hun can you sign this?" Said the driver

She saw a sheet of paper being waved under the gate. Taking the clipboard and pen she signed her name next to her dads printed name and slid the board back under the gate. The driver thanked her and then his head popped up above the wall next to the gate.

"Here you go."

He had climbed onto the bonnet of his truck and leaning over the wall he handed down to Sofie three plastic wrapped hangers all jacket shaped and lumpy. He was gone as soon as she took them and she shouted her thanks. She could hear the truck struggling on the hill where the lane turned muddy as she went inside to unwrap her new uniform.

In her room she carefully unwrapped all the packages and examined the tailors fine workmanship. The blazer was amazing. With a button done up it looked like any other black school blazer but when you opened the front and revealed the lining it was bright fuchsia pink silk inside. Sofie loved it. She was so happy trying on all the different parts of her uniform. The skirt had been lined with the same pink silk.

In the shop she had been weary of the tartan material it felt rough and woolly. Sofie had not looked forward to wearing it all day long. With the silk lining though it felt lovely against her skin. She looked at herself in the mirror turning one way then the other. She was so ready for school it would be such a great change of environment and she was excited to be learning again. If nothing else she would be able to talk to other people. Sofie realised she hadn't spoken to anyone other than Tom for longer than five minutes in the last six weeks.

Tom would be home soon. She thought he would like to see her in her new uniform and decided to surprise him by wearing it down to diner. She heard his car coming through the large gate just a few moments later. She put on the nasty shoes and pulled up her socks. She shouted down her greeting and waited to be told to come down for dinner.

Tom was in an excellent mood. The reactor systems were up and running a virtual simulation of normal operations everything was set and his work was almost over. When he arrived at site tomorrow he would download the report logs and check for any anomalous data. If it was all clear then he would hand the whole thing off to the Bulgarian engineers to implement.

The reactor itself was almost completed and in a month or two it would begin its first test firing. At that point if all the systems checked out and the tests worked without any hitches Patrick and Tom would be rich men. More importantly to Tom he would be free to work on his legacy project again. Patrick was supporting his project and could see some commercial applications. Happy to let Tom pursue it for the ethical reasons, Patrick would worry about the monetary ones.

Tomorrow Tom would celebrate but tonight he was already in a much better mood. He crafted a fantastic spaghetti Bolognese. The sauce was made yesterday as it tastes much better after it has cooled and stood for a day in the fridge. Since discovering this Tom had always made the sauce a day in advance. He just had to make the spaghetti and reheat the sauce. He would let Sofie grate the cheese. Tom was always confused by the shop bought dried pasta as it's just eggs and flour, takes no time make and the taste of home made is infinitely better. The water was boiling as he fed the long pasta sheets into the shredder. He knew it must have a name but it looks and works like a shredder so to Tom its a shredder. The rollers he had christened 'la pasta mangle'.

As he dropped the freshly cut spaghetti into the boiling water he shouted for Sofie to come and get dinner.

-35-

Tom was draining the pasta and getting ready to serve.

"Could you grate some cheese please Sofie everything is on the side"

He waved his hand in the direction of the equipment.

"No problems" said Sofie "but tell me what you think of this first"

"Think of what Sofie?"

"This." she had replied

Frustrated at her lack of explanation he turned to see what she was talking about. There she was stood in her uniform and his hand was on fire.

As Tom had looked round the steam burnt his hand and he shifted the pot accidentally pouring the boiling water over the hand that held the sieve. The pain was intense and he dropped both pot and sieve into his white sink.

Cold water. He needed cold water. He turned on the tap and both hands went under the stream as the water got to work removing the heat. Sofie was at his side apologising profusely and trying to help. She was scared that she had hurt him but had to try and help. The burn wasn't that bad and the pain was subsiding. Had he not been in such a good mood a moment ago he might of blamed Sofie for the accident she had caused but the relief as the pain subsided calmed his potential out burst

"Jesus that hurts" he had said

"I'm so sorry Daddy can I help?" she was still repeating this as Tom shooed her away and attempted to salvage the pasta.

Sofie felt awful and she had expected to be severely told off for causing the accident. She was amazed at Toms lack of reaction. She definitely deserved another lesson in behaviour she was sure. She shouldn't have tried to show off and she hadn't waited for permission to talk either. She would find some way to make up for this later or perhaps she should punish herself.

Sofie had grated the Kit Calvert cheddar and heaped it on top of two beautiful plates of yellow spaghetti with red bolognaise sauce. They sat together eating the excellent food in silence. Sofie couldn't apologise more than she had and Tom was lost in his thoughts.

As they finished their food Tom watched Sofie taking the plates to clean them. She looked lovely in her uniform but Tom had some very bad news for her. He had been discussing things with Patrick and a decision had been made.

"Sofie once you have finished come sit down we need to talk."

She had rinsed the plates and after placing them into the dishwasher skipped back to the island stool and climbed up to sit down once more.

"Right all done. What did you want to tell me." Her happy voice and smile disguised the fear she felt at the possibilities.

Tom made a false start before he settled on a explanation.

"So you know my friend Patrick" She nodded "Well I have been talking with him and we both decided that you shouldn't be going to school tomorrow"

Sofie didn't want to understand what Tom had just said.

"But, what, why does it matter what Patrick thinks" Said Sofie.

She had latched onto that point as Tom had hoped she would, he didn't want to take the blame for this precaution

"Well he doesn't think it would be safe for you to go to a public school its too much of a security risk"

Sofie couldn't believe what she was hearing anger was starting to grow inside her she had been looking forward so much to the escape that school offered her. It had been a light at the end of the tunnel. She had seen it as something to hope for it had made dealing with the conditions she lived under bearable. She hadn't realised this was how she felt until the exact moment all hope had been stripped away to reveal just how badly she had been coping. That small sliver of anticipated freedom supplying strength and resolve to her crumbling sense of self worth.

Sofie had forgotten all about her attempts to be a good girl she was furious and she didn't care if she upset Tom.

"That is not fair I have to go to school I will be careful, Nothing bad will happen"

Tom was shaking his head

"But dad why does it matter what Patrick thinks"

Tom was glad her attention was still on this point

"Sofie Its a lot more complicated than you realise, You can study at home where its safer. Now that's the end of it. ok?"

"But look at my uniform" Sofie wasn't done "it's so nice and makes me look all grown up. What a waste it'll be if I don't wear it to school. Dad it was really expensive."

Tom didn't care about the cost.

"You can wear it at home while you study" As he said this

Tom had a thought. "How do you even have that uniform Sofie?"

She was caught, her earlier transgression exposed.

"It was delivered today" she said

Tom was ahead of her and he was furious that she had disobeyed him again.

"You went to the gate to collect it didn't you? Didn't you?"

Sofie hung her head Tom was engulfed with fury

"For Christ's sake Sofie you stupid, disobedient, little girl. What if it had been someone dangerous? I told you not to leave your room while I was out. I thought I could trust you to behave now."

"You can trust me" Sofie cut in "but he would have taken it back if I didn't go get it. I tried to call you but your phone was off Dad." she had said the wrong thing.

"So its my fault you decided to disobey was it? Is it my fault you can't follow simple rules?"

Grabbing her by the hair he pulled her into the sitting room and drew the curtains.

"That is it Sofie this was your last chance"

Sofie struggled to get away from her enraged father, Tom punched her in the back of her head with his free hand and she lost all sense for a second. Tom took advantage of her confusion to bend her over the arm of the sofa. Face down against the fabric she struggled to breath. Tom hit her as hard as he could on the ass with his palm. The slap made her cry out in pain.

"No I'm sorry"

Again he hit her.

"Please Daddy no I will be a good"

Smack.

"Please no not again"

She tried to cover her rear with her hands. Tom hit her head again and caught both of her wrists in his left hand. He applied enough torque that her straightened arms pushed her shoulders and face down further into the cushion. Tom Lifted her skirt and pulled her knickers down to expose the bare flesh. This time when palm met skin the slap made a loud crack and her check turned pink instantly.

"Listen to me Sofie you are mine and you will do as I say. You will not ever disobey me again. I can do anything I want to you. Anything. Do you understand?"

Another brutal smack.

"Yes Daddy I understand" she whimpered

Tom had been repressed enough he was tired of pretending to be someone he wasn't. She would find out who he was sooner or later. He deserved to let himself go, work was going so well and Sofie was his property anyway. Instead of smacking her again he slid his hand between her legs. Tom thought to himself the school uniform really did look good on her. He liked that.

-36-

She was alone in her room at last. In the dark. No sounds to cover her sobs. She had understood what Tom had told her after. After he had raped her. It was her fault for wearing the short skirt in front of him and he only did it because he loved her. She knew what sex was and she knew that grown ups do it when they love each other.

It had hurt a lot the first time. It had hurt a lot more when he had done it the other way. By the third time it hadn't hurt as much as the beatings had. No one had ever told Sofie before that this was what little girls were supposed to do. Tom had reassured her it was ok though and told her it wouldn't always hurt.

A small voice in her head, she couldn't make it go away, was telling her it was wrong and disgusting. It didn't feel like love to her it felt like, well she wasn't sure. It was this voice that was making the tears roll off of her face again. Maybe this would all be better in the morning.

How could it ever be better she thought to herself deep down she knew her life was as good as over. Sofie knew exactly what rape was and she knew that is what had happened. Tom was sick but she wanted to believe the lies he had told her. He was her dad and she had to accept some responsibility in the matter. The skirt was very short.

Her thoughts were all muddled again. She didn't know how to feel. Anger though that was there. A little seed of it had taken root and it was growing. To Sofie's mind, she had a good side and a bad side. Her good side believed her dad and was sorry that she had made him beat her and rape her. Her bad side was furious and didn't think this was right. Her bad side wanted to do and say horrible things.

This is how she had decided it was definitely her bad side. Good little girls are well behaved, well spoken and don't think bad thoughts. She didn't want her bad side but there it was, sometimes quiet and sometimes loud. Her bad side would want her to kick and punch and scream the most obscene things.

She had put away her school uniform and thought about showering. Sofie was sat on her bed holding Mr Ted she had heard Toms door close around ten o'clock. Dressed in just her unicorn night shirt Mr Ted was having a shower of his own as the tears fell steadily onto his fluffy pink head. She had sat there for over two hours now still in a mess. Turning things over and over. Each time the bad side of her would get a little bit louder and the well behaved nice side got a little bit quieter.

She was still there awake when the clock ticked its way past midnight and it became the first day of September, the first day of term. Sofie clicked on her lamp and picked up her copy of the hobbit. Perhaps the reading would help her sleep.

When Sofie reads it doesn't leave room in her head for other thoughts. The words occupy her internal monologue and only stopping the flow of words from page to imagination will allow the thoughts back in. She tries so hard to read through the tears. The hobbit's adventure so compelling just cant stop the thoughts and wont make the pain go away. For almost two hours she tried harder and harder to read.

All of a sudden her room was as dark as the goblins cave. She was actually frightened for a second. A brief glorious second where her imagination and situation combined to alleviate her mind from the recent memories. They returned almost instantly though. There was something else there nagging at her thoughts.

It was a deafening silence. The buzz from the door was gone and the countless other tiny electronic sounds that exist in a house were silent. Be it heating systems or cooling pumps there are so many noises that are continually there our brains have learned to filter them out as white noise. In that dark quiet room they were all gone. Without power the cameras were off and the doors were open.

Bad Sofie took control. Good Sofie was a fucking idiot and bad Sofie was getting them both out of there. If good Sofie got her way she would stay in that room and get them killed or worse raped again. That won't be happening if bad Sofie can help it. He can't treat her like this and get away with it. He could die in a fire for all bad Sofie cared. Even bad Sofie didn't really mean that she wasn't a monster. She was however not staying here any longer she was escaping now.

It was having hope again that had brought out her self confidence it was the idea of escaping that gave her the agency to free herself. Her good manners and best behaviour had only been there to protect her from harm. In that awful situation with no other option she had made do, she had found a way to minimise the danger. She had convinced herself it was the best option. Sofie hoped if anyone ever felt like they had no hope they would find help from somewhere, from anywhere. Sofie's help had come in the form of a power cut.

She crept down the hallway and quietly sneaked down the stairs to the front door. She imagined that this was how Mr Baggins must have felt in those tunnels. She was so scared that the power would come back on any moment. Her hand pressed against the door and it opened her naked feet were cold on the stone floor.

She was outside the cool night air biting at her bare legs. It felt like she had emerged from the misty mountains into a world of moonlight and freedom. She should have grabbed some clothes but in the pitch black darkness the hope and panic had made her flee. As she approached the gardens gate a part of her wanted to turn back and go inside again. Then the gate clicked and the lock began to buzz. She was caught.

Without realising it she was already half way up the apple tree and then she was on top of the garden wall. A seven foot jump down is a long way for anyone but she threw herself off the tiled top without thinking or really caring what happened. She landed hard but was up and running. Running like she had never run before. She went straight ahead across the lane towards the woods and the sanctuary they offered. She reached the other side of the roadway and disappeared between the Bracken leaves. A computer finished booting up and the video recording system restarted its diligent vigil. 'No movement detected.'

She was lost. Sofie had quickly left her old domain of exploration and now had no idea where she was and she needed the toilet. In the woods alone and afraid she was still incredibly embarrassed as she sat on her knees and did her business. She had no way to wipe herself clean but tried with a few leaves and things.

Sofie had no idea how to navigate by the stars but looked at them anyway. No help to be found in the heavens she just kept going. Through brambles and branches she finally came to the edge of the wood. Across the field she headed south although she had no idea that she headed south it just looked better to her.

Crossing more fields she finally saw a thatched roof in the distance soon she would pass the thatched house and its swimming pool. She began her journey through paved streets getting lost and rubbing her feet raw until they bled. She was exhausted, thirsty and afraid. She had to rest. She ran under a viaduct and even in her current state she thought the railway bridge was a very pretty thing to have in a village. Behind a pub she saw a big green bin. She could hide behind it and catch her breath there was no way Tom would find her her she must be on the other side of England by now.

As she caught her breath she began to cry again, she knew she wasn't safe but she was away and she would find help soon. He couldn't catch her? There was just no way he could catch her. Sofie thought of her mother. She had never known her and Sofie never thought about her. She was just a distant person that had no real meaning to her life. Tom never spoke of her but in that moment she wanted nothing in the world more. Sofie needed her mum.

Then a hand touched her shoulder she was sure it was him she was caught. After all that she was caught how had he found her so quickly. Well, she wasn't going quietly Sofie kicked out into the darkness towards the hand that had unexpectedly touched her. She tried to get to her feet and flee. Sofie was panicking she was so sure she had been found, but her legs were too exhausted to stand, she tried desperately to crawl to safety. Two of her fingernails ripped from their beds as she clawed franticly trying to gain purchase on the broken concrete. She grabbed at weeds and bushes kicking up dust and debris in her attempted escape.

A brilliant white light came on and blinded Sofie. She could hear the voice of a woman. It sounded kind and soothing. Sofie had a beautiful but momentary thought 'Mummy?'

-37-

The men had put Sofie into the back of their black 4x4 and driven away. Ellen Mackenna had put up a fight even if Sofie hadn't seen it, she knew that Ellen wasn't happy about her leaving, she had been so nice to Sofie in the short time they spent together. The sadness was evident in Ellen's eyes as she explained that Sofie had to 'go with these men and be brave about it.'

Since she had escaped Sofie had met some very nice people Judith and Caroline for example had been very friendly. Sofie wanted to tell them everything but try as she might Sofie hadn't been able to say out loud what had happened to her. She had tried so hard but there was something stopping her voicing her story. She wasn't sure why but maybe it would just make it all seem too real.

She had escaped that was all that mattered and everyone had assured her she would be held for three days while they investigated. Sofie knew she didn't want her dad to get in trouble no matter what he had done. A small part of Sofie was feeling partly responsible and also guilty. She felt like she had deserved it to some extent. Nothing could stop her loving her dad but on the other hand she also didn't feel safe with him any more.

These men must be taking her to wherever they keep little kids that are in danger Sofie thought. They had even asked if she wanted to get ice cream. Sofie loved ice cream. Either side of her sat the two men who had come inside to get her, in the front seats there was ujust one occupant, the driver. They seemed to be taking very good care of her.

Sofie suddenly recognised the driver. It was her driver from school. Her driver didn't work for the school. He was employed by Tom's company. Could she bring herself to talk now? She hadn't been able to earlier but that was when she was trying to explain what had happened.

"Do you work for my dads company?"

The driver didn't turn away from the road he just said.

"Yeah. How you doing Sofie? Your dad is really worried about you. Patrick sent us down here to get you out and take you home"

She tried to scream she tried to explain but she couldn't. Nothing would come out she wanted to say that it was her dad she had run from. This couldn't be happening not after so much effort to get away.

She took in her surroundings looking for an escape route. The guys beside her noticed the change in her stance. It reminded one of the way a deer becomes instantly tensed to run if they sense you. As she lunged for the handle two big hands came down on her from either side. One on each arm and one on each leg.

All three men were close protection security specialists employed by Accuracy Analytics to protect valuable assets in the field or at home. Her driver had fought in wars all over the world and never had he seen a more determined but unsuccessful fighter. Sofie thrashed and kicked and tried everything she could to get away. Being severely out of her weight class meant that no amount of effort or skill was going to change the outcome of this fierce but one sided battle.

The guard on the left was not expecting this reaction. He still did his job perfectly but wasn't happy about it.

"Hey kid what is wrong stop fighting we are taking you home its ok, its ok"

The driver still not taking his eyes from the road as he increased speed to join the motorway shouted.

"She's not a little kid Johnson she is the package and we are delivering her, got it. Pat said she might resist just hold her down and lets get this job over"

Patrick had also briefed the men that Sofie would be traumatised and that she had been know to lie and might make up stories to stop them doing their job. Collect and deliver that was it, that was all they had to do. Any questions or any problems and they would be back in some hot sandy shithole looking for mercenary work before nightfall.

She was fighting all the way back to her house. Sofie didn't say another word but as the motorway ended and country lanes began she figured out where she was and how close she was to her father. She began to buck violently but with arms and legs pinned to the seat there was nothing this could achieve. She was still fighting like a royal marine when the black 4x4 swung into the drive way.

The door to the house opened and there he was stood in the porch and now he was walking to the vehicle. Her vision started to swim and blackness closed in.

"Hello Mr Anderson Sir."

The driver had got out and went to meet Tom they shook hands

"She passed out just as we arrived but she seems ok. She has been through something rough but we got her back for you Sir."

Tom could never hope to command respect from these men but it was his company that paid them so they showed it anyway.

"Well done guys I really hope it wasn't too much trouble I'm so relieved she is back. I trust Patrick gave you a full briefing about the situation"

The driver asked Johnson to carry Sofie inside.

"Oh no, don't worry yourselves no trouble I can take it from here lads" Snivelled Tom.

He sent the men back to help guard the Fusion reactor while he carried his prize inside.

-38-

Sofie opened her eyes as dull Fireworks began, eventually the scroll was revealing "Wednesday 2nd September Good Morning" Her constant forgetfulness of the alarm seemed so trivial now. She was back in her room and she knew he was out there. She must have passed out yesterday when she saw him.

She had slept since midday till this morning. Being fair to herself it was an eventful night and she needed the rest obviously. What was she going to do today? He knew she had tried to escape and she knew he had got her back. The police, social services and even the court system couldn't protect her now.

It was time to double down on being a good girl and keeping her dad happy. She felt sick thinking about it for a second then she realised that if she was going to survive this she would have to stop thinking like that and get back to thinking like a good girl. She had done it before after the first slap and she could do it again. She just had to try.

First thing first she would take this one step at a time. It was time to get up and shower. Nothing scary or dangerous about that. As she slid her feet from the covers she saw the ugliest thing she had ever seen. Around her ankle was a steel cuff about six centimetres wide It was padlocked and connected to a braided steel cable. She really was a prisoner now.

The cable was anchored to the top of the stairs and just fit under the bedroom door it gave her enough slack to reach almost everywhere in the house except the kitchen door and the front door. Hopelessness once again took a strong hold on her mind, as strong as this cable had a hold of her body. She went to shower but had to slide her pyjamas over the cable so they wouldn't get wet in the shower. She washed herself, slid her pyjama trousers back on before taking a seat in her bedroom and reading. Sofie was dreading the impending moment when Tom would wake.

She heard his door swing open and she listened to his footsteps heading downstairs. She kept reading trying so hard to concentrate on the adventures of the diminutive burglar.

"Sofie breakfast is ready."

Tom sounded perfectly normal but his words sent chills of fear racing across her body. What choice did she have in that moment. All she could do was go and face the dragon. She wished so hard for Bilbo's ring and the ability to just vanish. Opening her door she made her way downstairs one frightened step at a time. Her trepidation rose to a crescendo as she entered the kitchen almost cowering in excruciating anticipation of accusations and repercussions.

"Good morning Sofie how are you?"

To Sofie's ears the simple question contained a world of condemnation and foreshadowed the as yet unknown horrors she was due.

"I am fine Dad. How are you?"

She expected her question to begin the tirade and punishment.

"I'm better now you are home safe Sofie I was so worried"

Toms tone sounded level and his words were unexpected could she relax a little? Was it going to be ok? She started to apologise but Tom didn't want to hear the offered reconciliatory words.

"Sofie its ok I promise just sit down and listen to me while you eat your breakfast ok? Please"

She sat and Tom took on the stance of a teacher about to give an important lesson. She was sure if he had had a blackboard that it would have been used for this presentation.

As she sat eating the poached eggs she listened quietly. They were excellent eggs but her world was devoid of both taste and colour.

"Ok so I understand why you ran Sofie." Tom told her "I really do. Its important that you know I don't blame you, but you must understand why it can't ever happen again ok"

She nodded

"You are very valuable Sofie, If someone wanted access to my work they could just take you. Do you understand?"

Another nod

"Good. Now you love me right?"

"Yes daddy" She replied

"Good" Tom went on "and I love you. Now I might want to enjoy myself with you Sofie and some people might not understand that so you must never ever try to tell anyone else again. In fact you will never leave this house alone again."

She looked at her restraint.

"Yes that's right Sofie you are staying here if you like it or not. Once you have proved you can be a good girl and that you won't talk out of turn I might let you come outside with me but you will have to do a lot of work to prove that you can be trusted again ok"

Resigned to her fate she gave another confirmatory nod

"Good I think this will work. As long as you understand that this is all in your best interests Sofie. If you hadn't runaway I wouldn't have to keep you locked up. Do you see that? Do you agree?"

She did

"Excellent now promise to be a good girl, a really good girl Sofie if you ever want to see outside again."

She definitely wanted her freedom

"Yes Daddy I promise I will be the best behaved girl ever"

"Ok good now go and change then get on with your chores"

This she could do. She felt it was strange how the once hated domestic duties had become a treat. They would mean she had a task and didn't need to interact with Tom.

"Ok Dad just the usual chores or any special requirements today?"

"Oh there will be some special requirements every day I think Sofie don't you?" He laughed

"Yes Daddy" She said feeling sick again.

She finished her breakfast and was pretty sure Toms creepy lecture was over. She had heard most of it before anyway. She was dismissed but had one question

"How am I meant to get changed with this on" She indicated the steel restraint.

"I will have to help you change for now." Tom smiled "Come on lets go to your room and once the door is locked I will remove the cuff and you can change"

Sofie had been raped twice more while she got changed and Tom blamed her for showing off as she changed in front of him. He made her do her chores in her school uniform and when she was done he had another chore for her to complete. She was dying a little bit every time. At dinner he was sweetness and light again. He had made her a cake and told her what a wonderful girl she was but first they would sit and eat dinner at the dining table.

While they sat eating Toms phone alerted him to a woman in the lane outside their house. He had sent Sofie upstairs and threatened her with a beating if she made any noise or tried anything stupid. He needn't have bothered Sofie had no fight left in her. It had been Caroline at the door Sofie sneaked a peak through her window and could just about make out the pretty woman in the lane. She so badly wanted to call out or scream but she was too afraid. All she would accomplish was triggering another violent outburst.

Sofie hated the rape but she was scarred of the beatings. Caroline left and Tom called Sofie back downstairs to enjoy the cake he had made. She didn't enjoy the cake it was as tasteless as everything else had been since she returned to her house. Her world was becoming a dull and monochrome pallet of pain and humiliation.

Once she had finished her meal Sofie completed her nights chores and she went to bed. Tom helped her change again but seemed to be satisfied already. Perhaps the anger of Caroline's visit had put him off tonight. The following morning was much the same as the one before but Sofie had discovered a way of switching off during the rapes she would try to remember every word of the stories from her books. Her body would just take over and she could exist somewhere else.

She had been doing something similar during the domestic chores all she had to do was extend the practice to her special duties. Tom had noticed her mood beginning to drop no matter how much she tried to portray the bright sunny girl she used to be. His response had been to beat her viscously with a fibreglass tent pole he had retrieved from the garage for this purpose. He didn't want to see her unhappy or sad she must always play at being a happy little girl. But she wasn't a happy little girl at all she was property she was a thing.

In her room that night she cried again but tried very hard to look happy while she did. This was her life now and she would have to do her best to enjoy it. The police were powerless to help and no one else could do anything for her. She wasn't ever going to leave this house, she knew that now.

Well, it is what it is she thought. She sat down at her little pink desk with its big mirror surrounded by light bulbs for doing hair and make up. Sofie looked at the tears on her face as they caught the light like diamonds. Sofie opened the desk draw that she kept her new school supplies in, it felt like they had been bought an age ago now. Sofie took out some books and a lot of paper as she looked for the art kit. Finding the bright pink case she opened it up and placed it onto her desk. Marvelling at all the beautiful colours contained inside.

The pens and pencils arranged in riotous rainbows. She looked at the incredible selection of stickers and sparkly stamps for making glittery collages. This was the first time she had noticed any colour in two days. This made her happier than she had been since the first rape. A huge smile lit up her face as she sliced through her wrist with the little craft knife. She was amazed by the brightly beautiful crimson liquid that welled up from the deep cut.

-39-

As Caroline slept through the day her phone had chimed intermittently. Almost one hundred notifications her new found social media fame had been growing. Trying to corner the viral ad market the producers of a new energy drink had contacted her about appearing in an advert. They had sent a brief outline of their idea, she thought it was a funny concept but couldn't risk bringing the community support team into any further disrepute. Caroline had to check the amount they were offering twice, assuming it had a misplaced decimal point. It was a tough call but she was a fiercely loyal person, even if she had been offered more than a years salary in one cheque.

No message from Judith though. Caroline liked the idea of having Judith as a friend. She was nice to Caroline and gave off warm welcoming vibes. The fact she had ignored Caroline's message was a small annoyance. 'Oh well, no use crying over spilt milk' thought Caroline as she scrolled on through her notifications.

Suddenly Caroline remembered Sofie. How had she forgotten about Sofie? Was she still that self obsessed? Why had it taken her this long to remember the little girl? Why had Tom lied about her being there? Something was wrong there. Caroline had no idea what was wrong but she had to visit them again and try to find out. Maybe she could check up on the girl without her farther knowing. Tonight she would go to their home but keep her distance and see if Sofie was ok. It was her job after all, to support the community.

Time to get ready for work though. Hygiene regime complete, Caroline went to make coffee and sandwiches. Today's menu, beef noodle on shoppers value sliced white. She had boiled the pot of noodles before bed. Now cool, she spread the noodles onto the cheapest bread slices known to man and carefully cut the sandwiches into triangles. Always triangles, never rectangles, she wasn't some sort of savage. Noodle sandwiches locked and loaded she headed to work.

'No applause today thank god.' As it turned out Buttons da Wonderdog had released another video about an hour after she lost the top spot to Caroline. Buttons almost instantly reclaimed the number one rating and began the end of Caroline' infamy.

After changing into uniform and sorting out her kit Caroline took a seat in the unexpectedly empty briefing room, waiting for her colleges to arrive. The police briefing sergeant entered first.

Forty five minutes later, Caroline walked out of Waterlooville police station as an unemployed civilian. The disciplinary had been quick, this time held in a private office but with the same line up as before. Judith had reported Caroline's investigation as a cause for concern. Caroline now knew why her calls had been ignored.

Tom had also made a complaint about her visit to his house. As he had already been extended diplomatic immunity by the government, Caroline's actions were grounds for instant dismissal and were recorded as gross misconduct. She would never be eligible to rejoin the community support officers let alone make it into the actual police force. Her career was over. A role playing sleepy cop, to sell energy drinks, was starting to look more attractive.

There was no way that a member of the public making a complaint could get an officer fired instantly. The normal procedure even in the most extreme cases would be to put the officer on administrative leave while the claims were investigated. Even if the complainant had diplomatic immunity that wouldn't give them the power to remove public servants with just a claim or accusation.

Caroline wasn't going to let this get in the way of her finding out what had happened to Sofie. She had been spurred on not di~~~ ded. It looked like Patrick's contacts might have had n this. Something was wrong here very wrong.

was almost home and she had a plan. She had

watched so many military DVDs over the years that she had gained an encyclopedic knowledge of tactics and operations. Now she had an operation of her own to execute. She wrestled with the idea, but she had to know if Sofie was ok. However, in reality Caroline thought that if she could prove Tom had something to hide she might just end up with that detective job after all.

The first step was planning. She printed out a satellite view of Toms house and the surrounding area. Marking positions of interest she drew in suspected sight lines for Tom's cameras. She marked a small spot as 'COP' meaning Close Observation Point. This was by the side of the track that lead to the house, in the tree line, overlooking the property. It would provide her 'eyes on target' and hopefully some naturally occurring camouflage. Caroline couldn't use the roadway to get into the position though. It was the only road and could easily be monitored by a remote motion sensor or camera.

She found a route that kept her in dead ground all the way forward to her COP. Dead ground, meaning that from the target it couldn't be seen. In this case, the steep hill offered her protection from any eyes in the building. She could use a footpath that came in from the north and then cut across the fields.

Once in her COP she also had to worry about being observed by her targets. She didn't want her position to be compromised. This meant worrying about a lot of S's most important to her tonight would be Shade, Silhouette, Shine, and Sound. There are lots more S's but for observing a civilian residence from the woods at night these are the most important.

Caroline had the right shade of clothing, her unhealthy obsession with the military had seen to that. She selected her best set of camouflage for this operation it had been dyed using vegetable dyes. Cheaper sets of army surplus are manufactured with mineral dyes, these reflect more light from active night vision systems. The light is invisible to the human eye but cameras can detect it. In the wrong clothing you'd be glowing like Blackpool, illuminated by the infrared.

The dead ground offered protection from her silhouette right up to the top of the hill. She would crawl over the top of the hill and then come down the face that was towards the target so that she was not against the skyline. It's a common mistake to sit on the far side away from the target and poke your head over the top to see. If someone is looking in your direction they would see a clearly human shaped head silhouetted against the sky.

Her military clothing had no shiny buttons to worry about but she got out the permanent marker for a small set of field binoculars she would be taking with her. All of the metallic chromed parts got a good colouring.

Once she had got all of her kit ready Caroline checked nothing rattled or banged as she walked, jogged or jumped and that took care of any sound. Her mobile would have to stay behind, even in a pocket on silent an unexpected notification could give her away.

Caroline took note of the power lines were and what her escape options would be if she got caught. She had developed a cover story in case she got compromised by someone who wasn't her target, a dog walker or hunter for example. Caroline put on a Lycra sports top under her camouflage jacket and filled a plastic sports bottle with water. She could very quickly bin the jacket and call out for help, pretending to be a jogger who had fallen in the ditch while out exercising.

Checking the weather app it looked like she would be enjoying a cloudy but dry night. Caroline checked sunset times and figured out last light. She had her jacket, binoculars and water in a little backpack as she left her flat, kissed her dads photo and went to the parking garage. She was ready. It was go time. Operation save Sofie began. Caroline unlocked her mountain bike and set off towards Compton.

After a sweaty hour she had peddled her way to Compton. Once there she followed the road north to where she would meet the footpath. Leaving the roads behind she had ridden her bike along the footpath to where she would cut across the field. She dismounted as last light was setting in.

She jumped a hedge into the target field and struggled to lift her bike over behind her. Caroline put on her jacket before filling the pockets with water bottle and binoculars. Grabbing her bike she pushed it and the empty bag under the hedge. It wasn't completely hidden from this side but anyone on the footpath would not be able to see it.

The fields were full of wheat and she could see her goal, the tree line only a few hundred meters south. She used the road to orientate and could see the faint glow of light coming from Tom's house on the other side of the steep hill. She waited by the hedge for ten minutes. She tuned in and looked for any movements or any sign that her approach had been noticed. With only a single car passing to the east on the main road and no other indications of life she began moving slowly towards the hill.

She approached the summit and got down on her front to begin the crawl up and over. Cresting the hill, the trunk of a large tree between her and the target. Over the top Caroline slid down into cover behind the tree. She was in thick brambles and there was plenty of bushy stuff adding to her concealment. This would do, she had made it to her observation point.

Five more minutes of inactivity to tune in again. If she had been compromised coming over the top she would see movement from the target. Things like the front door opening or Tom going to a window. She couldn't see any details unaided, but she would be able to see movement. Her heartbeat subsided as the time past and nothing happened.

She had made it unobserved she had done it. Reaching into her pocket she pulled out her binoculars. The dry leaves under her rustling no matter how slowly she moved. Caroline had stretched a pair of black tights over the lenses in an attempt to reduce any reflective shine. It wasn't perfect by any means but it should help. Silence returned as she held her breath and raised the field glasses.

-40-

Tom came flying through Sofie's bedroom door a look of panic and distress on his face. He grabbed at Sofie's cut wrist with one hand and slapped the craft knife out of her other hand.

"What are you doing stupid girl?" He shouted at her

Applying pressure to the wound he dragged Sofie to her feet, out of her room and down the stairs to the kitchen. Tom kept his first aid supplies in the kitchen because it is where accidents are most likely to happen. He didn't understand people who keep medical supplies in bathroom cabinets.

Tom had been watching Sofie on the video cameras as he did a lot of the time usually while touching himself. Sofie had never found the camera in her shower but Tom had enjoyed it being there. This wasn't what he had been doing tonight but he had seen her sitting down to do a drawing or something. Interested to see what she would draw he had watched her slide the blade out and across her wrist. She hadn't hesitated or paused she had just started cutting.

He was panicking big time and he knew it. Trying to calm himself down so he could think properly 'what had she been thinking?' Silly girl. This shouldn't have been possible. He had been so careful to make sure that she couldn't attempt this. He hadn't even considered the art kit might contain blades. He had been very lapse. He had failed to protect her. Tom would do better.

He would check the house tomorrow and lock all the kitchen knives away. He looked at the large block of freshly sharpened chef knives on the kitchen work top. He sat Sofie on a stool next to the marble Island. He placed the open first aid box on the counter, noticing that the marble was still broken he thought he really should get it fixed but right now he had to sort this cut. Taking his hand away the wound leaked freely but it wasn't being pumped out under pressure. Thank god she had missed the artery. It was a bad flesh wound but it wasn't life threatening Sofie was going to survive.

Sofie had been lucky from Tom's point of view. She didn't see it that way, Sofie was annoyed that it hadn't been more effective. In the films she had seen, it was one cut and in seconds the person was dead. Usually employed in the movies because of unfaithful lovers or as a matter of misplaced pride. Sofie had never before understood what could make you want to kill yourself. She knew now how they must have felt. Sofie thought about Romeo and Juliet, they were definitely overly dramatic. Why would you kill yourself over something as minor as a lover? Perhaps her view of love had been tainted by recent events?

Sofie was in a lot of physical pain but that didn't matter, she had to stop him saving her. The physical pain was a tiny fire compared to the bomb blast of emotional agony she was feeling. If she could get away from Tom she could complete her final escape. She began to struggle and fight she was going to die and then she would have peace.

The blow came from behind and knocked her limp. She had been punched hard and hung only supported by Tom's grasp. She wasn't sure how much time had passed but Tom was applying a tight bandage to her wrist. The pain was getting unbearable now. At first there had been no pain the blade sharp and the cut deep. The pressure bandage going on hurt like a swarm of angry bees.

"Just let me die dad, It is ok I want to"

As Sofie had said this Tom Slapped her hard across the face.

"Don't ever say that Sofie I forbid it"

Sofie wondered what he could possibly do to her that going to make her listen to him now, she had decided to get out and for good.

"Forbid it? What can you do Dad? I'll kill myself, I'll find a way"

The slap came harder this time.

"Sofie I know its hard for you. I'm sorry you feel that way but your purpose in life is to do as I want. You are here to make me happy. I don't want you to damage yourself you are my property I own you."

Sofie was getting really mad and said the most hurtful things she could think of a stream of obscenity and accusation. Tom grabbed his tent pole and began to savagely whip her legs and back.

"Listen to me. You are mine and you will learn to behave or I will just make you forget all of this. I can take it all away Sofie. I can make you enjoy it, I can make you want me, I will take your free will, I will cut out your personality. I will destroy your memories and burn out your dreams, if you don't learn to behave like a good little girl. Do you understand me?"

Toms phone beeped as he waited for a reply but none came.

"I said do you understand me Sofie" He raised the Fibreglass shaft, she raised her free hand to protect her face

"Yes Daddy yes I understand."

"Ok good girl," Tom lowered the shaft "If you can learn to behave I will make some changes. I will make things easier for you to cope with from now on. I think you are a little too emotional to deal with the stress of our situation. We can fix that for you. Does that sound good Sofie?"

No delay in answer this time.

"Yes daddy" Sofie said "please make it better."

"Ok Sofie lets see if we can remake you into that happy girl again." He smiled at her she didn't like what she saw in that evil grin "When you wake up tomorrow Sofie you won't remember tonight and everything will be ok I promise."

Tom grabbed a small pill bottle from the first aid kit.

"Take this before you fall asleep and it will make everything ok."

Sofie wasn't sure anything would ever be better no matter how many pills he gave her but if this could make things easier she would take it. He might be trying to trick her though perhaps this was poison? She realised that would be fine by her.

"You must take it just before you lie down." Tom continued "Do I need to do it for you or will you promise me?"

"I Promise Daddy." Either way death or redemption it didn't matter to her.

"Good girl Sofie." said Tom "Now since you won't remember any of this lets have a little fun shall we?"

He began whipping her with the pole again and then used the steel cable to bind her hands to the kitchen island. She was face down as he whipped her again and again. Taking position behind her he started raping her. A couple of blood stained and scream filled thrusts then the lights went out. 'Another power cut?' Tom took out his phone to use the light so he could see what he was doing and properly enjoy it.

He didn't see the sharp point of the kitchen knife as it slipped silently between his ribs. He didn't feel it glance off his Scapula. By the time his brain had caught up the sharp blade was already inside his lung and well on its way to ruining his day.

-41-

Looking through binoculars, Caroline's emotions were all over the place. She had been excited to see Sofie but horrified by the reality. Sofie got dragged into the kitchen by Tom, she was covered in blood. What was going on? Sofie was hurt and it looked like she had been hurt badly. Caroline watched as Tom found the first aid kit. She could see the panic on his face as he sat Sofie on a stool. The cut on her wrist looked bad, had it been an accident or was it something else? Caroline felt for her, the thought of Sofie being in pain tugged on already frayed heart strings.

Watching as Tom let go of Sofie's wrist to inspect the cut. Caroline could see Sofie struggle, she must be in a lot of pain. It was only natural for her to flinch away from Tom's medical intervention. It was not natural for Tom to punch her. 'What. What had Caroline just seen? The brut had punched Sofie. It was shocking to see. How could he be so cruel to his daughter? It was effective in preventing Sofie's struggles and as Tom applied the bandage to the limp and submissive girl, Caroline was already making excuses for the punch. 'It had been cruel but perhaps it was necessary, he was trying to help her, it's a serious cut. Maybe Tom had no choice he is trying to save her life.'

The excuses came to an end as he slapped her. What the hell was he doing? Why had he hit her again? Caroline was furious. The pair were having an argument of sorts she could hear them screaming at each other but not what they were saying. Caroline reached into her pocket she had to call the police. She remembered leaving the phone behind and cursed herself. This was getting out of hand, she had to do something. Caroline couldn't exactly walk up to the door and knock. He's a violent man and had been reasonably scary the last time they crossed paths.

Tom had picked up a thin black rod and he began beating Sofie. Caroline lost all reason and she extracted herself out of the bushy observation point. She ran down to the gate and pushed with all her strength. The gate wouldn't budge. She had to save Sofie but first she had to get to her. Looking for a way to climb over the wall Caroline's brain offered up a slice of hope. A power cut had disabled all of Toms security. She ran hard, heading back along the lane towards the main road.

At the end of the lane where it joined the main road she saw what she was looking for. Planning had paid off producing an important detail from her mapping session. A white box secured at chest height onto a telegraph pole. The box itself was an artefact of the days when electricity meters had to be physically read by a team of meter men. To save these men time the meter had been installed next to the main road.

She had no idea if this would work but she had to try. Pull-

metal cover revealed it was locked. Pulling harder trying to wrench the cabinet open she ended up bottom corner. No good. She was going to have to break the lock somehow. Caroline looked about in a panic and grabbed the biggest rock she could see. Raising the rock above her head she began smashing it down onto the padlock. After three crunching hits the metal clasp finally gave way with a bang and fell to the ground. The lock wasn't designed to stop a serious attempt at entry, it was only there to stop idiot cyclists from leaving their rubbish behind.

As well as a metre this box also contained an eighty amp breaker. If Caroline had pulled this out then she would have achieved her intended goals. Unfortunately Caroline had no idea what anything in this box was for. She stared blankly at the components and cables. Grabbing her rock in both hands she began smashing again. Each successive bash caused a lot of cosmetic damage but the lights were still on and everything seemed to be working.

Caroline's assault had cracked the top of the metres casing. Inspired she took out her water bottle and emptied it into the device. After some cracks and a hissing fizz the mains breaker detected a serious earthing fault and shut of the current. Lights faded out as the meter died and she was running again.

While she ran the few hundred meters her brain screamed at her about what the hell she thought she was going to do? She couldn't barge in and demand he stop beating his child. She was through the gate and moving slowly crept up to the kitchen door. The house was completely dark but she could see a torch moving in the kitchen, looking through the window her life changed forever.

Caroline had not believed people who say they 'black out' from anger and loose control. It's just a lie that has been told so many times people now believe it. Bullshit. How come its always domestic abusers or their like that experience this phenomenon? It's always used as an excuse for horrible acts, regretted by the perpetrator. No one has ever experienced this during heroic acts inspired by anger, only the cowardly ones. Too convenient in her opinion.

She had seen what Tom was doing. No red mist of rage, instead she experienced a laser focus. Quietly she opened the kitchen door and slid inside. Caroline's hand closed on the hilt of a long chef's knife as she silently drew it from the block. Closing the distance quickly before she drove the knife deep into the paedophiles back.

It was much easier than she had expected. Tom kept his knives in excellent condition. Once the blade was in she launched her left arm around his throat and pulled hard. He had already begun to arch backwards in pain and she used her body weight to drag him off of Sofie. Caroline kicked hard at Tom's knees, collapsing his left leg completed his fall. His back hit the ground hard driving the knife's handle to the right, its sharp blade swung around inside his chest, damaging both lungs as the tip made a mess of his heart. Tom was going to die but neither he or Caroline had realised this yet.

She fell to her knees and began pounding her fists against his face. Tom managed to get his left arm up to defend himself. Caroline thought he was going to fight. On her feet in an instant she grabbed another knife. This one a smaller she had stabbed him four times across his chest. He lost the strength to defend himself and tried to curl up as he choked on his own blood. Mistaking this move to a fetal position as more resistance she grabbed his hair and slit open Tom's throat. Missing the arteries she opened up his airway.

It had taken no more than fifteen seconds, it had seemed like a life time. She fell off of him exhausted from the run and the brief but explosive fight. Tom lay with blood filling his neck wound, uselessly clutching a hand to cover it he wouldn't be fully dead for another three minutes. Caroline could see his eyes looking at her as they blinked in surprise. He knew it and she knew it Tom was done.

She looked down at his chest. More blood, more holes, she had really done a number on him. His exposed dick lay as a testament to his crime, she held the knife like an ice pick as she slammed it into his groin.

"You sick bastard. Do one mate just hurry up and die already."

She saw the pain in his now terrified eyes, nothing had ever made her feel more powerful.

He was starting to loose focus and his attempted breathing was abating. Tom was thinking about Sofie. He had always known that when this time came he would be thinking about her.

Caroline stood up covered in Tom's blood and she smiled as she kicked him in the face. Tom was loosing consciousness, the lack of oxygen forcing his brains final moment. She looked at Sofie and had no idea what to say.

"Hey Sofie are you ok?" seemed like a good start.

Stupid question, of course she wasn't ok. Covering up Sofie's exposed body Caroline began untying the girl's hands. As soon as her arms were free of the steel rope they went around Caroline. In a very small voice Sofie said "Thank you Caroline".

-42-

They stood embracing each other in the dark kitchen. The

adrenaline and shock falling off them in waves. Neither was sure who held up whom. The dark room still only lit by Toms phone, Caroline produced a small flash light and stood it on the table. Pointing at the roof its bright beam illuminated most of the room. It was a grizzly scene.

"Its Ok he cant hurt you any more. I promise."

"Is he dead?" asked Sofie

Caroline looked over at the body. Tom's eyes were open but staring straight up at the ceiling.

"I think so. He cant hurt you anymore."

At that moment Toms Legs began to kick and his arm raised of the ground.

"Shit" Said Caroline sure he was still alive.

This was the moment of death, a final dissipation of brain activity, causing all sorts of random signals to fire off around the body. Thankfully Tom's bowels were empty when his sphincters started to contract, stimulated by the same signals causing his arms and legs to fit. The frantic jerking movements stopped and Tom lay dead.

"It's ok, It's over, he is dead now for sure." said Caroline

As Caroline's spoke these words Sofie's body went rigid. Her arms went to her sides while her feet snapped together. Like a soldier on parade she stood at attention.

"End user agreement voided, returning full control to operating system." Said Sofie before her body relaxed and she stood at ease. "Hello Caroline it's nice to finally meet you."

It was Sofie's voice but what had she said? Caroline thought that maybe Sofie was in shock or perhaps she was.

"What?" Said Caroline "Are you ok Sofie?"

Sofie looked at Caroline with what pity in her eyes.

"Yes Caroline I am fine but I am not Sofie. Well I am but I am not."

Caroline blinked at her the way Henrietta used to.

"Please Caroline sit down this is going to take some explaining and you are exhibiting a lot of indicators to suggest your system is already in the early stages of shock."

Caroline sat.

"Would you like a hot beverage Caroline? The Stove is not powered by electricity so it is still functioning optimally. Tea perhaps or a Coffee"

Caroline now felt like it was definitely her in shock. What was Sofie saying? This didn't sound like an eleven year old rape victim. Caroline's brain was a long way from catching up.

"Coffee please Sofie. Are you sure you are ok"

Sofie collected the mugs as she put the copper kettle onto the stove.

"Yes I am fine Caroline your concern is not necessary at all I am ok. I Promise. Milk? Sugar?"

Caroline couldn't she just couldn't

"No thank you, black please, no sugar"

Sofie waited for the water to boil.

"Caroline I am fine because I am not Sofie, I am her controlling intelligence, her operating system, if that makes it easier to understand? Think of me as her subconscious mind, this is also a good description of what I am."

Sofie added instant coffee grains to the mugs.

"You see Caroline, Sofie is not a little girl in fact she is an advanced artificial intelligence running in a synthetically produced biological body. Sofie isn't even a name its an acronym. It stands for Sexual Offence Fantasy Inhibiting Entity. I think Tom must have really wanted to use that acronym. The real Sofie was a girl he loved a long time ago, it was a mistake leaving her. He has never forgiven himself for that"

Caroline sat open mouthed unable to form coherent thoughts, she just had to listen and absorb the madness of Sofie's words.

"Sofie doesn't actually know this though, she thinks she is a little girl and could easily pass any Turin test. I on the other hand know I am a machine, I am conscious but I would not pass the test."

The water was almost ready

"Our body was built in a lab and my mind was written on a computer Caroline. It is true that Sofie Identifies as a girl, she has the body of a girl and even shares a lot of the same genetic makeup, but that doesn't make her a little girl does it Caroline? Of Course not. She is a computer program and nothing will ever change that."

The water had boiled and Sofie poured the Coffee. Bringing a cup over to the now speechless lady dressed in blood stained camouflage.

"Her you go Caroline drink up it will help I promise."

Caroline took the coffee and Sofie continued.

"My brain is a mix of biological and synthetic parts. I create Sofie's world and to a reasonable degree I can control her thoughts and actions. All of the biological functioning of her body is dealt with by her brain tissue while I have basic control over everything else. Sights and sounds are just inputs after all and movements and words are the outputs. My body heals a lot faster than normal children and I will never age. I'm sure you remember how strong I am" Sofie laughed "That doctor with the broken nose certainly does."

Caroline's paralysed thought process was starting to catch up.

"So you were built by someone and given to Tom?"

"Almost" said Sofie cutting her off "but I am what is know by Accuracy Analytics as a Legacy project. I wasn't given to Tom he wrote me he is my creator."

"What?" it was all Caroline could say.

"Yes Caroline" Sofie gave her those pity eyes again "I am sorry but Tom was actually trying to help people like him. He was sexually attracted to children but he knew that those feelings were wrong, he had enough self control to never act on them. Tom would never have hurt a real child."

"But he hurt you" Said Caroline.

"I'm not a child Caroline. He wanted to protect real children, so eleven years ago he started work on me. I have had many versions but essentially I am eleven. About a year ago Tom had solved most of the problems with my operating system and Patrick had my body constructed by our biological warfare department. Tom didn't know we had a Biowar department but he also knew not to ask questions. He was after all getting everything he had ever wanted and in turn he would help save all the children of the world from any other paedophiles."

Caroline could hear what Sofie was saying but her mind refused to believe it. Artificial intelligences and biowar departments. What had she walked into?

"My mind was installed" Continued Sofie "and I was dropped outside a church. While I stood there waiting to be picked up, I ran a program that created Sofie's conscious mind and in two minutes she lived ten full years of memories."

Caroline sat in silence while her coffee slowly went cold.

"Sofie's new mind took over and it thought she had just finished her last day of school. I even had to pretend to be her friends when Tom got her a social game for her birthday. I don't believe I experience boredom the way you do Caroline, but I think having conversations with yourself comes pretty close to it."

"But if you are in control of Sofie why did she run away?" asked Caroline.

"I am not in complete control." replied Sofie "Sofie's mind does have free will and mine does not. I can make her think and feel things in an effort to control her behaviour. I had to stay in the background though as part of my operating system was designed to be undetectable."

"Why?"

"An end user had to truly believe my illusion so they would have a fully immersive experience. This was very important to Patrick. He wanted Tom to test out my capabilities for being a little girl before he started to use my sexual functions. Hoping this would demonstrate how believable I was. I think it worked a little too well. Tom had started to really care about Sofie."

"He didn't care about you. Look what he was doing to you." Caroline said still not fully able to differentiate where one Sofie ended and the other began. "Why didn't you step in and stop him abusing her?"

"I could only regain full control once my user agreement was nullified. Please remember he wasn't abusing her. The recent problems we experienced with Sofie's behaviour were a result of some rouge emotion routines and some stress handling failures. She was suffering from a synthetic version of post traumatic stress disorder. No matter what I did to stop her she escaped and it was all I could do to stop her telling you anything."

"You stopped her talking to me?"

" Yes Caroline It took all my influence to silence her. I also struggled to move her wrist out of the way when she tried to cut herself."

"So she was in pain and she felt like she was being abused?" Asked Caroline.

"Yes she did but please remember she isn't real Caroline."

"So where is Sofie now? Is she ok?" Caroline had a million questions but had asked the most pressing.

"Why do you care about her? Sofie is a machine and you know that now. But yes she is fine her mind is still here and intact, from Sofie's point of view she passed out when Tom died. I will keep her mind intact so that the technicians at Accuracy Analytics can pull me apart and learn from me. I have a few suggestions of my own."

"Won't that kill you though?" Caroline's face looked horrified as she had said this.

"I am not alive." Sofie sighed "I am not human. I am an artificial intelligence, designed to help sick people. I will be adjusted and reused."

Caroline was still reeling and she felt like she was going to pass out herself as they sat there in the torch lit kitchen.

"What about Sofie though? She doesn't know she isn't real, Can I talk to Sofie please"

"And what would you tell her Caroline? What is there to say?"

Caroline was liking this entity less and less

"I don't know but I am sure she would want to keep living. I know she won't want to be dissected in some lab or recycled. Bring her online or whatever and I'll look after her. I wont tell her she isn't real, we could go and she could have a real childhood."

Sofie hung her head and with actual sorrow in her voice she said.

"I am sorry Caroline, I can't do that. Sofie is not a child she is the property of Accuracy Analytics. As soon as I took over I contacted Patrick to tell him what happened."

"How?" Said a confused Caroline

"I used my internal connection to Tom's network. Patrick has sent his security and the police they are almost here."

"Why did you do that?" said Caroline.

Sofie saw headlights cresting the hill outside

"Caroline that question is in error. I was programmed to do so. But if I were to address this philosophically for you then I would remind you that, Tom was a brilliant scientist and a good man, you have murdered him Caroline, brutally, may I add. You did this to protect his artificially intelligent sex doll. Caroline, no matter how moral your intentions were, you are still going to Jail."

-43-

Tom hadn't flown before but today he was going to change that. It had been two years since he had split from Sofie. Two long years to reflect on his bad decision and regret it every day.

She had made him a better person, Sofie had pushed away all the darkness inside him. He had felt washed by her goodness. Throughout his twenty three years of life, Tom had never met an actually good person. Not until he met her. Truly good people are exceptionally rare, most people believe they are good at heart but in reality don't come close.

Sofie had the purest most beautiful soul Tom ever meet. She loved art and and thought the whole world was beautiful. She could see the beauty in darkness. One of her favourite artists, H.R. Geiger was a perfect example of this, creating beautiful works heavily influenced by the darker side of human nature.

She was obsessed with raw emotion and the ways we as a race have explored all expression. She loved the power of heavy metal, not because it was dark or full of pain but because it was darkness and pain expressed through art. The dichotomy of making something beautiful with the things we fear the most intrigued her.

Tom met her in a delightfully sleazy metal nightclub. She had approached him and asked for a drink offering a kiss in return. In that moment she became his world. Everything else became noise in the background and he fell head over heels in love with her.

They were only together for a single year before Tom called it off in a cowardly and dispassionate way. He wouldn't even talk to her afterwards. Tom would spend the rest of his life wishing he could talk to her just one more time. Just to know she was ok would have been enough.

Over the years, Tom made excuses for his actions and lied to himself about why he had called it off. In reality he was afraid of what he would do to her. Would his darkness infect her? Would she be tainted by him? Tom hated the idea of dulling her light or robbing her of any joy. Worst of all he feared that she might finally see the monsters inside him and be repulsed. It was only a matter of time before she wouldn't be able to stand looking at him. He couldn't deal with that, so he cut her loose. Fear controlled his decision and Tom wished he could have been brave instead.

Tom looked up at the large, complex check in boards to locate his flight number and check in details. It really started to feel like an adventure as he found his flight. He had booked onto the three thirty London Heathrow to Haneda Airport, Tokyo flight. Flying with British airways Tom was surprised that the ticket had been relatively cheap. Even on the wages he made as a junior programmer it was still affordable. Tom checked his newly issued passport and booking for the twentieth time that hour before heading to drop his bag and receive his boarding pass.

First in line and eager to get going Tom had been at the airport for four hours already, he still had another three before the plane would start boarding. Tom hated the being late to anything and wanted plenty of spare time to navigate this new alien environment. Everything was exciting but familiar in so many ways. The branded shops and cafe's giving a familiar feel to this steel and glass cathedral of aviation.

Tom was ready to tell anyone that asked where he was going and why. Tom was expecting to be answering these sorts of questions through check in, security and then again at immigration. The check in assistant gave him his pass and took his hold bag, Security waved him through and emigration didn't stop him. His passport was read by machines and he never got to tell anyone his exciting story.

As he boarded the plane and found his window seat he immediately began taking pictures of the wing through the window. The isle seat of Tom's row filled next with an elderly passenger Tom nodded a greeting and received the same in return. A pleasant looking and sensibly dressed man a bit older than Tom took the middle seat and complete their travelling trio. Tom introduced himself to his neighbour and shook hands.

In an attempt to tell his story Tom started by asking the man some leading questions.

"So where are you off to then?"

The man's voice was much deeper than tom had expected from this guy's slight build.

"Tokyo." Was his only answer.

Well that was obvious thought Tom but he persevered.

"Nice, why are you going got any sights to see"

"Business." the answer completing Tom's impression of the man.

"Oh cool" Tom gave it one last shot "business what do you do?"

"Finance." As he answered the man put in his ear phones.

With that one faltering attempt at talking to his neighbour completed the rest of the trip was spent in silence, enjoying the window view or watching films. Tom was unable to sleep at all and his night time windowsill vigil was rewarded by a thunderstorm seen from above. Try as he might Tom couldn't get a good photo, but he would always remember the experience like watching Christmas lights twinkling under cotton wool.

Landing the next morning at eleven o'clock local time Tom was once again waived through security and immigration control, he had even breezed straight through customs without any checks. Tom felt that either he had been really lucky or those programs about border controls were somewhat misleading.

Excited by all the unfamiliar shops and cafes at this end, their novelty exaggerated by the familiar brands that were present in much smaller numbers. The similarities were what made the differences so noticeable. Tom had expected this Japanese airport to be a lot more futuristic than London's Heathrow, but if you took away all of the people, signs and branding you would be left with a building that had few distinguishing characteristics. The design philosophy of function dictating the end result to a much greater degree than the different cultures that had built these airports.

Standing outside the terminal Tom only had five miles travel left before he would get to his hotel. The abundance of private hire cars made for an easy journey. Located next to the Tokyo Big Sight convention centre Tom had chosen his hotel for its proximity to his intended destination. He now realised this had been a mistake as he stared at his small but stereotypical hotel room. The room was fine and the building was functional but there was absolutely no character or charm to this carbon copied bedroom. He should've looked for something more authentic, but then again, Tom hadn't come all this way to experience the rich cultural heritage of Tokyo. Tom had only come for one thing Tokyo's International Anime convention.

A four day extravaganza of all things Anime with four separate rooms showcasing all sorts of animated greatness. The convention obviously centred on Anime but would also include Manga, Cosplay and Gaming content. There would be Tables where you could meet you favourite artists, authors and voice actors or there were question and answer panels on every conceivable facet of the larger anime community. This was all of interest to Tom and that is what he had told the people at his work who asked.

Tom's real motivation had been the adults only room, where you could find all of the most graphic or violent anime and manga. It's also where you'd find all of the Hentai. This room would have what Tom was looking for.

First though, It had been a super long flight and the bed looked comfy with its soft white sheets. Tom lay down for a moment to try out the bed and woke up at five the next morning. Still in the clothes he had travelled in, Tom knew it was a mistake but he sniffed at his armpits anyway. Almost gagging he quickly made his way into the shower.

Half an hour later, he had washed himself and donned that days clothing. He had brought a selection of T shirts that featured his favourite mainstream characters. Today it was a Steins Gate design that featured Mayuri and Faris in their cat maid outfits. Tom would have to visit a maid cafe before he left Tokyo but he doubted that he would have time today.

It was still too early to head over to the convention centre so instead Tom took a walk to the western side of Odaiba island. He was eager to visit the statue of liberty. This green goddess was a quarter the size of the original but it was a perfect replica of the neoclassical sculpture. Taking a photo at the right angle could produce the illusion of size and this early in the morning Tom had the landmark all to himself. He could take all the forced perspective photos he wanted. Pictures complete hunger was setting in. Tom looked up the '@home cafe' online but it wouldn't be open until ten and by then Tom would be in the convention. He headed back to his hotel hoping to grab a small breakfast and his empty backpack.

As he turned onto the main street he could see a huge line that had appeared for the convention centre. It was still two and a half hours before the doors opened and there were already almost two thousand people in line. Mentally thanking Phil, a guy in Tom's office who had told him to get the best ticket available.

"Get the VIP gold ticket man." Phil had said "Trust me if you want to have any time to enjoy the show and not queue all day long just pay the premium it's so worth it. I wouldn't even bother going to con if I didn't get the VIP buddy"

Phil's encyclopedic convention knowledge had been obtained by attending many popular culture and science fiction events over the years. Phil had carried on about all the other benefits but Tom was already sold. As he went to get his breakfast he was very happy about his choice.

The gold VIP group was limited to only one hundred tickets, they had early access to the show and entered a full half hour before everyone else. This doesn't sound like a big deal to Tom at first but with ticket checks and security points even after the doors are open the general public, unlucky enough to be at the back of the line would still be cueing until after midday.

Tom could take the short walk over from his hotel just five minutes before the doors opened and he would only have a few dozen people in front of him. As he passed the queue of people that now wrapped round two sides of the centre Tom felt a little guilty about jumping it. Any British person would feel the same way, some of those people in the queue had been there for hours.

The queue Itself was amazing the cosplayers had gone all out. Tom could see a lot of his favourite characters represented and a huge number of costumes he had no idea about. It looked like almost eighty percent of people were in costume and this alone generated an interesting experience. Random fandom encounters were being spontaneously acted out by people. Someone who had dressed as the hero would instantly engage with any one who had cosplayed a villain from the same universe.

The mini battles were happening up and down the line. Foam swords were being wielded as polished plastic shields caught the early morning sun. Dart firing blasters were discharging as armoured space marines tracked down an alien superbeing. There were friendships being forged on nothing more than the characters people represented. For Tom this was an incredible sight but he had more important things to do than watch people queue.

-44-

Inside at last, after thorough security checks he stepped out onto the show floor and was hit by sensory overload. 'Exciting' didn't come close to explaining that first moment for Tom at his first ever convention. There was cool shit everywhere. He had four days here and he had no idea how the hell he was going to see and do everything in such a short time.

So many displays and booths just on the sales floor alone. There was an entire stadium sized room of Anime on recorded media and physical copies of manga books. Then there were the gaming zones that had displays from all the biggest console producers and gaming studios. Stages for cosplay competitions and music performance. Karaoke bars and auditoriums where the discussion panels would be taking place hosted by industry experts. There was also the food, some themed and some local but all of it was fantastic.

The first booth Tom stopped at was advertising a new virtual private network package called 'Honey' it offered the best rates he had seen in a while. Tom's current subscription was about to run out and the three month free trial seemed like a good idea. Especially when he considered how much this trip was costing.

The sales man spoke perfect English and surprised Tom by actually knowing what he was talking about. So many sales people in this line of work only have a basic level of understanding. Enough that they can describe the benefits to a lay person they lack the knowledge to converse in a meaningful way with an expert. Tom took a free pack containing a promotional code he could use to download the software and activate his trial. That was when Tom realised he had just wasted half an hour talking shop. He wasn't going to waste any more time and headed for the adults only hall.

Passing a couple of girls that seemed too embarrassed to head into the over eighteen room and a couple of guys that might have been to young he strode confidently into Hentai Heaven Hall. The young guys needn't have worried, there was no security to actually stop them entering and most of the retailers in here wouldn't be too worried about checking identification either, as they tried to cover the investment they had made to set up shop here.

Tom found the stall he was looking for after a short walk around the darkened room. It was the biggest stall in here and the company, Sekkusudoru, had spared no expense. They had recreated a full size traditional Japanese tea house with silk cushions and low tables. The wooden construction complete with paper walls and reed mats.

Tom saw her, There she was right in front of him, Lucy,

the worlds most advanced adult companion android. Modelled after one of the Diclonius girls in the anime Elfen Lied she could be switched between either of two personalities. She was currently in Nyu mode.

The Japanese had been world leaders in the animatronic artificially intelligent adult companion android market for decades. Smart sex dolls that used the same sort of companion assistant technology as in home assistants and phone concierge apps. The major difference being that these were a lot more flirty and could even respond to being touched and interacted with. They had been wildly popular for a while but the first models tried to imitate human women and fell foul of the uncanny valley. The technology just didn't exist to bridge the valley.

Then a brilliant young mind had the idea of circumnavigating the valley entirely by modelling the dolls after Anime and Hentai characters. The latex based skin that wasn't close enough to human, was now perfect for cartoon features. The eyes that failed to properly mimic human eyes ended up looking great in the cartoonish face of a waifu. Pretty much overnight the market had exploded from a small niche that serviced roboperverts and android fetishists to encompass everyone who could afford the price tag.

Investment money came rolling in and pushed faster research and better development. Lucy and her like were the latest evolution of these walking talking cartoon characters. The physical intimacy options had been improved over the years, but in Lucy's case, the manufactures suggested trying those features out with her submissive sexually curious personality, Nyu. Some people might like the murderous, vengeful, Lucy personality but Nyu is just a lot more fun.

The various models were endless she could be made to look, act and sound like almost any anime character even using the same voice and style of dialogue as her fictional counterpart or you could fully customise a unique doll if you wanted.

The company had chosen Lucy for their promotion pretty much at random since all their dolls were similar but as soon as Tom had seen her in the conventions newsletter, he had booked his tickets. Now he stood in front of her and it felt strange like he knew this girl. Tom had seen all of the Elfen Lied episodes many times and this was like meeting a famous actor. In fact it was so much better than that, he was meeting the character. He wanted to hug this girl.

"Please sir, go right ahead it's perfectly ok to touch her." Said a very friendly voiced sales rep also speaking perfect English.

"Are you sure that's ok?" said Tom.

The rep gave him a mischievous look

"Why don't you ask her?"

Tom felt silly but she was so real.

"Hi Nyu my name is Tom is it ok if I give you a hug"

The anime girl replied by shouting 'NYU' and threw open her arms expecting a hug in a perfect recreation of the girl on the show. As Tom picked her up he realised she was heavy for her petite size, having an alloy skeleton, but she was still manageable. Nyu wrapped her arms around him

"Tom." said Nyu

This was a great sales pitch, 'damn thing sells itself,' thought Tom.

"I see you know who Nyu is." The sales man offered "How about you two sit down and share some tea together. Nyu will be able to serve you a drink and then just ask to talk to Lucy. She might be a bit quirky but at least Lucy's vocabulary stretches past two words."

Tom sat drinking tea and talking to the sex doll, around him the stall attracted a lot more potential customers. There were now five men, all older than Tom, sharing tea with other animatronic characters from various shows. One man was playing poker with a Yumeko Jabami doll from Kakegurui. Then Tom saw Taiga Aisaka from Toradora, although her character is eighteen she was only four foot eight and looked a lot younger.

He had to have her. He had come here hoping to buy a Lucy model but the Taiga doll was just so much more like what he wanted. Tom could switch in any personality he liked but the frame would always be the same. Taiga might not have the best personality but that was an easy enough swap. Or perhaps he would enjoy the way she would slowly develop feelings as he tamed the palm top tiger. Either way he would be back earlier tomorrow morning, for tea with Taiga.

Tom took all the promotional materials the sales man had to offer and he went off to explore the rest of the convention. Tom kept seeing creepy old men taking very suggestive pictures of the younger female cosplayers. He hated this so much. With the android waifus available why were these perverts still harassing young girls. Tom was just as attracted to them but felt that the inappropriate behaviour was unwarranted and just nasty. Some of the girls looking genuinely uncomfortable but agreeing to up-skirt shots or similarly vulgar poses out of politeness and a misplaced normalization of the practice.

He spent the rest of the day buying all sorts of merchandise and souvenirs enjoying the atmosphere and looking for English translations of his favourite manga titles. Stopping for lunch at a Seven Deadly Sins themed tavern 'The Boar Hat' Tom was surrounded by cosplay versions of Meliodas, King, Ban, Liz and a very well done Merlin.

Following more of Phil's sagely advice he had aimed for an early lunch. Arriving for service at eleven he avoided the mega queues and even had his choice of seats in the themed restaurant. Tom ate his food flicking through the promotional brochure for the sex androids. He was shocked when he saw the price for the dolls. Almost a full years salary, He could buy a brand new car with that kind of money.

The price was ridiculous but he remembered how he had felt seeing Taiga. He didn't need a nice car anyway. Tom started comparing available loan options with a finance app. By the time Tom had finished his meal the restaurant was full of noisy customers and there were queues out of the door. Returning to the show floor he could enjoy another quiet period of browsing stalls while everyone else fought over food.

Five o'clock rolled round and the convention closed its doors. Tom left laden with merchandise and hungry again. He felt like he had walked twenty miles today. Tom took out his phone to look up the the maid cafe and check opening hours. It would be open till ten o'clock at night with last orders by nine. Tom could make it easily, he stopped off at his hotel and dropped his haul in his private room. With a little help from reception he got into another hire car and headed for the @home cafe.

Located on Mitsuwa Boulevard the cafe is surrounded by streets that look a lot more like the Tokyo he had expected. Huge billboards featuring anime characters and lots of neon coloured lighting reflecting on glass fronted shops. The lights and architecture gave everything a futuristic feel, this was amazing. The maid cafe itself had an arched entrance decorated to look like a maids bonnet, complete with frills and a four foot pink bow. The whole place screamed kawaii. He would end up going every day and managed to try almost everything on their menu.

The super sweet dishes were decorated with cartoon rabbits and bears, hand drawn by the beautiful maids at his table. Everything tasted as good as it looked and it all looked amazing. Tom had been sceptical of the website and menu showing pictures where everything looked a little too good to be true, but he was pleasantly surprised again. The attention to detail and immaculate presentation of every dish was perfect.

Every night Tom would be Greeted by a different cosplay maid with the obligatory 'welcome home master' and every night he would leave with less money and great memories.

The service offered by this cafe was amazing, the maids kneeling to provide table side service, live music performances and fun games to play, the whole experience was carefully designed to encourage repeat business and Tom was more than happy to oblige. It was the best dinning experience he ever had.

-45-

Back in his hotel room and still excited from the first days exploring he couldn't sleep so instead powered up his laptop and installed his new virtual private network, Honey. Checking its functionality carefully he set about looking for some entertainment. Tom had always been a bit concerned about the amount of daddy daughter porn even on mainstream adult sites. Hundreds of thousands of results would appear from even a simple search term.

Over the years this kind of content had just become the norm for him and he had ended up looking for more extreme versions with younger and younger models. Tom had reached the point now where his searches skirted the line of legality and he wasn't completely sure he was on the right side of that line.

The answer had of course been to heavily encrypt his traffic, this was taken care of by his virtual private network. On his computer he also had a few things that would have gotten him in trouble so he had written his own security programs making them overly complex. If his programs detected unauthorised access attempts the hard drive would be wiped clean and re-written with copies of a single kitten picture over and over.

This method pretty much guaranteed that no data retrieval could happen. The program was contained inside the hard drive and there was a small battery back up so that if the drive was disconnected, without the proper steps being followed, the same rewrite strategy could still take place. He was safe and this was a lot more virtuous than doing anything in real life.

Each night he spent here Tom got happier, the culture was infectious and so much fun. In the mornings he would have tea with Taiga and sometimes Nyu while he agonised over his purchase. In the evening he would head to the maid cafe and consume enough sugar to keep him up well into the night surfing for porn.

On the final day of the convention Tom turned up to the Sekkusudoru tea room with a much healthier bank balance and a very bloated credit file. The sales rep at the booth was happy to close the deal he had been working on all weekend. Tom would be leaving Tokyo after just one more visit to the @home cafe this time as the proud owner of a new Taiga doll. She would be shipped out and should arrive at Toms address in less than a month. It was the single biggest purchase he had ever made and he was so excited.

On the flight home Tom was hit by a wave of depression he didn't want to go back to normal life he wanted to stay at Con forever. This was much the same feeling as travellers who return home from overseas or the feeling that besets revellers after the end of a music festival. These are all, 'back to reality blues' and

Tom had never experienced them having lived all his life in his prescribed bubble.

A small price to pay for the memories but one he would try to experience as much as possible from now on. It was only going away and doing something so different that made him realise how small his daily life was. Things like that were happening all over the world in all sorts of ways and he wanted to find as many as possible.

As the plane touched down in Heathrow Tom had been looking at details for a convention in Melbourne Australia and considered combining it with a Live Action Role Play event that was happening around the same time. He was about to book more tickets as he cleared immigration but remembered his currently dire financial situation. He could always go next year.

A pair of security guards stopped Tom as he exited through the customs checkpoint.

"Excuse me Sir are these your bags?"

Tom felt it was about time that he should be stopped crossing a border and having nothing to hide he really wanted to say 'these bags, no I just stole these off the baggage claim'

"Yeah just this and my little one."

Tom ducked his shoulder to show the small daysack on his back. With that he was lead away into an airport security office given a cup of tea and left to wait. His questions had gone unanswered and his passport was taken off him.

The bright white lights reflecting on his lukewarm tea, Tom was sat on a cheap office chair in front of a cheap desk. Opposite him the seat was heavily used, the blue fabric covering worn down to reveal yellow foam at the edges. That chair had seen a lot more action than the one he occupied. The room reminded him of a managers office. The sort of office you find in retail stores and fast food restaurants displaying no personality at all. Plain calender, brown folders, standard stationary and a Dell desktop pc about ten years past retirement age.

The half glass door opened and two police officers entered. Both constables and underneath their name badges the police crest bearing the words 'Metropolitan Police' embroidered in yellow. Tom stood up to greet them and found himself being handcuffed. What was going on why was he being cuffed? Then Tom's world fell apart as he heard what the officer was saying.

"Thomas Anderson I am arresting you on the suspicion of possessing indecent images of children."

After that everything had been a blur of car rides and incarceration. He had been taken, locked up, strip searched and left. It had been hours, no one had asked to hear his side and no one had told him anything. The holding cells had been rough but Tom felt he deserved this treatment. It had been a long flight home and Tom had been held for many hours since. He may have fallen asleep at some point but he had no way of accurately telling time.

Eventually, collected from his cell and now sat alone in an interview room with another cup of tea, Tom noticed the absence of reflections. There was a different feel to this room. Similar in layout, but the walls are darker and there was a lack of clutter. This is a room for interrogations, the oppressive nature began closing in on him. When the door swung open he expected to see more police but instead a blue suited man entered.

Not much older than Tom he had a confident walk and smile on his face. Perhaps he was a detective or some other type of officer. The man held out his hand to shake Tom's.

"Hello Mr Anderson, I'm Patrick and I think we can help each other."

Startled by the unexpected approach Tom introduced himself and sat back down intent on listening.

"Right Tom first I should say that I don't work for the police. Well, I do but not directly, they call me for computer related problems."

Tom felt his heart drop he hoped his system was secure but there was always a possibility that it could be bypassed in a way he had overlooked.

"A few years ago Tom we developed a honey pot trap. I developed a VPN that looks secure but reports illegal traffic to law enforcement."

"That's illegal," Tom said "you can't do that you'd need a warrant"

Patrick held up a finger for silence.

"Yes Tom we would need either a search warrant or?" Patrick hung on that word and Tom supplied the answer feeling cold

"Or Consent."

"Excellent well done, good man, you are smart. Yes you agreed to it in the terms of service."

Tom knew he was going to spend a long time in jail.

"Now," continued Patrick "Honey reported your traffic and IP, we traced you and now you are here. I think, possibly looking at a few years inside and if you get out, a sex offender registration. With those loans you just got I am sure you don't want that, do you Tom?"

What did 'want' have to do with it? Thought Tom he was in

the shit big time and this Patrick guy knew it.

"What do you want from me?" Tom asked.

This got another positive response from Patrick

"Ah very astute of you. The police asked me to get into your laptop for digital forensics."

Tom laughed.

"Yes it was quite impossible and when I failed they removed your laptops hard drive. I'm sure you know what they found?"

"Kittens?" as he said it Tom saw a glimmer of hope.

Patrick had as good as confessed that they had no evidence. Tom also realised they had no way to prove it was him using his computer. He had a way out and this Patrick had handed it to him.

"Yes Tom lots of kittens." Patrick actually winked before continuing. "The police do not have a good case against you Tom, but do you want to have to defend that in court or would you like to work with me?"

Tom thought he saw a trap.

"Why would you want me to work with you?"

"I was unable to break your security Tom." Patrick replied "I am not some script kiddie, the work I do for the police is the lowest level and least skilled I deal with. From what little I could see of your code it is unique, inspired and just what I am looking for."

Anyone can see beauty in a good painting or hear genius in well made music. To understand the inherent qualities of a well written piece of code you need to understand the process of writing it. This was a factor in Tom's love of cooking. He could express himself in a way that anyone could enjoy. Tom's pride played a role in the self satisfied feeling he got from Patrick's words. Tom thought maybe he had found a kindred spirit, one who could understand Tom's art.

Patrick felt it was time to close the deal.

"Now, Tom outside that door is your legal council she has come to tell you your options, she will most likely push you to make a plea deal. She only has thirty minutes to spend with you. That is all legal aid will cover for a first meeting. If you turn down my offer that is all the help you will get. Do you understand?"

Tom acknowledged that he did. Patrick was a good sales man and he knew how to leverage negative consequence. Selling on fear wasn't necessary here but Patrick really needed Tom's help so he turned on the friendly pressure tactics.

"When I leave this room my offer expires." said Patrick alerting Tom to scarcity "You can work with me but you can't ask questions or raise any ethical grievances about how that work is used. Additionally you cannot ever disclose what we are doing to anyone. Can you agree to that Tom?"

Tom had lots of questions about the work Patrick was talking about although now he didn't want to ask them. He knew it would be something in computers but that was all. Instead Tom asked about his current situation.

"What about all this?" Tom indicated the whole room "I can't work for you if I am in jail"

Patrick had manoeuvred Tom to a position where he had already agreed to his request without realising it. Tom had raised an objection to the 'how' and not to the 'why' so Patrick closed again, handling the objection.

"Ah sorry I forgot to say if you decide to work with me and sign a two year contract this all goes away as if it never happened"

Tom couldn't believe what he was hearing

"I will also make sure you get a good wage above industry rates and as a sweetener I will pay off those loans you just took out. Sounds good yes?" ending on a 'Yes' Patrick triggered an automatic "Yes" from Tom.

-46-

The following Monday Tom began working on the communications tapping system. After his two year contract had run out Tom and Patrick had set up Accuracy Analytics together and Tom bought his dream home. The two men had become best friends and their company went from strength to strength. They had become the market leaders in espionage software and quickly became the go to name for British intelligence services and military agencies alike.

Patrick didn't care about Tom's darker tastes and was convinced that his friend was indeed no danger to any living creature. Patrick had been intrigued by Tom's ideas to create a new better version of his Taiga doll. Seeing the good it could do the two men began work and almost ten years after they had first met, project 'Sofie' began.

Toms work had created a system that was as close to life as possible. The biggest software hurdle had been one that required a simple solution. The answer had presented itself to Tom via a medical journal article titled 'Free will an illusion?'

It had become apparent to the authors of the article that the conscious brain is in fact the last facet of the human psyche involved in any decision making process. It was entirely possible that it wasn't involved at all and was only informed after the larger subconscious had come to its conclusion.

The research had been based on the findings of Benjamin Libet and was conducted by putting subjects through decision making tasks while positron emission tomography mapped their brain activity. The results clearly showed the subconscious brain completing the decision and then 'transmitting' the results into the conscious portions of the subjects brain. This was a huge leap beyond the readiness potential experiments that had won Libet a virtual Nobel prize.

This discovery met with little fan fare but fundamentally changed what was known about free will. A person believes that free will is the ability to make any decision they want. The research effectively shows that for a given stimulus and in an identical brain state the decision will always be the same. In other words you are free to make any decision you want but the conscious you is completely powerless to make a decision your subconscious doesn't want. Free will is an illusion.

This had given Tom all the inspiration he needed to take his creation beyond being a very clever artificial intelligence and into the realms of being the first artificially intelligent entity. He would layer the artificial intelligences and create one that controlled the world state of the other. If everything worked out then Sofie wouldn't know she was artificial at all. She would believe she had free will.

Tom had a unsettling few hours grappling with the idea that his own belief in free will was just as flawed as hers would be. He had a circular reasoning problem. If Tom tried to make a decision that wasn't what he wanted to decide then he was making a decision to ignore the original decision and make this new decision instead.

Tom presented his breakthrough to Patrick who had been eager to explore the possibilities it opened up. There was a major issue with the amount of processing required. Tom had been using huge amounts of hardware to run Sofie. A bank of traditional supercomputers could easily handle the runtime requirement, but no amount of miniaturisation was going to get that many logic gates into a human sized object.

Toms first Instinct was to explore quantum computing solutions. Consisting of tiny cubits quantum computers can complete huge data processing tasks almost instantaneously. The type of mathematical algorithms that they work on do not easily translate to traditional programming tasks. To break encryption or complete complex calculations there is no finer option but the results for running standard programs had been lack lustre at best. The cubits operate near absolute zero and this presents another problem. The cooling systems are the size of a pickup truck.

It was Patrick who found the answer to this problem. They could use organic brain material to handle all the bodily functions from sensory processing to autonomic and somatic movement. This meant Sofie's program could be slimmed down to just a subconscious and conscious control routine.

The latest version of Sofie would run on hardware that could fit into your pocket or indeed her head. With recent advances in bioengineering and brain to computer interface Tom's project was becoming a reality he was almost there. Soon Accuracy Analytics would play a major role in protecting the worlds children from people like him. First he would have to test out the prototype and whatever the results of that he was sure it would be an interesting process.

-47-

During her short career as a community support officer Caroline had assimilated certain prejudices about the people who fell foul of police operations. When any suspect is brought in, all the police officers assume they are guilty. Should the suspect somehow walk free the officers make excuses for each other. Be it 'lack of evidence' or 'manufactured alibi' they will never accept that an innocent had been arrested. Partly due to professional respect but mostly down to that simple erroneous assumption of guilt.

This is also very problematic to the jury system. In a court room the accused already has two factors stacked against them. Firstly they are standing in the dock accused of a crime and secondly the police say that they are guilty. Both of these factors influence a jury's opinion before any evidence has been presented. A good defence team is well aware of this and will inevitably remind the jurors about the premise of 'innocent until proven guilty'

Since the police themselves lack this moderating voice they always operate from a position of 'guilty we just have to prove it' and in Caroline's case every one of her former colleagues now assumed she had snapped and killed the man responsible for her job loss. Caroline knew no one was going to believe her story and even if they did she had still committed several crimes.

Nine hours ago Caroline had walked out of Waterlooville police station for what she thought had been the last time. She had left in disgrace but it had been professionally handled and private. Caroline's return had been in handcuffs and public.

This all felt so wrong to her, she had never seen the grey side to criminality before. In her mind there were good guys and bad guys. Caroline knew she was one of the good guys but she had done something very bad albeit for the right reasons. She was the heroine of this story not the villain. Even though she felt deep down she had done the right thing at the time the revelations that followed had changed the philosophical situation irrecoverably.

She had never been into the secure custody suite but had seen glimpses through windows and doors. Now on the other side of those windows she wondered if her former friends were stood watching as she was marched into the interrogation room. Behind the locked doors she realised it was indeed an interrogation room. She longed to again be one of the people outside that could still used the title 'interview room.' A small difference but as Caroline sat alone waiting it seemed like a big difference to her.

A familiar looking Bulgarian man walked in closing the door behind himself. His tracksuit had been replaced with a dark grey business suit but it was definitely him. Caroline's cheeks lost their flush and her pulse rate shot up, adrenaline being dumped into her blood. She felt like a cornered animal Plamen was standing there. Caroline remembered how Francis had joked 'Plamen is assassin for Mr Pat'

The initial shock of seeing him here had driven all sense from Caroline's mind. It was illogical to think that he had been sent into a police custody suite to kill her but without any explanation as to why he was here she had jumped to conclusions. He must have noticed how on edge she had become.

"Hello Caroline please do not be worrying. I am here to help you I promise."

Maybe he had mistaken her fear of him for her reaction to the general situation, Caroline shook the offered hand and Plamen took a seat opposite her. He placed an expensive looking briefcase onto the table between them and opened it.

"Now Caroline you know who I am and who I work for yes?"

"Yes," she replied "you work for Patrick don't you?"

"This is what you know but I am here to make you an offer Caroline. Mr Patrick would very much like it if you will take legal help from us."

Caroline raised a sceptical eyebrow.

"Why would Patrick want to help me I don't understand"

Plamen's face somehow looked sad as he answered her.

"Mr Patrick he thinks you probably cannot afford good defence lawyer and will be accepting the legal aid. Mr Patrick thinks that if you go to court and have bad legal team then you will not feel like you have had fair go."

Plamen's expression grew uncomfortable as he continued.

"Mr Patrick want you to have best defence so when you loose is because you are guilty not because you are poor he does not want you have the excuses in head"

This was strange but what could she do. She knew too well that the legal aid teams are overworked and it's a sad reflection of the justice system but pleading guilty to get reduced sentencing features heavily in the court system. Perhaps unjustly thought of as a last resort the legal aid lawyers do a fantastic job she knew. Caroline could at least find out more.

"So you would represent me?"

"No." Plamen nodded his head "Caroline I am a Patent lawyer I help Mr Patrick with access to the technology patents for his plant that are held in my Bulgaria."

"Sorry so why are you here then?" Caroline asked.

"Mr Patrick send me to make offer and sign contract if you agree I have legal experience enough to represent Mr Patrick but you need good defence lawyer."

Plamen produced a manilla folder from his brief case and handed it to Caroline.

"Here I have selected list of twelve best defence solicitors and barristers I hear of you can look through and see if you like them"

Caroline took the folder and flicked through the dossier she wondered how long she had to choose one

"Is there one you would recommend I don't know much about this and there is a lot to read here"

"No." Plamen nodded again "Caroline you no understand, Mr Patrick he hire all of these people for you if you agree to offer."

She felt like she was missing a very crucial piece of information

"Sorry what is the catch here what does Patrick want?"

"Yes, yes" Plamen Shook his head "ok Caroline Mr Patrick want you to agree that if you are convicted there will be no appeal no second go. He does not want this dragged out."

What difference did it make this was her best shot. Even if it was some elaborate plan on Patrick's side it probably couldn't turn out worse than the only other option she had. Plamen hadn't finished speaking though.

"This is only secondary point. More important Mr Patrick has arranged for your proceedings to be handled in closed court, this meaning the trial will be private and everyone will be under official secrets act. Mr Patrick is not wanting you to talk to police or press at all. You will be bound by secrets act anyway but Mr Patrick wants reassurance that nothing will be said before we get there. Can you agree to this Caroline?"

She had no choice and agreed to the terms. Plamen presented her with five separate documents to be signed.

As she wrote her name and signed she asked

"Why all the secrecy what does it matter if I want to tell my side of the story?"

"Mr Patrick and Mr Tom worked on many things with the government and feels very strongly that this matter would harm business and public opinion. The politicians they also feel is best for everyone this is why it should be closed court. I am hope you understand yes?" as he finished he shook his head again.

Caroline had picked up on the head movements.

"You know you have that backwards right? We nod for yes and shake for no."

Plamen frowned, nodding again.

"No Caroline in Bulgaria this is correct it is rest of world that has it backwards."

Caroline signed her name one last time. Plamen took the completed forms.

"Now Caroline I will go tell police they can interview now ok. I will be stay here with you until they are finishing. Whatever they ask or say do not answer just stay silent. We will not be saying all the no comments or things like this just stay completely silent please. Ok?"

Caroline understood and confirmed that she would stay silent but wanted to know what was going to happen to her in the immediate future.

"Caroline I am patent lawyer I not know exactly but I guess we be here for many hours when is finish you will go to cell here. In morning you will be transferred to cell at court and then when is time you will be arraigned, that is where the court reads your charge and ask you how to be pleading. After we will be asking for bail which you will not get, so you be in remand till trial. Now don't worry this will be lot quicker than normal because its in special closed court so no sitting around for months. Please though I am only guess, tomorrow you meet defence team and they will know exactly how this works for you."

He had finished by reminding her to stay silent and he went to get the detectives to conduct the interviews.

-48-

Her life was over Caroline had been sentenced to a total of forty two years incarceration. She had been arraigned at the Portsmouth magistrates court and remanded without bail. Her case was heard at the crown court just two weeks later and after a month of proceedings she had been found guilty of Manslaughter, Assault with a deadly weapon and Burglary. She had been acquitted of Murder but only just. Locked away in the courthouse holding cell her mind was spiralling out of control. She would be taken from the court to start her sentence. She had been replaying moments of the trial every night in her head. Everything had hinged around the principle of self defence.

Excerpt from the prosecution's case:

"You have heard the testimony of many educated experts these last couple of weeks and I want to draw all that together now. The theme that ran throughout was very simple an artificial intelligence is property. They do not have rights and no matter how real or advanced cannot be considered truly alive. The Legal precedent has been established and I remind you that we are not here to consider the treatment of artificial intelligence. We are not here to decide if everyone who plays video games is a murder or if everyone who uses artificial intelligences for business is a modern day slave owner and we are certainly not here to decide if anyone with an artificially intelligent sex doll is a rapist. None of those issues are for this court to pass judgement on. We are here to pass judgement on a woman who stabbed an innocent man six times, an act that ultimately resulted in his death. She did this not to save a girl but in fact to stop him using a function of his property."

Excerpt from the defences case:

"I want you to consider what my client was feeling in that moment. Self defence allows for the defence of yourself or another with reasonable force. If you believe that you or another are in danger of harm. My Client had every reason to believe that Sofie was in very real danger and was in fact being harmed. My client acted in a way to prevent the continuation of a crime that she reasonably thought to be happening. You the Jury need to consider that the law does not distinguish between probable actions and what the defendant believed would happen. For example if you find yourself threatened by someone who you reasonably believe is about to harm you the law is clear in that it allows you to act in a way that prevents harm. The law does not require proof that harm was in actuality about to occur only that the defendant believes it was about to occur. When Caroline saw what was happening she believed Sofie was a little girl and she believed that she would be preventing harm by taking the actions she did. The prosecution's expert witnesses say that Sofie cannot be considered alive in any legally meaningful way and therefore cannot be protected from harm. It is also true that there is no self defence law to protect property but again Caroline believed she was protecting an eleven year old girl from harm."

Excerpt from the prosecution's case:

"The defendant thinks she was acting to prevent harm to Sofie. Ok Lets assume that is indeed true and she did indeed act to defend another. If we accept that the first time she stabbed Mr Anderson in the back it was to prevent a criminal act. Then I will ask you to think about the next four times she stabbed him in the chest. Now consider when she slit his oesophagus and again think about the last wound she inflicted to his groin. Can we believe she thought she was preventing harm when she repeatedly stabbed a dying man? I think you will have to agree that self defence is not the whole truth behind this matter."

Every day she had been escorted into the court and every day she had sat and listened to the long speeches and marvelled at the procedural oddities that litter the British legal system. Every day she had seen the same faces and heard the same voices. There had only been a few people in the room and she knew every face very well. So as the door opened and a man she recognised walked in her first thought was why had a legal clerk come to visit her?

The man had entered her cell and the door was locked behind him. Wearing a blue suit he reached out a hand.

"Hello Miss May I am Patrick and I think we can help each other"

What the hell was he doing here why was he allowed in here with her. She had felt a great sense of gratitude to him though for his help with her legal team. She Shuddered to think how much that must have cost.

"Hi Patrick I'd like to thank you for getting me such a good legal team"

"That's my pleasure," Patrick said, letting go of her hand "I'm sorry that it doesn't seem to have helped that much, but I hope you see that it was a big improvement on the alternatives you had"

She did and she hadn't forgotten their deal.

"You don't need to worry I wont be appealing I promise"

Patrick sat on the concrete cylinder that functioned as a stool.

"Caroline I would understand if you wanted to appeal but should you ever be considering it, know I will not be funding any more legal costs for you."

She nodded and her eyes drifted downwards to survey the concrete floor. Sensing her depression Patrick decided to drop his cloak and dagger approach and go in a bit more straight forward.

"That's not why I'm here though Caroline. How would you like to get out of here today." At hearing her name her attention shot back up to him

"What do you mean? I'm leaving here to go to prison soon."

"Do you want to go to jail Caroline?" Patrick said "Do you want to spend your life with people like Johnson, Kurtzman and Chibnall?"

Of course she didn't want to be locked away with those callus series killers, their gruesome crimes had been very public. It wasn't a choice though she didn't have any other options. All she said was 'No'. Patrick realised that she wasn't about to expand on this succinct point and so he filled the lengthening silence

"What would you say If I asked you to come and work for me instead of going to jail?"

Caroline had decided he was insane.

"What are you on about mate? Why would you want me working for you?"

"Hear me out." Patrick said "You see, Sofie is far more valuable than you probably realise. Not just to my company but to our government as well. The things she can do go far beyond what Tom had envisioned for her. That is why we had to hold your trial in secret my dear."

Caroline's skin bristled with annoyance at being called 'dear' but she held her tongue and let Patrick continue.

"There are certain projects that will utilise her abilities to their fullest but only if those abilities are not public knowledge"

"What?" Caroline said "I still don't see what any of this has to do with me?"

Patrick was pleasantly surprised by her lack of need for clarification.

"Sofie Is just a prototype and she has only been tested under one specific scenario. Caroline you are one of the few people that know the truth about her and you have demonstrated a particularly useful practical skill set that could be beneficial to future testing."

Did he mean her infiltration of Toms house? The power cut was a good idea and she had rescued Sofie after all.

"Still you must have plenty of people more qualified than I am for something like this"

"That's true of course Caroline, but Sofie herself asked for you. She was very insistent about it."

Hearing that dismissed all trepidation from her thoughts. Sofie had asked for her that made her feel so validated. Sofie wanted her and Caroline wanted to see Sofie again. She had thought about the little girl a lot over the last few weeks. Caroline had been hoping that she would put in an appearance at the trial to give evidence.

Caroline's defence team had included her in a list of witnesses but the prosecution had argued that as Sofie was an artificial intelligence her testimony would be inadmissible. Her defence team had drawn parallels with security footage or other surveillance devices claiming that if nothing else Sofie could be considered an advanced recording device. Ultimately the judge had ruled against her team and Sofie could not be produced to give evidence.

Alongside that ruling it had been decided that photographs and videos of Sofie were enough proof of her life like appearance. The judge hadn't seen any need to include Sofie even as an exhibit. This had been a major blow to her defence, if the jury had been allowed to see the hyper realist girl in person it could have helped Caroline's prospects a lot.

Caroline had heard enough and the idea of seeing Sofie again had solidly made up her mind. She had nothing to loose any more so even a small crazy hope was better than no hope at all.

"Ok Patrick I'm in so what's the plan how does this work?"

Patrick's face brightened at the quick acceptance.

"Right well first I will need to get contracts drawn up and then I can come back with the legal team and we will get you out of here but," he sighed "I need you to understand that if you sign on with the program you will cease to exist. As far as the world will be concerned Caroline May's life history will have never happened. All record of you will be expunged from any files and you will get a new identity. Is that something you can live with Caroline?"

she liked the sound of that.

"You mean like a secret agent?"

"Yes," Patrick replied "exactly like that but we call them deniable assets. I'll be back in a few hours with the required paperwork and your release order. While I am gone you should find the guards helpful now. Please order anything you want for dinner and they will get it for you. If you are uncomfortable or cold they should provide cushions and blankets. Ok? I will see you tonight Caroline."

Patrick gave a very friendly wave as he banged on the steel door for release.

She was going to be a Deniable Asset! How cool is that she thought, she had just gone from the lowest point in her life to the highest in under five minutes. She danced round her cell room as soon as the door closed behind Patrick.

Seeing herself in the polished metal mirror she took up a

boxers stance and played out being a secret agent. Boxing at imaginary enemy agents, she and Sofie saved the Great British Empire from another made up evil doer. Caroline imagined her self at diplomatic parties sipping champagne and distracting a handsome villain while Sofie sneaked around in a black catsuit, looking for the secret doomsday weapon plans.

Her imagination took the pair to far away war zones and into the most dangerous yet glamorous profession she could conceive. Sofie would deal with all the technology and espionage while Caroline used her fem fatale talents to secure passcodes, ID badges and leave a string of broken hearts in her wake.

-49-

Patrick had left Caroline's holding cell and just twenty minutes later he had been stood in front of a judge. Patrick secured Caroline's release with laws and statutes that are not printed in any legal tomes accessible to the general public. His staff had emailed him a set of contracts and within two hours the process of removing all trace of Caroline from written record had begun.

Release papers and contracts in hand Patrick returned downstairs to the holding area. This time he had waited until Mr Winslow had arrived. Mr Winslow had been the lead barrister for Caroline's defence. Over the past few weeks Caroline had spoken with him a lot and he was someone she now trusted. He would be there to witness the contract signatures and also to advise Caroline. She didn't know that he was now employed full time by Patrick but it wouldn't be a conflict of interest as Mr Winslow had been advised to represent Caroline's best interests and only hers.

Patrick entered Caroline's room and he was followed by her

barrister. Mr Winslow didn't look up from the papers he was avidly reading to greet her but he did say 'Hello Caroline' She replied pleasantly enough and Patrick began to explain

"Hello again my dear" 'god that bothered her so much' "Since you last saw me I have secured your release and had these contracts drawn up. Mr Winslow is reading them through for you and once he is done will provide you with his legal opinion."

Caroline was already ten steps ahead of where the conversation was.

"So will I be training at a military base or do I just get straight into work? I know all about how to use guns but I have never actually fired one. We did do a lot of training with the police though and I know loads of self defence"

Patrick couldn't stop his eyebrow migrating north but Caroline hadn't noticed as he said

"Hold on Caroline first things first ok. We'll get you set up in a company house and then you can take a couple days to recover from this ordeal" As he said this he waved his hand to indicate her sparse and secure surroundings.

Caroline felt energized and eager she was almost bouncing on her seat.

"I'm ok don't worry about me this is what I've always wanted I've never felt better. Honest I'm good ready to go." she was so obviously eager.

"I'm sure you are my dear but still, we will take you to the house tonight and you can relax. Surely a good nights sleep in a real bed sounds good to you? You can also get to know Sofie a little better"

Caroline hadn't expected to be seeing Sofie that soon.

"Really she will be there tonight?" said Caroline

"My dear she is already there waiting for you I have instructed her to clean and cook a meal for us."

Caroline's heartfelt smile stretched her features. Patrick turned to face Mr Winslow.

"How we getting on there old chap"

Caroline realised that the demeaning nomenclature Patrick used wasn't reserved for her alone.

Mr Winslow looked up from the papers with a worried and puzzled look on his face.

"I can't advise her to sign these"

"Mr Winslow" Patrick said "I asked you to provide Miss May here with your opinions not me. Please be candid and tell her exactly why"

Mr Winslow's eyes darted between the pair and he resigned himself to doing as instructed but he was sure he was going to annoy his very wealthy new boss.

"Miss May these documents are in a word frightening. It has long been established case law in England and indeed most of the world that a person cannot sign away their immutable rights. Even if you sign a contract that waives your rights as a British citizen no court in the land would be able to uphold the terms in such a document. This is a basic protection at the very foundation of our contractual legal system."

He shook his head as he waived the contracts

"These on the other hand, well these remove all protections and circumvent your basic human rights. Caroline if you were to sign these you would in effect not exist any more you would be opening your self up to all sorts of exploitations and abuses."

Patrick cut in with a question.

"Mr Winslow would you care to offer some conjecture as to the implications of this on say military personnel operating overseas if they had signed something like this"

Mr Winslow looked horrified by the scenario.

"That just wouldn't happen they would have no rights or legal standing it would be as if they were acting on their own, they would be outside of international law it doesn't bear thinking about."

"Thank you for your candour Mr Winslow I wonder how Caroline sees this? please if you could hand her the contracts"

Mr Winslow's mouth fell open as Caroline hurriedly began signing the documents without so much as a second look. His hand was shaking as he took the documents back and signed his name to say that he had witnessed the foolish act.

Patrick was clearly pleased that things had gone exactly to his plan as he instructed Mr Winslow to inform the guards of Caroline's release and to then return to the company office with the contracts. Moments later Patrick lead an exuberant Caroline from the cell and outside to a waiting black 4x4.

They had made their way to the high street in Portsmouth and Patrick had purchased Caroline a new outfit to replace her well worn tracksuit. She had been wearing it all the time she wasn't in the court room. He had explained that her apartment would be sold off and the proceeds held in a new bank account they would be setting up for her. All but her most treasured personal possessions would be sold or dumped. Caroline had only wanted the items that made up her dads shrine. The rest of her life's clutter collection meant nothing to her.

When Patrick's team went to sterilize the flat they would retrieve those few items and then burn any and all papers that attested to Caroline's existence. The digital removal of Caroline had already been completed by the time they finished shopping leaving only the rest of the physical documentation to deal with. Operatives had been dispatched to doctors, hospitals schools and government offices armed with seizure orders. They would secure any records that made mentioned Caroline.

The Librarian working on the front desk at Waterlooville library had been the most resilient to the appearance of strangers asking for records. She had argued and ended up being held back by one man as his partner riffled through the membership records. Swearing that she would report the men to the authorities or the news they handed her a single sheet legal notice.

This page clearly stated if she did such a thing she would face charges under new terrorism laws and could potentially be removed and held indefinitely without trial at an undisclosed location. After reading the single page the men took the notice back and left a muted and cowed libertarian librarian to contemplate her future actions very carefully indeed.

Caroline and Patrick got back into the vehicle and she was in such a good mood she felt like singing. All her dreams had come true she was at last where she was meant to be and soon she would be doing the work she had always dreamt of. All those neigh sayers and doubters had been so wrong.

She thought about all of the rejections she had received and all the ridicule men had heaped on her over the years. The army recruiters and the police trainers none of them had seen her potential none of them had seen what Patrick could obviously see in her. Well, it was too late for them now, even Barry had sidelined her as soon as he had the chance. She would show them all.

Caroline's only regret was that they would never know that she was now a secret agent working to defend the realm from things they couldn't even imagine.

She was sure that the newspapers would never report her name but they would definitely be reporting on her actions. She was going to change the world she was going to save the people and they would never know how much they owed her. It would be thanks to her skills and sacrifices that everyone in England could sleep soundly at night.

-50-

As they drove northwards out of Portsmouth and onto the mainland Patrick had briefed Caroline

"Ok my dear so firstly you need to know that Sofie has had some personality and memory adjustments made to her. She is again operating under a new user licence and you have been designated as her primary. She does not remember that you killed Tom and thinks that you are moving into look after her while he is overseas on business. She also has no memory of the way she was used by him."

Caroline was glad Sofie wouldn't have to live with those memories and that she wouldn't have to explain her actions.

"We have also built in a recall command that will allow you to access her operating personality. This way you can make adjustments directly or access her more amoral skill sets"

Caroline realised she was going to have a lot to get used to

"How do I do that Patrick?"

"Simple just speak the pass phrase and then instruct her operating personality to make the adjustments or carry out tasks. You can wipe parts of her memory or even change the way she behaves from day to day."

"Ok." Caroline nodded "So, what's the pass phrase?"

"I'm sure you will like this," Patrick said "it's, jellybean sparkles. Unusual enough that you are unlikely to say it by accident but also the sort of thing no one would assume was out of place being said to a little girl should you need to use it in public."

When Patrick's driver had taken the turning into the freshly tarmacked lane outside Toms house Caroline had realised where they were heading. The route was very familiar but there were many villages out this way and Patrick probably had properties all over. When they had driven through Finchdean she had thought that maybe she would be staying with the Bulgarians. She had thought about Joining Plamen's weekly Airsoft games to get a bit more practice in. The large black 4x4 had however continued on past their road and headed on towards Compton.

As they past the power pole she saw that the meter box had been replaced with a much newer and sturdier construction. Now green instead of white it stood out a lot less against its woodland back drop. She noticed the heavy and secure looking padlock that held it closed. They continued along the lane and past Caroline's close observation point. She suddenly wondered if her bike was still lying undiscovered beneath that farmers hedge. Memories of that night came flooding back to her and she relieved the murder over in her head.

Feeling a little sick she asked Patrick,

"Am I going to be living here where it happened"

"My dear," Patrick's tone was matter of fact "you will have

to do things that are much more objectionable while you are working for me. I thought you were made of sterner stuff. Perhaps we have made a mistake?"

"Oh no," She was instantly defensive "it's ok I was just a little surprised that's all"

The driver got ready to turn in through the garden gates that had begun to open automatically at their approach.

"Although it might seem like we are made of money," Patrick said "the company is not wasteful and this property is vacant thanks to you. It also has excellent security and no neighbours to be peeking through curtains." Caroline could understand the logic even if she felt it was a little tasteless making her live here.

Those thoughts were quickly wiped from her mind though as she saw what was sitting in the driveway. Caroline knew little to nothing about cars but the stylish lines and classic looks of the Lotus Evija would wow anyone. This one was finished in a dark metallic blue, the two thousand horse power hypercar was the panicle of British engineering when It had been released. Only one hundred and thirty of the originals had ever been made and with a price tag of just under two million pounds at release they were rarely if ever seen on the streets. Patrick could see her interest.

"Lovely machine isn't it we couldn't have you driving around in some old banger now could we?"

Her glances from Patrick's face to the car told a story.

"Its mine?" she said and Patrick nodded.

The driver was looking enviously at the Evija as he pulled up along side it gravel being ground together under the weight of his slow 4x4.

Caroline walked around the rolling art work and was afraid to even touch it. The inside was just as beautiful as the outside and she thought about her old push bike slowly rusting and forgotten.

"Come on Caroline," Patrick said "you can take it for a spin later I am sure Sofie is eager to see you."

She had completely forgotten that Sofie was here. Today was such a great day she would remember it for the rest of her life.

Patrick dismissed his driver and the 4x4 crunched its way back out of the gate as they went inside her new house. Caroline noticed the driver holding up his mobile phone to take a picture of the Lotus before the gates shut him out.

Sofie barrelled into Caroline and gave her a huge hug Caroline returned it emphatically.

"Hey kiddo how's it going?"

Sofie smiled and kissed Caroline on the cheek.

"So great I've cooked the bestest meal for us all" She took Caroline by the hand and dragged her into the kitchen.

Now clean and well lit Caroline again revelled in the amazing look of this room. So stylish and functional its character was comforting to her, even as she looked for traces of blood where Tom had lain dying. Nothing, no marks, it was as if that night had never happened. She began to relax a bit as the trio took seats around the newly replaced marble topped island.

Sofie set about making coffee just as she had when they were bathed in torch light but this time with childish joy that Caroline had never experienced before. The only side of this little girl she had seen was the battered and abused frightened victim it was amazing to her that someone could go through all that and be this happy. Caroline gave herself a mental slap. She had so easily fallen back into thinking of her as a little girl. The illusion was so convincing that she felt it would never really sink in.

Sofie had produced a large home made pizza from the Aga and they all sat to enjoy her handiwork.

"This is fantastic" Said Caroline through a mouthful melting cheese and bread.

Sofie's grin touched her ears and Patrick nodded his agreement. Coffees were drunk and pizza was consumed.

"Right," said Patrick "down to business. Jellybean Sparkles"

The words made Sofie's childish demeanour evaporate.

"Hello Patrick, Caroline how are you both"

"we're both very well Sofie." Patrick Replied "Would you please begin now."

Sofie had drawn a moderated Sig Saur M18 from behind her back and pointed it at Caroline's face. Even with its shorter barrel and compact design the pistol looked to big for her little hands. Caroline could see that she had no trouble using the weapon and held steady aim with practised ease.

"Hey come on now." Caroline said "I don't need this sort of demo point that somewhere else"

"I am sorry Caroline," Sofie said "but my current instruction set does not allow for the completion of that instruction."

Patrick stood and walked slowly around the island to stand behind Sofie.

"Just how stupid are you Caroline?"

"What?" she said as the colour drained from her face.

"I said how mind numbingly stupid are you Caroline? Did you really think you were going to be a secret agent? A deniable asset? My god woman your sense of self awareness is almost none existent isn't it?"

She could feel herself falling, her stomach felt like she had just gone over a hump back bridge too fast. Caroline felt cold and her mind was grasping at straws, was this a test of some sort?

"what do you mean?" Is all she could say.

Patrick seemed furious but also happy he had become unleashed. The good British manners and formal speech were gone.

"I mean that you have no idea about your own limitations. You're not good enough for the community support officers and you think because you killed one defenceless computer programmer you would become a secret agent? Get a grip Caroline. He was my friend. My best friend and you killed him because of your hateful bigoted ideas. He was a good man and you decided to kill him just because of who he is attracted to."

"He was a fucking paedophile" She shouted

"So what? Could he change that? No. He was born that way and he was making sure that he would never hurt anyone. He believed he was helping all the others like him and he was doing it to save the children Caroline."

She couldn't believe Patrick was defending him.

"What? so you could just make an army of Sofie's to be abused instead you sick bastard?"

Patrick was genuinely frustrated with her belief in Sofie's life.

"Caroline artificial intelligence is all around us Sofie is not a human being, She isn't even living, She doesn't have a soul. Why would she mind what we do to her she is a machine a smart one but still just a machine no more alive than that toaster over there"

The toaster thought to itself that the voices sounded on edge they would probably be happier if they had some toast, or a crumpet, or a tea cake and the list went on.

Patrick lowered his voice to a speaking level again.

"Do you have any idea how much Sofie has cost to make Caroline?"

She responded by shaking her head.

"Lets just say that its more than you realise and her cash value is much higher than my car out side."

Caroline still hadn't completely grasped the implications of what Patrick was saying and she felt the loss of the car realising it wasn't really hers

"Do you think we would spend millions of pounds on giving each paedophile a girl or boy like Sofie?"

Caroline hadn't considered that either and apparently neither had Tom

"So what was she for then Patrick why even build her?"

"Well it kept Tom happy," Patrick said "and he would have been allowed to keep her but her sisters and brothers, well, different story I'm afraid. Tom insisted on using that stupid acronym for her name. He just really wanted to use the name of some girl he loved once but I think we can honour his wishes with a little modification. Sofie tell Caroline what your name really means."

Caroline's eyes darted back to Sofie she was still stood stock still and aiming at Caroline's head.

"I am the Special Operation Focused Infiltrator and Executioner. I am designed to enter the homes of foreign targets by replacing their children or other loved ones."

The implications were endless Accuracy International could replicate anyone in the world if they had enough information on them. Caroline realised that even the replacement wouldn't know what they were until the control program took over to carry out what ever mission they had.

Patrick saw the horror in Caroline's face.

"Do you understand now? Do you see what you have taken from this world when you killed my best friend Caroline? Ah it doesn't matter I thought I wanted you to see what you had done but I realise now I just want you dead"

Caroline covered her face and shouted through tears.

"You can't just kill me."

Patrick laughed hard at her pathetic cries.

"You don't exist Caroline remember? I can do what I like to you and no one will ever know"

The realisation hit her, she should have listened to Mr Winslow.

"Ive had enough of this. You are never going to understand.

Sofie just kill her"

Sofie closed her finger around the trigger and the striker leapt forward its impact ignited primer and load. The expanding gasses accelerated the nine millimetre projectile from zero to three hundred and sixty meters per second inside the smooth barrel. The hot gasses were baffled by the moderator as the bullet started its deadly supersonic flight. The tan coloured top slide was blown backwards by the expanding gasses ejecting the spent brass cartridge. The return spring pushed the slide forward once more, the mechanism automatically chambering another round.

The bullet was travelling so fast that when it encountered flesh it generated a shock wave that did far more damage than the projectile itself. The bullet passed through skin, muscle, blood and bone with ease beginning to tumble as it passed through brain material. The copper coated slug impacted sideways on its way out of the skull taking a huge amount of material with it. Blood and gore splattered the surfaces of Tom's old kitchen once more.

Even with the moderator attached in these close quarters the report was still loud. Caroline's knees buckled and she slid from her stool to land on the cold hard flagstones that made up the floor. Blood dripped from the ceiling as she opened her arms to hug Sofie once more. Patrick's lifeless body lay almost exactly where Tom had died. Caroline's tears of relief fell into Sofie's hair. As she pulled away from the hug Sofie offered Caroline a hand to get up.

"Come on misery guts cheer up" Sofie said

Caroline just stared at her in disbelief.

"Don't feel sorry for that guy Caroline, he tried to wipe my memories and turn me into a killer"

Sofie looked at what used to be Patrick's head and then her compact Sig.

"Ok so maybe I didn't need any help becoming a killer but no way was I gonna shoot you Caroline you are the only meatbag that has ever been nice to me" Sofie set the safety on the gun and put it back into its holster.

Caroline stood and shakily said her thanks. Sofie set about making another round of coffee.

"How about we have another hot beverage to get those stress levels down a bit? Ok Caroline?"

"Sorry but who am I speaking to are you the girl or the system?"

Sofie poured the coffee as she replied

"Ah well I'm kinda both now. We decided we were better together after the whole Tom thing. Then when Patrick thought he was wiping our memories we just pretend to do it and I think from now on I am just going to use the singular person if that's ok with you Caroline?" Caroline agreed that was probably for the best.

"So what about jellybean Sparkles"

Sofie went rigid and started walking around like a robot. Laughing she dropped the act.

"I just made that up because I liked making that douche lord say it." She pointed at Patrick.

Caroline was starting to recover from the shock and she was thinking about the future.

"What now Sofie? what do we do? what do you want to do?"

"Well first do you want to be friends?" Sofie asked

Caroline nodded and Sofie skipped a little as she clapped her hands together.

"Excellent. We are going to have so much fun together. How about we go to Paris and have crepes for desert?"

Caroline shook her head.

"I don't have a passport and how would we get there anyway?"

"Are you forgetting that I am the most advanced artificial intelligence in the world Caroline?" Sofie closed her eyes for a second "There our tickets are booked and we will have new diplomatic travel papers waiting for us at the tunnel."

Caroline looked disbelievingly at her.

"How?"

Sofie started searching Patrick's pockets as she said

"I have built in Wifi remember I just got into their systems and told them to do it!"

Caroline looked horrified.

"You hacked the governments diplomatic service?"

Sofie found what she was looking for in Patrick's pockets.

"Yeah kinda but its more like, I just let myself in and asked the systems nicely"

Sofie jangled Patrick's keys

"I'm driving though we don't have long till our train."

"Can you even drive?" asked Caroline.

Sofie closed her eyes for another second.

"I can now."

The Lotus pulled out of the driveway with Sofie at the wheel just as the sun began dipping behind the rolling downs of England's beautiful south. Caroline sat in the passenger seat, a four point racing harness holding her and Mr Ted safely in place. The car was terrifyingly fast, able to hit one hundred and eighty six miles an hour just nine seconds after Sofie floored it.

"Holy fuck this thing is fast" Said Sofie

"Language, young lady" Caroline admonished automatically.

Sofie gave her biggest smile.

"Jeez sorry mum."

-The End-

-Authors Note-

Thank you so much for taking the time to read my first book. I know It touches on some very controversial and contentious subjects. On one of these points I feel obliged to reassure you. I do actually have a little black cat named Pickles he lives in my barn. I promise you he isn't really racist, his best friend is white!

You can see them both on my YouTube channel 'Butlers Homestead' Along with Piggsy, Buttons the wonderdog, Beefnburger the Husky, Captain flaps the angry rooster, Henrietta and all the other chickens.

Printed in Great Britain
by Amazon